The Betrayal

W0010324

BEVERLY LEWIS

The Betrayal

BETHANYHOUSE
PUBLISHERS
MINNEAPOLIS, MINNESOTA

THE BETRAYAL

Copyright © 2003
Beverly Lewis

Cover design by Dan Thornberg

Note to Readers: Although *Martyrs Mirror* is an actual book, the account
of Catharina Meylin is a creation of the author.

Published by Bethany House Publishers
11400 Hampshire Avenue South
Bloomington, Minnesota 55438
www.bethanyhouse.com

Bethany House Publishers is a Division of
Baker Book House Company, Grand Rapids, Michigan.

Printed in the United States of America

ISBN 0-7642-2331-3 (Paperback)
ISBN 0-7642-2807-2 (Hardcover)
ISBN 0-7642-2806-4 (Large Print)
ISBN 0-7642-2808-0 (Audio Book)

Library of Congress Cataloging-in-Publication Data

Lewis, Beverly
  The betrayal / by Beverly Lewis.
    p. cm.   (Abram's daughters ; 2)
    ISBN 0-7642-2331-3 (pbk.) — ISBN 0-7642-2807-2 (hardcover) —
ISBN 0-7642-2806-4 (large print)
    1. Lancaster County (Pa.)—Fiction. 2. Sisters—Fiction. 3. Amish—
Fiction. I. Title. II. Series: Lewis, Beverly, 1949- , Abram's
daughters ; 2.
    PS3562.E9383B48   2003
    813'.54—dc21   2002008665

Dedication

For

Pamela Ronn,

my "shadow twin"

and wonderful-good friend.

By Beverly Lewis

ABRAM'S DAUGHTERS

The Covenant
The Betrayal
The Sacrifice
The Prodigal

❖ ❖ ❖

THE HERITAGE OF LANCASTER COUNTY

The Shunning
The Confession
The Reckoning

❖ ❖ ❖

The Postcard
The Crossroad

❖ ❖ ❖

The Redemption of Sarah Cain
October Song
Sanctuary*
The Sunroom

❖ ❖ ❖

The Beverly Lewis Amish Heritage Cookbook

www.BeverlyLewis.com

*with David Lewis

BEVERLY LEWIS, born in the heart of Pennsylvania Dutch country, fondly recalls her growing-up years. A keen interest in her mother's Plain family heritage has led Beverly to set many of her popular stories in Lancaster County.

A former schoolteacher and accomplished pianist, Beverly is a member of the National League of American Pen Women (the Pikes Peak branch), and the Society of Children's Book Writers and Illustrators. She is the 2003 recipient of the Distinguished Alumnus Award at Evangel University, Springfield, Missouri, and her blockbuster novel, *The Shunning*, recently won the Gold Book Award. Her bestselling novel *October Song* won the Silver Seal in the Benjamin Franklin Awards, and *The Postcard* and *Sanctuary*, (a collaboration with her husband, David) received Silver Angel Awards, as did her delightful picture book for all ages, *Annika's Secret Wish*. Beverly and her husband have three grown children and one grandchild and make their home in the Colorado foothills.

August 9, 1947

Dear Jonas,

Honestly, you spoil me! I've saved up a whole handful of your letters, and only a few months have passed since you left for Ohio. It's all I can do to keep from running to the kitchen calendar yet again to count up the days till your visit for our baptism Sunday next month. How good of your bishop to permit you to join my church district. The Lord above is working all things out for us, ain't so?

Your latest letter arrived today in the mail, and I hurried out to the front porch and curled up in Mamma's wicker chair to read in private. I felt you were right there with me, Jonas. Just the two of us together again.

It's easy to see the many things you describe in Millersburg—the clapboard carpenter's shed where you're busy with the apprenticeship, the big brick house where you eat and sleep, even the bright faces of the little Mellinger children. How wonderful-good the Lord God has been to give you your *heart's ambition, and I am truly happy for you . . . and for us.*

Here in Gobbler's Knob (where you are sorely missed!), there isn't much news, except to say I know of four new babies in a short radius of miles. Even our English neighbors down the road have a new little one. Soon we're all going to Grasshopper Level to lay eyes on your twin baby sister and brother. I have to admit I don't know which I like better—feeding chickens and threshing grain, or bathing and playing with my sweet baby sister, almost three months old. Lydiann is so cuddly and cute, cooing and smiling at us. Dat laughs, saying I'm still his right-hand man. "Let Mamma and your sisters look after our wee one," he goes on. But surely he must know I won't be called Abram's Leah for too many more months now, though I haven't breathed a word. Still, I'm awful sure Mamma and Aunt Lizzie suspect we're a couple. Dat, too, if he'd but accept the truth of our love. Come autumn, the People will no longer think of me as my father's replacement for a son. For that I'm truly happy.

Oh, Jonas, are there other couples like us? In another village or town, hundreds of miles from here or just across the cornfield . . . are there two such close friends who also happen to be this much in love? Honestly, I can't imagine it.

I miss you, Jonas! You seem so far away. . . .

Leah held the letter in her hands, reading what she'd written thus far. Truly, she hesitated to share the one thing that hung most heavily in her mind. Yet Jonas wrote about everything under the sun in *his* letters, so why shouldn't she feel free to do the same? She didn't want to speak out of turn, though.

Should I tell Jonas about the unexpected visit yesterday from his father? she pondered.

Truth was, Peter Mast had come rumbling into the barnyard in his market wagon like a house on fire. In short order, he and *Dat* had gone off to the high meadow for over an hour. Sure did seem awful strange, but when she asked Mamma about it, she was told not to worry her "little head."

What on earth? she wondered. *What business does Cousin Peter have with Dat?*

Part One

♦ ♦ ♦ ♦

The daisy, by the shadow that it casts,
Protects the lingering dewdrop from the sun.

—William Wordsworth

♦ ♦ ♦ ♦

Never praise a sister to a sister,
in the hope of your compliments
reaching the proper ears.

—Rudyard Kipling

Chapter One

Dog days. The residents of Gobbler's Knob had been complaining all summer about the sweltering, brooding sun. Its intensity reduced clear and babbling brooks to a muddy trickle, turning broccoli patches into yellow flower gardens. Meadowlarks scowled at the parched earth void of worms, while variegated red-and-white petunias dropped their ruffled petticoats, waiting for a summertime shower.

Worse still, evening hours gave only temporary pause, as did the dead of night if a faint breeze found its way through open farmhouse windows, bringing momentary relief to restless sleepers. Afternoons were nearly unbearable and had been now for weeks, June twelfth having hit the record high at ninety-seven degrees.

Abram and Ida Ebersol's farmhouse stood at the edge of a great woods as a shelter against the withering heat. The grazing and farmland surrounding the house had a warm and genial scent, heightened by the high temperatures. Abram's seven acres and the neighboring farmland were an enticing sanctuary for a variety of God's smaller creatures—squirrels, birds, chipmunks, and field mice, the latter a good enough reason to tolerate a dozen barn cats.

Not far from the barnyard, hummocks of coarse, panicled grass bordered the mule road near the outhouse, and a well-worn path cut through a high green meadow leading to the log house of Ida's *maidel* sister, Lizzie Brenneman.

Ida, midlife mother to nearly three-month-old Lydiann, along with four teenage girls—Sadie, Leah, and twins Hannah and Mary Ruth—found a welcome reprieve this day in the dampness of the cold cellar beneath the large upstairs kitchen, where Sadie and Hannah were busy sweeping the cement floor, redding up in general. Abram had sent Leah indoors along about three-thirty for a break from the beastly heat. Ida was glad to have plenty of help wiping down the wooden shelves, making ready for a year's worth of canned goods—eight hundred quarts of fruits and vegetables—once the growing season was past. Working together, they lined up dozens of quarts of strawberry preserves and about the same of green beans and peas, seventeen quarts of peaches thus far, and thirty-six quarts of pickles, sweet and dill. Some of the recent canning had been done with Aunt Lizzie's help, as well as that of their close neighbors—the smithy's wife, Miriam Peachey, and daughters, Adah and Dorcas.

The Ebersol girls took their time organizing the jars, not at all eager to head upstairs before long and make supper in the sultry kitchen.

"I daresay this is the hottest summer we've had in years," Mamma remarked.

"And not only here," Leah added. "The heat hasn't let up in Ohio, neither."

Mary Ruth mopped her fair brow. "Your beau must be keepin' you well informed of the weather in Millersburg, *jah?*"

To this Hannah grinned. "We could set the clock by Jonas's letters. Ain't so, Leah?"

Leah, seventeen in two months, couldn't help but smile and much too broadly at that. Dear, dear Jonas. What a wonderful-good letter writer he was, sending word nearly three times a week or so. This had surprised her, really . . . but Mamma always said it was most important for the young man to do the wooing, either by letters or in person. So Jonas was well thought of in Mamma's eyes at least. Not so much Dat's. No, her father held fast to his enduring hope of Leah's marrying the blacksmith's twenty-year-old son, Gideon Peachey—nicknamed Smithy Gid—next farm over.

Sadie stepped back as if to survey her neat row of quart-sized tomato soup jars. "Writin' to Cousin Jonas about the weather can't be all *that* interesting, now, can it?" she said, eyeing Leah.

"We write 'bout lots of things. . . ." Leah tried to explain, sensing one of Sadie's moods.

"Why'd he have to go all the way out to Ohio for his apprenticeship, anyway?" Sadie asked.

Mamma looked up just then, her earnest blue eyes intent on her eldest. "Aw, Sadie, you know the reason," she said.

Sadie's apologetic smile looked forced, and she turned back to her work.

The subject of Jonas and his letters was dropped. Mamma's swift reprimand was followed by silence, and then Leah gave a long, audible sigh.

Yet Leah felt no animosity, what with Sadie seemingly

miserable all the time. Sadie was never-ending blue and seemed as shriveled in her soul as the ground was parched. If only the practice of *rumschpringe*—the carefree, sometimes wild years before baptism—had been abolished by Bishop Bontrager years ago. A group of angry parents had wished to force his hand to call an end to the foolishness, but to no avail. Unchecked, Sadie had allowed a fancy English boy to steal her virtue. *Poor, dear Sadie.* If she could, Leah would cradle her sister's splintered soul and hand it over to the Mender of broken hearts, the Lord Jesus.

She offered a silent prayer for her sister and continued to work side by side with Mamma. Soon she found herself daydreaming about her wedding, thinking ahead to which sisters she might ask to be in her bridal party and whom she and Mamma would ask to be their kitchen helpers. Selecting the hostlers—the young men who would oversee the parking of buggies and the care of the horses—was the groom's decision.

Jonas had written that he wanted to talk over plans for their wedding day when he returned for baptism; he also wanted to spend a good part of that weekend with her, and her alone. But on the following Monday he must return to Ohio to complete his carpentry apprenticeship, "just till apple-pickin' time." His father's orchard was too enormous not to have Jonas's help, come October. And then it wouldn't be long after the harvest and they'd be married. Leah knew their wedding would fall on either a Tuesday or Thursday in November or early December, the official wedding season in Lancaster County. She and Mamma would be deciding fairly soon on the actual date, though since Jonas didn't know precisely when he'd be returning home for good, she had to wait to discuss it with him. Secretly she hoped he would agree to choose an earlier rather than a later date.

As for missing Jonas, the past months had been nearly unbearable. She drank in his letters and answered them quickly, doing the proper thing and waiting till he wrote to her each time. It was painful for her, knowing she'd rejected his idea to spend the summer in close proximity to him out in Holmes County—a way to avoid the dreaded long-distance courtship. But for Sadie's sake, Leah had stayed put in Gobbler's Knob, wanting to offer consolation after the birth and death of her sister's premature baby. In all truth, she had believed Sadie needed her more than Jonas.

But Jonas had been disappointed, and she knew it by the unmistakable sadness in his usually shining eyes. She had told him her mother needed help with the new baby, the main excuse she'd given. Dismayed, he pressed her repeatedly to reconsider. The hardest part was not being able to share her real reason with him. Had Jonas known the truth, he would have been soundly stunned. At least he might have understood why she felt she ought to stay behind, which had nothing to do with being too shy to live and work in a strange town, as she assumed he might think. Most of all, she hoped he hadn't mistakenly believed her father had talked her out of going.

Today Leah was most eager to continue writing her letter the minute she completed chores, hoping to slip away again to her bedroom for a bit of privacy. When she considered how awful hot the upstairs had been these days, she thought she might take herself off to the coolness of the woods, stationery and pen in hand. If not today, then tomorrow for sure.

No one knew it, but here lately she'd been writing to Jonas in the forest. Before her beau had left town, she would never have thought of venturing into the deepest part, only going as far as Aunt Lizzie's house. But she liked being alone with the trees, her pen on the paper, the soft breezes whispering her name . . . and Jonas's.

Growing up, she'd heard the tales of folk becoming disoriented in the leafy maze of undergrowth and the dark burrow of trees. Still, she was determined to go, delighting in being surrounded by all of nature. There a place of solitude awaited her away from her sisters' prying eyes, as well as a place to dream of Jonas. She had sometimes wondered where Sadie and her worldly beau had run off to many times last year before Sadie sadly found herself with child. But when Leah searched the woods, she encountered only tangled brushwood and nearly impassable areas where black tree roots and thick shrubbery caused her bare feet to stumble.

Both she and Sadie had not forgotten what it felt like as little girls to scamper up to Aunt Lizzie's for a playful picnic in her secluded backyard. Thanks to her, they were shown dazzling violets amid sward and stone, demanding attention by the mere look on their floral faces . . . and were given a friendly peep into a robin's comfy nest—"but not *too* close," Aunt Lizzie would whisper. All this and more during such daytime adventures.

But never had Lizzie recommended the girls explore the expanse of woods on their own. In fact, she'd turned ashen on at least one occasion when seven-year-old Leah wondered aloud concerning the things so oft repeated. "*Ach,* you mustn't think of wandering in there alone," Lizzie had replied quickly. Sadie, at the innocent age of nine, had trembled a bit, Leah recalled, her older sister's blue eyes turning a peculiar grayish green. And later Leah had vowed to Sadie she was content never to find out "what awful frightening things are hiding in them there wicked woods!"

Now Leah sometimes wondered if maybe Sadie truly *had* believed the scary tales and taken them to heart, she might not have ended up the ruined young woman she was. At the tender age of nineteen.

At the evening meal Dat sat at the head of the long kitchen table, with doting Mamma to his left. Fourteen-year-old Hannah noticed his brown hair was beginning to gray, bangs cropped straight across his forehead and rounded in a bowl shape around the ears and neck. He wore black work pants, a short-sleeved green shirt, and black suspenders, though his summer straw hat likely hung on a wooden peg in the screened-in porch.

Before eating they all bowed heads simultaneously as the memorized prayer was silently given by each Ebersol family member, except baby Lydiann, who was nestled in Mamma's pleasingly ample arms.

O Lord God heavenly Father, bless us and these thy gifts, which we shall accept from thy tender goodness and grace. Give us food and drink also for our souls unto life eternal, and make us partakers of thy heavenly table through Jesus Christ, thy Son. Amen.

Following the supper blessing, they silently prayed the Lord's Prayer.

Meanwhile, Hannah tried to imagine how the arranged seating pattern might look once Leah was married. She worried her twin also might not remain under Dat's roof much longer, not if she stayed true to her hope of higher education. How Mary Ruth would pull off such a thing, Hannah didn't know, especially now with Elias Stoltzfus making eyes at her.

She gazed at her sisters just now, from youngest to eldest. The table *would* look mighty bare with only five of them present, counting Dat, Mamma and baby, Sadie, and herself. It wouldn't be long till Lydiann could sit in a high chair scooted up close. That would help round things out a bit . . . that and if Mamma were to have another baby or two. Anything was possible, she assumed, since Mamma was approaching forty-three. Not too terribly old for childbearing, because on the Brenneman side of the family, there were plenty of women in the family way clear into their late forties—some even into the early fifties. So who was to say just how many more Ebersol children the Lord God might see fit to send along? Honestly, she wouldn't mind if there were a few more little sisters or brothers, and Mary Ruth would be delighted, too; her twin was ever so fond of wee ones and all.

This made Hannah wonder how many children young and handsome Ezra Stoltzfus might want to have with his wife someday. She could only hope that, at nearly sixteen, he might find her as fetching as she thought *he* was. Here lately she was mighty sure he had taken more of a shine to her, which was right fine. Of course, now, he'd have to be the one to pursue her once she turned courting age. She wouldn't be flirting her way into a boy's heart like some girls. Besides, she wasn't interested in attracting a beau that way. She wanted a husband who appreciated her femininity, a man who would love her for herself, for *who* she was, not for attractiveness alone.

Hours after supper, alone in their bedroom, Leah offered to brush Sadie's waist-length hair. "I could make loose braids if you want," she said.

Sadie nodded halfheartedly, seemingly preoccupied. Leah tried not to stare as Sadie settled down on a chair near the mirrored dresser. Yet her sister looked strangely different. Sadie's flaxen locks tumbled down over her slender back and shoulders, and the glow from the single oil lamp atop the dresser cast an ivory hue on her normally pale cheeks, making them appear even more ashen. A shadow of herself.

Standing behind Sadie, she brushed out the tangles from the long workday, then finger combed through the silken hair, watching tenderly all the while in the mirror. Sadie's fragile throat and chin were silhouetted in the lamp's light, her downcast eyes giving her countenance an expression of pure grief.

Truly, Leah wanted to spend time with Sadie tonight, though it meant postponing the rest of her letter to Jonas. Tomorrow she would finish writing her long letter to him— head up to the woods to share her heart on paper.

She and Sadie had dressed for bed rather quickly,

accompanied by their usual comments, speaking in quiet tones of the ordinary events of the day, of having especially enjoyed Mamma's supper of barbecued chicken, scalloped potatoes with cheese sauce, fried cucumbers, lima beans, and lemon bars with homemade ice cream for dessert.

But now this look of open despair on Sadie's face caused Leah to say softly, "I think about him, too."

"Who?" Sadie whispered, turning to look up at her.

"Your baby . . . my own little nephew gone to heaven." Leah's throat tightened at the memory.

"You do, sister?"

"Oh, ever so much."

Neither of them spoke for a time, then Leah said, "What must it be like for you, Sadie? Ach, I can't imagine your grief."

Sadie was lost in her own world again. She moaned softly, leaning her head back for a moment. "I would've let him sleep right here, ya know, in a little cradle in this very room," she whispered. "I would have wanted to raise him like a little brother to all of us—you, Hannah, and Mary Ruth. Lydiann, too."

If Sadie's baby *had* lived, the disgrace on the Ebersol name would have been immense. But Sadie didn't need to be reminded of that at the moment.

Gently finishing up with her sister's hair, Leah began brushing her own, letting it hang long and loose, down past her waist. But quickly Sadie reached for the brush and said, "Here, it's *your* turn, Leah. Let me . . ."

Later, after Sadie had put out the lamp, they continued to talk softly in bed, though now about Mamma's plans to visit the Mast cousins soon. "I used to think it would be fun to have twins," Sadie said. "What about you?"

"If I could simply play with them all day, maybe so. But to cook and clean and garden, and everythin' else a mother must do, well . . . I just don't know how I'd manage."

"Oh, Leah, you're too practical, compared to me."

Leah had to smile at that. "I guess we *are* different that-away."

After a lull in their conversation, Sadie brought up the snide remark she'd made earlier in the day. "Honestly, I didn't mean to taunt you about writin' to Jonas," she said. "It was wrong of me."

"'Tis not such a bad thing to write about the weather, jah?"

Sadie lay still next to her. "I'm thinking a girl oughta write whatever she pleases to a beau."

Whatever she pleases . . .

Inwardly Leah sighed. Wasn't that Sadie's biggest problem? Doing whatever she pleased had nearly destroyed her young life.

In the past Leah and Sadie had been like two pole beans on a vine, growing up under the same roof together.

What's happened to us? she wondered. Tender moments like tonight's were few and far between.

Sadie rested her head on the feather pillow just so, being careful not to muss her pretty braids. Tomorrow her hair bun would be a fairly wavy one, something Mamma wouldn't take too kindly to. Neither would Dat if he happened to notice. But Leah's fingers and the gentle brush on her hair had soothed her greatly. Sometimes it felt like old times, as if nothing had changed. A fond return to their friendlier days of sisterhood when they had shared every detail of each other's lives.

Her chin trembled and tears sprang to her eyes. Leah had always been a true and compassionate sister, but even more dear this summer. Forfeiting her own desire to spend time with Jonas, Leah had stayed home to comfort *her*.

Turning over, she fought hard to compose herself, lest she be heard sniffling again tonight. She did not pray her silent rote prayers. The desire to do so had long since left. She honestly believed the Lord God had seen fit to take away her tiny son instead of allowing her to love a baby conceived in sin, and the thought made her heart cold with aching.

Yet nearly every night—in a dream—she was with her own wee babe, who was ever so alive. And she and Derry were still desperately in love, sometimes even married, and always completely taken with their new little one, holding him . . . cooing baby talk at him.

Alas, upon waking each morning, Sadie was hit yet again with the ugly, hard truth. She had been punished for the sin of youthful lust. More than a hundred times she had recalled that hideous night, how Dr. Henry Schwartz had kindly said he would "take care" of the baby's remains. Now she regretted there was not even a small burial plot under the shade of ancient trees. Not a simple, respectable grave marker had been given her child, no grassy spot to visit in the People's cemetery, where she could grieve openly beneath a wide blue sky . . . where she could lie down under a tree and let her body rest hard against the earth. Her precious son had come into the world much too early, with "no breath in him," as the doctor had sadly pronounced.

Sometimes during the daylight hours it almost seemed as if the birth itself had never occurred, though she lived with a gnawing emptiness that threatened to choke her. Not having a place to mark the date and the event made the memory of that dark April night ofttimes shift in her mind, even distort itself. Sadie was back and forth about the whole thing—some days she treasured the memory of her first love; at other times she despised Derry for what he'd done to her.

Often she would stop what she was doing, painfully aware of a newborn's whimper. Was her imagination playing tricks? She would look around to see where her baby might be. Could Lydiann's frequent crying trigger this? She didn't know, yet the alarming sense that her baby still lived persisted no matter where she went these days—to Preaching service, to Adah and Dorcas Peachey's house, or to any number of Ebersol and Mast cousins' homes. The lingering feeling haunted her through every daylight hour, as acute as it was bewildering.

In spite of her depression, Sadie tried to look to the future, hoping someday she might have another baby to love, one whose father loved her enough to marry her in the first place. One with no connection to the Gobbler's Knob grapevine and who had no inkling of her wild days. Yet to meet a nice, eligible Amishman like that she would have to leave home, abandoning everything dear to her. It would mean enduring the shun.

The only other choice she had was a kneeling repentance

before the church brethren, but how could that ever solve her problems? It would never bring her baby back, nor Derry— neither one. Repenting could guarantee her only one thing: a lonely and miserable life.

Chapter Two

Leah hadn't realized before just how vulnerable she felt walking through the tunnel of trees that comprised much of the hillock. Even in the full sun of late morning, the light filtering through the webbing of leaves and branches seemed to die away the farther she headed into the woods.

Her best stationery folded neatly and pen in hand, she plodded onward, hoping to rediscover the same grassy spot where she'd spent a sun-dappled hour a few days ago. Beneath the feathery shade of a rare and beautiful thornless honey locust tree, she had written one of her love letters to Jonas. Never once did she think she'd have such difficulty finding the exact location a second time, so lovely it had been. Yet with hundreds of trees towering overhead, confusing her, how could she?

At the moment she thought the sun had set prematurely over distant green hills, she came upon a most interesting sight. She stopped in her tracks and wriggled her toes in the mossy path. "Well, what is this?" she whispered.

There, in a small clearing, a tiny shanty stood, though just barely. In all truth, it was leaning slightly to the left, and as she stepped back to take in the strange place, she could see it was quite old and in dire need of repair. Walking gingerly around its perimeter, she decided the wood shack was probably safe enough to enter. She did so and quickly, too, because the wind had suddenly come up, blowing hard from the north with an edge to it.

The sky *was* growing darker now, even as she pushed hard against the rickety door and hurried inside. Much to her surprise, she found a rather cozy, if untidy, room with exposed plank walls and overhead beams. Several wooden benches were scattered round, the only places to sit. A waist-high, makeshift counter stood in the back, along with a metal trash can. Still, nothing inside really hinted at what purpose the shack served.

Placing her writing paper down on one of the benches, she stood in the center of the little room and curiously looked around. It was in need of a good redding up, as Mamma would say. Both Mamma and Lizzie required cleanliness in all things, and had they come with her today, they would have immediately set to work picking up the paper debris and whatnot littering the floor. Never mind that the shack wasn't part of someone's house or barn; it needed some tending to. Even Mamma's potting shed was far neater.

Going to stand at the window, she leaned on the ledge and looked out at the wind beginning to whip through the shrubbery, bending the trees something fierce. She decided she might as well stay put for the time being, what with a storm rustling things up so. Not that she would complain about a blustery rain shower—not since the Good Lord had allowed this heat wave to encompass the region. Thirsty crops would drink up a downpour like this in short order.

She was ever so glad for even this unsteady shelter. The rain intensified, hammering wildly on the ramshackle roof. Settling down on a bench, Leah picked up where she'd left off with her letter to Jonas, putting her pen to the cream-colored paper.

There's one thing I should tell you in case you hear it through the grapevine. (I hope you won't feel bad about this.) Here lately I've had to help my father outdoors more than ever, since Dawdi John's hip gave out a few days ago. It's a pity seeing Mamma's father suffer. My sisters and I take our turns keeping him company, as does Aunt Lizzie. Sometimes to help Mamma, I take him over to the village doctor, Henry Schwartz, who's as kind as he can be.

As for working alongside Dat again, I've always known I was meant for the soil. Called to it, really. And once you and I are married, Dat will simply have to hire some extra help. Soon I'll be tending my own vegetable and flower gardens and cooking and keeping house for you while you build oak tables and chairs in your carpenter's shop nearby. We'll be happy as larks!

By the way, there's a small house with a For Rent sign in the front yard less than a mile from here—set back a ways from the road, even has an outbuilding on the property. Maybe Dat and I will go see about it if you agree we should.

I'll send this off right quick, then wait eagerly for your next letter.

All my love,
Your faithful Leah

She reread the letter, then folded the stationery. Leaning back, she stretched her arms and noticed a leak in the highest peak of the roof. Within seconds the droplets turned to a trickle; then a near-steady silver stream intruded upon her refuge against the cloudburst. Not a bucket was in sight, only the trash can overflowing with refuse. She searched for something else to catch the water but was startled to hear running footsteps outdoors and rushed to the window to look.

What's Aunt Lizzie doing out in this? she wondered.

The door to the shanty flew open, and there stood Mamma's younger sister soaked clean through to the skin. Lizzie's face turned instantly pale upon seeing Leah. "Well, I never—"

"Hurry and come in out of the squall, *Aendi!*"

The brunette woman leaned hard against the door, shoving out the wind and rain. "What on earth are *you* doin' here?"

"Oh, I'd hoped to find a comfortable spot under a tree somewhere . . . before the rain was makin' down so suddenly." She glanced over at her letter. "Caught me by surprise, really."

Lizzie nodded her head. "Seems the woods have a climate all their own, ain't so?"

Leah knew how much her aunt, even at thirty-five, enjoyed exploring the forest—truly, Lizzie's own backyard. Drawn to small woodland creatures, Lizzie often amused Leah and her sisters with animal-related stories. Leah sometimes wondered how it could be that Aunt Lizzie seemed so at home in the very woods she'd always warned against, knowing the name of each tall and dark tree at first glance. Lizzie's heart was as tender as the petal blossoms she cherished, and she doted on her nieces beyond all reason.

Outside, the rain was spilling fast over the eaves in elon-gated droplets, like the delicate, oval pearls Leah had seen on the bare neck of a worldly English woman in a Watt & Shand's department store newspaper ad. But inside, the stream from the unseen hole in the roof had taken up a rhythm all its own, predictable and annoying.

"Do you think you could help me find one particular tree if I described it? I mean, after the rain stops."

Aunt Lizzie smiled, pulling on the soaked-through purple sleeve that clung to her arm. Her long black apron and prayer cap were also sopping wet. "Which tree's that, honey-girl?"

"One where the grass is soft and thick and grows right up to the trunk. I must admit to thinkin' of the forest floor beneath it as my piece of earth." She went on to tell about the curious honey locust tree. "It has no thorns. And if ever I could find it once more, I believe I might somehow mark it so I could return there again and again."

"Oh . . .'twas a wonderful-*gut* place to daydream, jah?"

"Not dream so much as write a newsy letter," she con-fessed. "My sisters are awful nosy sometimes. They'd just love to know what I'm writin' to Jonas."

"Well . . . so *that's* what brought you here." Lizzie seemed somehow relieved as she spoke. She went and sat down on the closest bench, and Leah did the same.

"I never knew this place existed."

"Well, I daresay it's 'bout to come a-tumblin' down. Which, if you ask me, might be a gut thing."

"Oh, I don't know. Maybe with a little sweepin' and pickin' up it could be a right nice spot to—"

"No . . . no." Aunt Lizzie shook her head, turning to face the side window. "Best leave it for the turkey shooters, come Thanksgiving."

With Lizzie's quick remark, Leah felt she understood. So . . . the lean-to had been built long ago to provide shelter for small-game hunters. Nothing more.

"Since we're up here away from everyone," Leah said softly, "I can tell you I'm terribly worried 'bout Sadie."

Aunt Lizzie stared hard at the floor. "Jah, I fret over her, too."

"Must be somethin' we can do."

Aunt Lizzie nodded, removing her wet prayer bonnet. "I have to say I do miss her perty smile."

"And I think Mamma does, too."

"A cheerful countenance comes from the joy of the Lord God rising up from one's heart."

Leah wasn't surprised at this remark. Aunt Lizzie often spoke of the Holy One of Israel as if He were a close friend or relative. "What more can we do?" she asked.

"Nothin' short of haulin' Sadie off to the preacher or the deacon, I s'pose." Aunt Lizzie's face dropped with her own words. " 'Tis awful frustratin'."

"Honestly . . . I never would've promised to keep mum if I'd thought Sadie would remain stubborn for this long."

For a time Lizzie was silent. "Your sister would never trust you again. And she might not forgive me, neither."

"We can't just let Sadie lose her way. Can we, Aunt Lizzie?"

"Indeed. Seems to me somethin's got to break loose here 'fore long. Either that or she'll make a run for it."

Leah gasped. "Sadie would leave?"

"I'm afraid it was my idea. Last year I'd suggested a visit to Ohio might do her good, but I fear now she might never return."

Leah felt limp all over. She didn't know what to make of it. Sadie hadn't mentioned a word.

Aunt Lizzie continued. "I pleaded with her to stay put until at least your wedding. Perhaps by then she'll come to her senses. I pray so." She rose and went to the window. "I've talked to her till my breath is nearly all . . . to no avail. Still, I won't stop beseechin' the Lord God heavenly Father for her."

A stark silence followed, and Leah was mindful of the calm outside, as well. The summer shower had passed.

Chapter Three

The ground was soggy beneath their bare feet when Leah and Lizzie left the safety of the hunter's shack to hike down the hill toward home. Birds warbled a chorus of gladness, and the overcast sky steadily brightened as the sun finally succeeded in peeking out of the slow-moving gray clouds.

Lizzie put her nose up and sniffed. "Does the air smell sweet to you after a shower?"

Leah inhaled the clean, mintlike scent. "We could stand to have moisture like this every single day from now till Jonas and I . . ."

Lizzie offered a gentle smile. "Well, go on, Leah dear. I can keep quiet about your weddin' plans. You can trust me with the day Jonas will take you as his bride."

"Jah, I would, but . . . well," she sputtered a bit.

Lizzie must have sensed the awkwardness and attempted to smooth things over promptly. "What do you 'spect we'll do 'bout all that parched celery, honey-girl? You and your mamma will have a whole houseful of folk to feed at the weddin' feast, with no celery."

Mamma's celery stalks *had* been looking altogether pathetic, what with the intense heat and lack of precipitation, even with the additional hand watering they'd been doing lately.

Leah spoke up. "Maybe Fannie Mast's vegetable patch is farin' better than ours." She could only hope that was true, although with infant twins, Mamma's first-cousin Fannie would be hard-pressed to keep her one-acre garden going without help from daughters Rebekah, sixteen, and Katie, thirteen, and occasionally nine-year-old Martha.

Aunt Lizzie pushed ahead on the unmarked path, Leah following close behind, aware of the People's whispered tittle-tattle surrounding the wedding tradition of serving celery.

Taking a long breath, she held it a moment before letting the air out. "Mamma says it's, uh . . . necessary for the young couple to eat plenty of celery at their weddin' feast."

"For the sake of fruitfulness," Aunt Lizzie replied over her shoulder. "The Lord God put every plant—vegetable, fruit, and herb—on the earth for a purpose. Some have healin' properties, others aid in digestion and, well . . . getting young couples off to a right good start, ya know."

And that was the closet thing to a lesson on the birds and bees she knew she'd be getting from either Aunt Lizzie or Mamma. Of course, Sadie could easily fill her in to high heaven if she chose to, but Leah didn't care to ask. Not the way Sadie had gotten the cart long before the horse. Better to discover such things later, after Leah belonged to Jonas and he to her in the sight of the Lord God.

They had reached the place where something of a me-andering dirt path appeared, descending into a grassy area with less underbrush to tangle one's bare feet. Lizzie's small house was in sight at last, up ahead on the left. This corner of God's green earth had a pungent fragrance, and its pleasantness made Leah suddenly think of Mamma—and an early-morning promise Leah had made. "Ach, I nearly forgot."

Lizzie turned quickly. "Forgot what?"

"Mamma's expectin' me home."

"Well, then, mustn't keep her waitin'...."

Leah glanced at the sky. "We're going to bake up a batch of cherry pies ... then after a bit Dat will be needin' me at milkin' time."

"You'll have to come visit me again soon."

Nodding, she said she would. "Or ... better yet, why don't you come down tonight and have a piece of my pie? I'm determined for it to taste wonderful-gut."

"You'll do just fine. And when your dessert turns out to be ever so delicious, we'll compare notes, jah?"

"Mamma scarcely ever writes down recipes, you know. It's all up here." Leah tapped her head.

"Your mamma's one of the best cooks round here. She takes the cake, now, don't she?" Lizzie said, a hint of sadness in her eyes. Sadie's unwillingness to repent seemed to tinge nearly everything.

Leah hugged her, then broke free and headed on down the mule road toward home, turning briefly to wave to her dear aunt. But Lizzie was already gone.

Ida had been standing at the open window upstairs, having put the baby down for an early afternoon nap. Grateful for the coolness after the rain, she stepped back to allow a breeze into the bedroom. She could clearly see Leah up there in the woods, waving a fond good-bye to Lizzie. Then, here she came, bounding almost deerlike out of the trees as her long skirt swept the damp ground.

What's my sister filling Leah's head with today? she wondered, suspecting the pair had gone walking together, picking wild flowers, making a fuss over every little plant and animal. That was Lizzie's way—always had been. She was bent on soaking up every inch of the woodlands, introducing each of Ida's girls to the vast world of flora and fauna. Sadie had been spending all kinds of time up at Lizzie's during the past few months. Nearly all summer, really, until just the past week or so. More recently, Lizzie had singled Leah out.

She supposed Lizzie had every right to spend her spare time with whomever she pleased, but it irked her to no end. Truly, she wished Lizzie might keep her nose out of Abram's and her family's business. Lizzie and Peter Mast both. They'd all lived this long just fine. Some things were best left unsaid.

She exhaled sharply and headed downstairs, refusing to dwell on her fears for another minute. In the kitchen she laid out the flour, sugar, and all the necessary ingredients for the mouthwatering pies. As she did she thought ahead to the next Preaching service to be held here this weekend. Two hundred and more church members would come from a four-square-mile radius to gather where Abram's own father—the respected Bishop Ebersol—had raised this stone house as a shelter for his family and as a house of worship amongst the People. Hopefully, by then Lizzie's urgency could be put to rest. Ida made a mental note to talk with Abram about it once again.

Sadie, with a bucket of soapy water in hand, set about to wash down the bedroom walls, helping Mamma cleanse the house as was their custom, creating a holy place for the Sunday Preaching. "Might as well get a head start on some heavy cleanin'," she'd told Mamma at the noon meal.

" 'Tis a gut thing to make hay while the sun shines, too," Mamma had said in passing, somewhat inattentive.

Sadie was relieved to have the afternoon alone. Her twin sisters were downstairs dusting, sweeping, washing floors, and whatnot. These days it was best on her nerves to have absolute solitude, though that was next to impossible with seven people in the house. She had been suffering such a peculiar dull ache up and down her forearms, confiding it only to Aunt Lizzie earlier this summer.

What a surprise to discover Lizzie's remedy was to carry around a five-pound sack of potatoes, much the size of a wee babe. Lo and behold, when she did so, Sadie found it truly eased her pain. Accordingly, she clasped the potatoes quite often and ever so gently while spending time at Lizzie's away from Mamma's eyes.

Aside from frequent walks up to Lizzie's place, Sadie preferred to spend her "alone" hours cleaning for Mamma or hoeing and weeding the vegetable garden, along with visits next door to the *Dawdi Haus* to chat with Dawdi John.

Today she wholeheartedly threw herself into her work, stepping back now and again to see if she'd covered every square inch of the light gray walls. The bedroom windows were next on her list of things to do. She'd already decided to wash them single-handedly. No need asking for help from Hannah and Mary Ruth, not when they had plenty to keep them occupied downstairs. As for Leah, she'd hurried out the back door and headed up toward the mule road, as if going to visit Aunt Lizzie.

But Sadie was *schmaerder*. It didn't take much effort to figure out Leah these days. All of them assumed she was going off to the woods to write to her beau. Just so she kept her promise and didn't reveal Sadie's wild rumschpringe to Jonas Mast. Both Leah and Lizzie had vowed to keep quiet, but Sadie had heard recently that her former sidekick, Naomi Kauffman, was said to be weary of flirting with the world. She was even taking baptismal instruction right along with Leah, preparing to join church. Of all things!

Sadie didn't appreciate Naomi setting herself up as "holier than thou," which she certainly seemed to think she was here lately. And why? Just because she'd been far more careful than Sadie—or plain lucky—and hadn't gotten caught. Besides, Naomi's unexpected turn had more to do with Luke Bontrager, who was awful sweet on her, than most anything else. Of this Sadie was fairly sure.

If Naomi *was* to become the bride of the bishop's grandson, she had some fast confessing to do. Now, wasn't that a howdy-do? It was all fine and dandy for Naomi to make amends, turn her life around, and plan for a future as an upstanding young woman, so long as she kept Sadie out of it. Hopefully, Naomi didn't know the half about Sadie's fling, but what *did* she know? And if she started spilling the beans, what then? After all, Naomi had continued to see Derry's friend Melvin Warner after that first meeting at the Strasburg café. Derry had told Sadie this on several occasions, and she assumed it was true.

When Sadie was finished with the three upstairs bedrooms, she moved to the hallway and commenced to do the same—washing down walls, scrubbing mopboards, and mashing a few stray spiders as she went. Her thoughts flew to Aunt Lizzie as she worked. The past few weeks, Sadie had been discouraged. Not only had her aunt changed her mind and become adamant about her staying put, Lizzie was now saying she didn't think Sadie needed a change of scenery after all.

"Don't you see?" Lizzie had insisted. "Your father's covering and blessing are mighty important. If you would but confess to Preacher and the membership, you'd be pardoned by the People." Aunt Lizzie went on to quote her favorite Scripture. " 'Godly sorrow worketh repentance to salvation . . . but the sorrow of the world worketh death.' "

Obliged to listen, Sadie felt hot under the bonnet when Aunt Lizzie talked so pointedly.

Chapter Four

Too warm to stay indoors a second longer, Mary Ruth stepped outside for a breather on the back stoop. King, the German shepherd puppy, came scampering across the yard to greet Leah. Her skirt was mud spattered as she stooped to pet the dog, a curious yet kindly gift from Gid Peachey last spring. Observing this, Mary Ruth smiled as Leah hurried toward the house, the dog panting as he followed close on her heels.

"Hullo, Mary Ruth. I missed you!" Leah said.

Mary Ruth hoped Leah wouldn't go running off to help Dat. Not when she had a question to ask. "Didja get caught in the rain?"

Leah's face reddened. "No . . . I found shelter."

Sighing, Mary Ruth decided not to beat round the bush. "Does it bother you that Dat doesn't approve of you marryin' Jonas?"

Leah seemed a bit startled by the question, but she met Mary Ruth's gaze with a gentle smile. "Does it bother *you*?"

Pausing there, Mary Ruth was aware of Leah's sweetness

once again . . . her fine hazel eyes with tiny gold flecks, the dark curve of her long lashes, the way her expression seemed to radiate trustfulness, even goodness. Yet Leah was intent on ignoring Dat's wishes in order to become Jonas Mast's bride. None of it added up.

"Doesn't bother me in the least," she replied at last. "I'm just tryin' to understand."

Leah burst into a full smile. "That's what makes you so special. You have a gift of understanding, I daresay."

Mary Ruth couldn't help herself; she actually choked a little and tears welled up. "Much good that does me . . ."

Leah was staring now, wearing a concerned frown. "What is it, Mary Ruth? Why are you cryin'?"

"Just thinkin', I guess." She forged ahead and stuck her neck out. "I hope you'll follow your heart. Have the courage to marry the boy you love."

Leah's eyelids fluttered. "Didja think I might not?"

Turning quickly, Mary Ruth looked over her shoulder, toward the barn. "Dat, well . . . he's made it mighty clear here lately that it's Gideon Peachey who's the right beau for you. He's said as much to all of us."

"Dat has?"

"He said 'if only Leah knew Gid the way I know him.' Things like that. And he said he was weary of keepin' it to himself any longer—after these many years."

"Jah, I know *that* to be true, the years he's stewed about it."

She felt she ought to say one more thing. "Mamma's not so much in favor of Gid, though. Just so you know."

"You sure?"

"Mamma prefers Jonas, seems to me." Now she struggled to keep a straight face. "She thinks your children will be mighty handsome if you marry into the Mast family."

"And why's that?"

"Jonas has a right fine nose. Gut-lookin' all round, he is." Mary Ruth sighed. "I don't mean to say Smithy Gid *isn't* handsome. He's just more rugged lookin', I guess you could say. Whereas Jonas is—"

"Both handsome *and* strong—in body and mind? Is that what you mean?" Leah had her now, and her sister's eyes shone as if with glee. Sadie and Mamma sometimes grew weary of Mary Ruth's too-talkative nature, but Leah never seemed to mind.

Leah continued. "When it comes to certain things, no matter how defiant a choice might seem to others, if you know in your heart you were meant for somethin'—or someone—then, I believe, 'tis best to be true to that."

"You mean it?"

Leah nodded. "I've seen how you throw yourself into your schoolwork. You're a scholar, ain't? When the time comes, you'll have the courage to make the right decision. You'll simply have to put your hand to the plow and refuse to look back."

Mary Ruth's emotions threatened to overtake her again. "You're a true sister and friend, Leah," she managed through her tears.

"Always remember that." Leah smiled, reaching to hug her.

◆

Sadie headed toward the kitchen for a glass of cold water, so awful hot it was upstairs. But before she stepped foot in there, she happened to overhear Leah talking to Mamma as they baked pies. Leah was saying she and Aunt Lizzie had taken shelter in a little hunter's shack on the hillock that morning. "The place was old and run-down like nothing you've ever seen," Leah said softly. "Right peculiar, I must say. Up there in the middle of nowhere, but it kept us safe and dry till the rain passed."

Sadie felt her throat constrict. Anguished memories rushed back and she was helpless to stop them. For all she cared, the shanty was good for one thing and only one: kindling.

Leah was frowning at Sadie now, catching her eye. "What? Did I say somethin' wrong?"

Himmel! she thought, not realizing how far she'd inched herself into the kitchen. There she was, standing in the doorway listening, evidently with a pained expression on her face. "Aw . . . no," she gasped. "I guess I'm surprised both you and Aunt Lizzie got caught in such a cloudburst, that's all. Usually, Lizzie can tell by smellin' the air if rain's a-comin'." She paused momentarily, then—"Looks to me like the bottom of your hem got awful grimy on your way back home."

Leah looked down at herself and seemed to agree she was in need of a good scrubbing. "But it won't do to wash up and change clothes now." She thanked Mamma for such helpful pointers with the pies, saying she hoped they tasted as good as they smelled, then scurried off toward the barn.

Sadie briefly followed after Leah. She stood in the open back door, staring out through the screen. She caught a glimpse of the bottom of her sister's bare feet as she ran to the barn. Milking the cows was something Sadie knew little about. Sure, she'd helped Dat here and there occasionally, but only in a pinch. Yet with Leah's wedding coming up soon, Sadie was worried sick she might have to take her tomboy sister's place outdoors with Dat. She was fond enough of her father, but there was no way she was willing to do the kind of dirty work Leah did—and cheerfully at that. Besides, *she* ought to have been marrying first.

Mamma broke the stillness. "Sadie, would you mind changin' Lydiann's diaper?"

She gasped inwardly. "Aw . . . must I, Mamma? I still have chores to finish. . . ." Her legs felt as rubbery as the inflatable tires on tractors, so forbidden by the bishop.

Mamma appeared to lapse into a gray mood, and her milky blue eyes seemed to look right through Sadie . . . to the dark of her heart. "Why is it you're not so lovin' toward your baby sister anymore?" Mamma's voice wavered. "When she was brand-new, you were ever so helpful then."

Back in May, when Lydiann was first born, Mamma had singled Sadie out as the elder sister most mindful of the new little one. At the time, she'd felt her mother truly suspected something was amiss and was hoping to force a confession. So Sadie had gone along with helping to care for Lydiann, hoping to hide the shocking truth.

Now, though, she went out of her way to avoid babies and the expectant mothers in the church community, especially during the common meals that followed Preaching service every other Sunday. At work frolics she sat on the opposite end of the quilting frame from the pregnant women. It just didn't seem fair other women were able to carry *their* babies to full-term. What was wrong with her?

Scarcely could she stand to be near Mamma anymore. She felt sure her mother was hovering and ready to report her to the ministers. If so, she would be required to offer repentance. *"Obey or be shunned"*—the People's endless refrain.

"A quick diaper change can't hurt none." Mamma's voice jolted her out of her musings.

"In a minute." She reached for a stack of plates to set the table.

When Mamma's back was turned, Sadie hurried outdoors, pretending to walk to the outhouse. She knew Dat and Leah were out milking and, more than likely, could observe her if they were but looking.

Once she reached the outhouse, she turned abruptly and ran to the meadow, dodging cow pies as she picked her way barefoot through the pastureland, muttering to herself all the while.

Kicking at a clump of wild grass, Sadie raised her head to the sky, studying the clouds and the way the sun shone too hard on the tin roof. Sniffling, she brushed away hot tears. *I'm the one black sheep of the family,* she thought.

The far-off clanging of the dinner bell gave her pause. She was sorely tempted to keep on walking, never to return. Simply walk away, just as she planned in due time.

Folding her arms tightly, she headed back toward the barnyard and the house, wondering which was worse— Mamma's disapproving mood . . . or her own restless heart?

Chapter Five

The liquid warble of several wrens out near the milk house awakened Leah. She hurried out of bed, whispering "time to wake up" to Sadie, who was still sleeping soundly. But Sadie only groaned and turned over, covering her head with the summer quilt.

Something was beginning to weigh on Leah's mind, and she wanted to talk with Sadie about it. It had to do with Naomi Kauffman and her outspoken new beau, Luke Bontrager, who had shown a different side than she'd expected. Especially here recently after the baptismal candidates had met with Preacher Yoder and Deacon Stoltzfus for the required instruction. Naomi had actually seen the error of her ways, making things right with the Lord God and Preacher Yoder— a mighty good thing. A girl just never knew when she might breathe her last lungful of air. Too many teenagers had lost their lives racing trains with horse and buggy or in farming accidents. Being Plain could be downright dangerous sometimes.

The deacon and the preacher had been admonishing them

mostly in High German that day, discussing at length the eighteen articles of faith from the Dordrecht Confession. Leah had a hard time understanding what was being taught, let alone how she should respond to the questions. She was brave enough to speak up—much to Luke's surprise—to ask if it would be all right for her parents to help her read the baptism chapter found in Matthew's gospel. Well, Luke had arched his eyebrows. "You ain't *studyin'* the Scriptures, now, are you?" he whispered her way.

"My father reads the German Bible to us in Amish each night, is all," she'd answered, not one bit ashamed. Besides, Dat's reading the Scripture aloud was far different than analyzing God's Word like some folk outside the community of the People were known to do. She might have added that Mamma often prayed without putting in many "thee's" and "thou's," like some Mennonites they knew who called upon the name of the Lord God. But by then she was cautious and didn't dare say that much. It wasn't anybody's concern how Dat and Mamma went about passing on the faith to their children, was it?

In the end Deacon Stoltzfus said he was in favor of Leah getting help from her parents, that it was all right for her to ponder these Scriptures—it wasn't as though they would be having an out-and-out Bible study like some church groups. "Your father can read you Matthew chapter twenty-eight, verse nineteen, as well as Mark chapter sixteen, verse sixteen . . . in English or Amish, either one. 'Tis long past time all you young folk understand fully the covenant making," said the deacon.

Preacher Yoder may have been less enthusiastic but gave

his blessing on Deacon's remarks. "Go ahead, Leah, speak with your father . . . if you have any questions about your kneeling vow a'tall."

Naomi had looked mighty eager to take Leah aside, which she did out in the barnyard after baptismal instruction. There Naomi had whispered to Leah that Luke had begun courting her, and to keep it quiet. "'S'okay for you to tell Sadie I'm getting married, though," Naomi said unexpectedly. "She might be a bit surprised. . . ."

Which would have been the end of it if Adah Peachey hadn't come walking up to the two of them and said, "Hullo, Leah . . . Naomi."

For a while they stood there engaging in small talk. Then Naomi lowered her voice yet again, saying she'd like nothing better than if both Leah and Adah would consider being in her bridal party. Leah waited, expecting Naomi to correct her self on the spot and say she in fact meant *Sadie*—surely she would. But the uncomfortable silence was broken by Adah, who, all smiles, said she'd be right happy to be one of the bridesmaids.

"Well, Leah?" Naomi turned to her. "What about you?"

"I'm thinkin' maybe you'd want to be askin' Sadie, jah?"

"No, I asked *you*," Naomi replied, big eyes shining.

"Then, I'd like to talk it over with my sister, seein' as how you and she—well, you're close friends and all."

"Used to be."

The words had sounded so final, it pained Leah to remember them. *"Used to be."*

Now here she sat in the quietude of her bedroom, with Sadie beginning to stretch, there in the bed. Waiting for her sister to rise and shine, she felt quite uneasy. She let a few more minutes pass; then she spoke at last. "I want to ask you somethin', Sadie."

Suddenly she felt it might be a mistake to address the touchy issue. Yet it was better now than for Sadie to hear it elsewhere. "How would you feel if I stood up with Naomi on her weddin' day?" she blurted.

"That's up to you" came the quick and sleepy answer.

"You don't mind, then?"

"Not any more than I mind you goin' to her weddin' at all."

Leah sighed. "Well, aren't *you* goin'?"

"Not if I can help it." Sadie sat up in bed. "Friends and relatives are expected to attend the weddin'. I daresay I'm neither of those to Naomi."

Leah paused, then asked gently, "Can you say . . . uh, what happened between you and Naomi?"

"She has no business bein' baptized, is all." Sadie turned her head and was staring out the window.

"Then why do you s'pose Naomi's goin' ahead with it?"

"One reason, I 'spect."

"To marry Luke?"

Sadie clammed up, and Leah went to the wooden wall hooks next to the dresser and removed her brown choring dress from a hanger. Standing there, she felt awkward, as if she didn't truly belong in the shared room. " 'Tis a sorry situation, Naomi's . . . if what you say is true."

"Why must you be judgin' everyone?" Sadie snapped.

Leah was startled at her sister's biting words, but the conversation ended abruptly with Mamma's knock at the door.

"Time to begin the day, girls" came her soft call.

Hastily, they dressed in their choring dresses and brushed their hair into low buns at the nape of their necks. Then they put on their devotional caps and hurried downstairs to help— Sadie with kitchen duties and Leah with the first milking of the day.

That evening when Leah and Sadie were preparing to dress for bed, Sadie brought the matter up again. "You surely think the same of me as you do of Naomi," she said. "Ain't so, Leah?"

Leah wasn't prepared for this, even though Sadie's accusation—*"judgin' everyone"*—had echoed in her ears all day. "You know by now what I think," she said, getting up the nerve. "I think God will forgive anyone for sin. And so would Mamma. She's all for you, Sadie. She'd forgive you if you'd but ask."

"Mamma might, but not Dat."

"Ach, Sadie, how can you say that? If you went through the correct channels, bowed your knee in contrition before the People—"

"Might be best to save your breath, Leah."

Sadie's comment pained her. She feared her sister was farther from the Lord God and His church than ever before. And for this Leah felt truly sad.

Sadie continued to seethe with anger as she picked up the lantern at the back door and walked out into the night, past the well pump and through the barnyard. The moon wore a silver-white halo, the sky black as pitch. She might've used the chamber bucket under the bed, but she needed to breathe some fresh air. The night was exceedingly warm, despite the afternoon shower, maybe more so because of the humidity that hung like a shroud over the farm. Both she and Leah had thrown off the covers before ever settling into bed. Of course, it could be the harsh silence between them that was making Sadie feel warmer than usual. Even her fingertips were hot as she walked to the wooden outhouse.

Who did Leah think she was, ordering her elder sister around? All this fussing between them had left Sadie emotionally drained. To think her best friend, Naomi, had bypassed her and asked Leah to be a bridesmaid, of all things! Well, she hoped not to be anywhere near Gobbler's Knob by the time Naomi and Luke tied the knot.

On the return trip from the outhouse she made a stop in the kitchen to wash her hands and eat some graham crackers and drink a glass of milk. That done, she felt a little better and headed back upstairs only to discover that, lo and behold, Dat and Mamma were still awake and having a discussion in their room, behind closed doors. Sadie had never encountered this in all her born days because her parents were often the first ones to head for bed, especially with Lydiann waking up at three-thirty for her early-morning feeding.

Dat was doing the talking. "No . . . no, I tend to disagree."

"We ain't never goin' to see eye to eye—"

"Have you thought it over but good, Ida? *Have* you?" Dat

interrupted. "Do you realize what an upheaval this'll cause under our roof?"

"Indeed, I have. And I believe . . . if you don't mind me bein' so blunt, it's time we tell her."

Sadie froze in place. What on earth were her parents disputing? *Tell whom? Tell what?*

The conversation ceased altogether with Mamma's pointed remark, and Sadie assumed her parents had decided to retire for the night. As for herself, she was wide awake and crept back down the steps, hurried through the kitchen, then let herself out the back door without making a sound. Sitting on the back stoop, she stared up at a thousand stars.

"Have you thought it over but good?" Dat's words came back to haunt her. *"What an upheaval . . ."*

She slapped her hands over her ears, pressing tightly against her head . . . hoping to halt the memory of what she'd heard. Could it be they had been talking about her?

King came wandering over from the barn and sat on the concrete next to her, his long black nose pointed toward the moon. She reached down to rub his furry neck. "Something terrible's a-brewin'," she whispered, trembling now. "I feel it awful heavy in the air."

Chapter Six

Mary Ruth finished hoeing and weeding her patch of the family garden Thursday, along with the girls' separate charity garden. Standing up, she arched her back and attempted to relieve her aching muscles. Gazing at the sky, she noticed a bank of clouds drift across the blue at a mercilessly slow pace and felt a strange connection to them. Ever so restless, she despised the slow-poke pace of her days waiting for school bells to ring. In a little over a week!

With both her and Hannah off at school, Mamma would indeed suffer with less help around the house. Still, the law was the law, and Mary Ruth was happy to be required to attend through eighth grade. In one more year she'd be eligible for high school. The thought gave her chills of both delight and dread. She held no hope of Dat ever giving her the go-ahead; it would be next to impossible to obtain his blessing. He would simply quote the Good Book to her if she were brazen enough to share with him her deepest longing. "'For the wisdom of this world is foolishness with God'"— this said with Bible in hand. And that would be the end of their discussion, though sadly, it would never reach the phase of true discussion at all.

Even the term *high school* was not without reproach. It represented high-mindedness and pride, and she'd heard many times growing up that *"self-praise stinks."* Yet what was she to do about the inner craving? Was *she* the only one smitten with the problem amongst the People?

Hannah wandered over, hoe in hand. "What would ya think of goin' to Strasburg with me?"

"To stop by the little gift shop?"

"I have a batch more handkerchiefs to deliver."

"Okay, then we'll go right after lunch. And 'bout the time Mamma and Lydiann are up from a nap, we'll be back home."

Hannah nodded, all smiles. "Just the two of us?"

"Sounds gut to me." Mary Ruth hoped to squeeze in a visit to the public library while Hannah handled her consignment shop transactions. Getting a head start on her studies was heavy on her mind. If she had to, she could easily hide the newly checked-out books under the bed. Hannah could be persuaded not to tell.

It was clear Hannah was already counting the years till she made her covenant with the People and God. Unassuming and on the bashful side, especially around strangers, her sister would make a fine Amish wife and mother someday, which was just as appealing to Mary Ruth as the next girl—getting married and having children, that is. It was the unceasing hankering for books that got so dreadfully in the way. The thought of committing the sum total of her life to the People was troubling at best, and she was grateful to have a few more years till she had to decide one way or the other.

———◆———

"You don't mind if I run across the street right quick . . . when we get to the gift shop?" Mary Ruth asked Hannah as they rode along in the enclosed carriage. She had chosen Dat's faster driving horse of the two, as well as the enclosed family buggy. With the gathering clouds and the increasing possibility of rain, it made good sense.

"Why not just say it outright?" Hannah said softly, almost sadly. "You're goin' to the library."

"Jah."

Hannah sat to her left, eyelids fluttering. "Truth be known, I prefer the summers. And you . . . well, you live for the school year."

"You know me awful gut." She paused, then added, "What do you think Mamma would do if she ever found my library books . . . hidden away?"

"Are you sayin' you honestly can't curb your appetite for readin'?"

"Books are like friends to me. Words come alive on the page."

Shrugging one shoulder slightly, Hannah said nothing.

"I s'pose I'm addicted, 'cause now I've started readin' other books, too," she ventured. "I don't mean *bad* books, don't misunderstand. But I must admit, I like readin' stories—things that are purely made up but that, well . . . *could* happen." She was somewhat hesitant for Hannah's reaction.

"Ach, I don't know what to think" was her twin's dismal reply. "I can accept you readin' geography books, imagining

61

what it's like to travel round the continent and all, but made-up tales?"

Sighing, Mary Ruth wondered how to explain. "Here. This is what readin' stories is like to me. It's findin' a spring in the midst of a barren land. Just when I think I might up and die of thirst, I stumble onto this fresh, cold water, and I'm suddenly given new life 'cause I can—and do—drink to my heart's content."

Now Hannah was beside herself, seemed to Mary Ruth. She was staring down at the buggy floor, eyes blinking and glistening to beat the band.

"Aw, what's a-matter, Hannah?"

"I wish I could understand what you mean. That's all I best be sayin'."

The fact they didn't share a great love for reading was beside the point. Hannah was clearly pained by Mary Ruth's revelation that she was obsessed with books, especially fiction. *I wish I'd never said a word,* she thought.

She leaned over and tipped her head toward her twin's, their white prayer bonnets forming a double heart as the horse pulled them toward Strasburg.

While Mary Ruth hurried across the street to the library, Hannah made a beeline to the gift shop with her basketful of newly embroidered handkerchiefs in hand. Happily, she received her payment from the owner, Frances Brubaker, a short, petite woman in her thirties, Hannah guessed. Then she counted out forty more cotton hankies, a third of which showcased embroidered bumblebees this time. The rest were birds' nests with pale blue eggs nestled inside, and there were tiny baskets of fruit, too—all colors. She had decided it was time to stitch something different than the birds and multi-colored butterflies of the last grouping.

While she was there, two English women came into the store, one more talkative than the other. Both were oohing and aahing over the various items, as if never having laid eyes on "handmade" things, which was the word they kept repeating, and this somewhat reverently. They spotted Hannah near the counter and took an immediate interest, peering over at her several times, unashamed at their curiosity. Each time, though, she had to look away, suffering the same uncontrollable feeling of shyness she had while tending to the roadside stand at home. Truth was, she felt self-conscious most of the time and wished Mary Ruth had stayed by her side, here at the store, instead of running off to her beloved books.

"An Amishwoman with several children in tow came into the shop the other day," Frances addressed her from behind the counter. "She was looking to buy a whole bunch of embroidered hankies. But she specifically requested *cutwork* embroidery, like the one she brought to show me."

Hannah was surprised at this. "What did it look like?"

"Well, it had a dainty emerald-and-gold butterfly sewn into the corner."

"And cutwork, you say?"

Frances nodded. "The customer was very interested in it, said nothing else would do. She said she wants to give a quantity of them away on her son's wedding day . . . that she'd stop by in a month or so. Could you duplicate a hankie like that to sell?"

"Maybe so if I could see it." Hannah found this more

curious than she cared to say. Truth was, she'd made only *one* such cutwork butterfly hankie in her life. *And awful pretty,* if she thought so herself. She'd given it, along with cross-stitched pillowcases, as a gift three years ago to Sadie on her sixteenth birthday. Sadie's reaction had been one of such joy Hannah decided it should remain extra special. Never again would she make the cutwork style on any of her other hankies, either for sale or for gifts, in honor of Sadie's turning courting age.

"I would make most anything else . . . just not a handkerchief like that." She wondered who the woman had been, asking about a handkerchief so surprisingly similar to Sadie's own. But she kept her peace and said no more.

Still, she couldn't stop thinking how peculiar this was and felt a bit crestfallen. *Had someone seen Sadie's special hankie and decided to copy it?* she wondered.

Back in the carriage on the ride home, Mary Ruth sat with her library books balanced on her lap as she attempted to hold the reins.

"How will you get all of them into the house?" Hannah asked, eyeing the books.

"Oh, I'll manage somehow, even if I have to sneak them in two at a time. Meanwhile, why don't you trade places with me?" She handed the reins over to Hannah, who promptly switched to the driver's seat.

They rode along for a time in complete silence. Mary

Ruth was glad to peek into the pages of the first book in her stack, *Uncle Tom's Cabin*. And by the time the horse turned off the narrow road at Rohrer's Mill, the water-powered grist mill, she'd already completed the first chapter. Her heart cried out with compassion for the slave girl Eliza and her handsome young son, Harry. With such strong emotions stirring, she wondered anew how she could ever give up this fascination with the printed page. Could she quickly devour oodles of books to satisfy her appetite, then join church, hoping that the wellspring of joy might linger on through the years, even though she'd never read again? She supposed it was one way to look at the problem, though she'd have to come clean to Preacher Yoder before ever taking her kneeling vow, especially with this new passion for fabricated stories.

She marked the page with her finger, then asked Hannah, "How old do you want to be when you get baptized?"

"Sixteen or so," Hannah said. "Seems to me we oughta join church together."

Just as she thought.

Hannah was quiet for a time, then she said, "If you end up goin' to high school—"

"Oh, I *will* go," Mary Ruth interrupted. "Somehow or other."

"Okay, then, what will you do 'bout Elias Stoltzfus?"

Mary Ruth paused. "I don't think that's somethin' to worry my head over, really, seein' as how neither of us is of courtin' age yet. Elias is just fourteen."

Hannah turned from her, looking away.

Mary Ruth leaned forward. "I'm sorry. Did I upset you?"

"It's nothin'," Hannah was too quick to admit. She sniffled

a bit, then straightened. "I just thought . . . well, that maybe Elias might change your thinkin', ya know. Maybe he'd make a difference in your future somehow."

Fact was, Elias *had* begun to upset the fruit basket. The more she ran into him at Preaching and whatnot, and the more she talked with him even briefly, the more she liked him. A lot . . . truth be told. It was like stepping barefoot on a nettle, seeing it tear away at the flesh of enthusiasm and desire. If she gave in to her attraction to him, and his to her, it wouldn't be but a few years and she'd be riding home from Sunday singings with him. He'd end up courting her . . . *and then what?* What if the same enormous hunger for books showed up in one or more of their children? Such a thing would bring heartache to both her and Elias's families.

No, she thought it best to nip her romantic interest in the bud, refuse his attention for the sake of her own ambition. She knew she was born to be a schoolteacher. In short, she could not deprive herself of the one true thing that mattered most to her on God's green earth.

When they arrived home, the sky had turned dark with threatening clouds. "It'll soon be makin' down," she said, working with Hannah to unhitch the horse from the buggy.

"A nice rain would help the crops," Hannah said, drawing in her breath loudly enough for Mary Ruth to hear. "Should I run inside and see where Mamma might be just now?"

Mary Ruth nodded, noting the look of dire concern on

Hannah's face. "Jah, go have a look-see. Meanwhile, I'll water and feed the horse."

Hannah strolled down to the house, calm as you please, but in a jiffy she returned with a big smile on her face. "Mamma's nursin' Lydiann upstairs," she whispered. "Best come now."

"Where's Dat, do you think?"

Hannah had a ready answer. "Both Dat and Leah are out back in the pasture, bringin' home the cows for milkin'."

"And Sadie?"

"Never mind her," Hannah replied, shaking her head. "She's nowhere round that I saw. Besides, she would hardly care, jah?"

So, confident as can be, Mary Ruth carried all seven books across the barnyard and into the house. Hannah led the way, glancing back at her every now and then as they hurried through the empty kitchen and up the long flight of stairs.

Once in their bedroom Mary Ruth separated the books and got down on her hands and knees, pushing a group of four, then three clear under the bed, far as she could reach.

"There," she said, rising up, "who's goin' to look *that* far under the bed?"

◆

After supper Mary Ruth headed out toward the back porch. On the edge of dusk, the evening was still light enough for her to go walking. But on second thought she decided to go swing in the hayloft a bit. The long rope hung high on the rafters as a constant reminder of happy childhood days, and it was easy to ponder one's life out there amidst baled hay and weary animals moving slowly in the warm, dusty stable below. The mouse catchers were sure to keep her company, too.

On the way to the barn, she spotted Dat and Gideon talking in the cornfield. Dat placed his hand on Gid's shoulder for a time, thanking him, no doubt, for his afternoon help.

Dat's reeling in the smithy's son closer all the time, she thought. She was almost certain her father had a trick or two up his sleeve yet. But if that was true, he sure didn't have much time left to botch Leah's plans to marry Jonas Mast.

Besides that, if Dat did *not* succeed in getting Leah's eyes on Gid, something would have to give with farm chores when the time came for Leah and Jonas to set up housekeeping. Dat would definitely have to hire someone nearly full-time—more than likely Gid Peachy. But what a thorn in the side to poor Dat, who preferred to have Gid as his son-in-law, not as a hired hand. She could tell by the look on her father's ruddy face that he was much too partial to Smithy Gid, the way he spoke kindly of the brawny young man—used to be in Leah's hearing—which he didn't do so much anymore.

Still, she couldn't help feeling Dat just might keep Leah from marrying the boy she loved, one way or another. Mary Ruth clenched her jaw at the very notion, wishing she and her sisters weren't so hog-tied around here.

Chapter Seven

Friday dawned much cooler, and Abram, Ida, and the girls were grateful for the relief. While Mary Ruth took her turn tending the vegetable stand out front, Leah, Sadie, and Hannah weeded the enormous vegetable garden, spraying for insects so the family, not the bugs, could reap the benefit of their labors.

Leah worked tirelessly for hours, harvesting summer squash, carrots, peppers, and pounds of cucumbers. They'd already put up a bounty of pickles, both sweet and dill, and Mamma suggested they take even more cucumbers out to the roadside stand to sell. "Or give 'em away if you have to."

While doing her backbreaking gardening, Leah intentionally forced her thoughts away from Sadie to the inviting spot in the forest. The mental picture was even more delightful because Sadie and she were at odds—terribly so. And now that she'd stuck her foot in her mouth over Naomi's wedding request, well, Leah was at a loss to know what to say or do next.

All morning she suffered troublesome feelings toward her

elder sister. The silence between them became worse than annoying. Sadie harbored resentment toward her, that was clear. The slightest reference to Sadie's need for repentance had been met with disdain.

Once the gardening was done, Leah hurried up to Aunt Lizzie's, wanting to go in search of the honey locust tree. She hoped she could talk openly with Lizzie while tramping through the woods on their search. Surely Aunt Lizzie would not see this as an excuse to gossip—heaven forbid!—but rather take to prayer the things on Leah's heart. Such perplexing emotions made Leah wonder if her prayers might simply bounce off the bedroom ceiling instead of wending their way to the Throne of Grace.

With a hug, Aunt Lizzie met her at the back door wearing an old black cooking apron. Newly scrubbed, the small kitchen was awash in sunlight. The familiar, welcoming smell of freshly baked bread drew Leah to sit at the table and savor the aroma. "Smells wonderful-gut," she said.

"Thought I'd bake a dozen raisin cinnamon rolls and a loaf of oatmeal bread for the Nolt family, down yonder," Lizzie said, bringing a glass of iced tea over to Leah. "How would you like to ride along?"

Leah didn't have the heart to bring up the hoped-for excursion to the woods and discourage Lizzie from her kind and generous deed, especially seeing the bright look of happiness on her face. "Jah, I'll go," she was quick to say, still hoping to go to the woods with her aunt later.

It was during the buggy ride down Georgetown Road that Leah opened up and shared her heart. She told Aunt Lizzie of her recent conversation with Sadie, all the while Lizzie's gaze remained fixed on the road as she gripped the reins just so.

"Sadie's not interested in attending Naomi's wedding. Doesn't that seem odd to you?" asked Leah.

"Sounds to me like Naomi might not want her there."

Leah pressed further. "How can that be?"

Lizzie was slow to respond, taking a deep breath first. "Sometimes friends don't remain close for one reason or another. Honestly, I 'spect we should be awful glad Naomi and Sadie aren't so chummy anymore."

"Maybe so, but I have a strong feeling Naomi's turned away from the world completely. If it's not too blunt to say so, I believe she is more receptive to the church than ever."

Lizzie brightened at that. "I trust and pray what you say is true."

Then they chattered of this and that, especially of the flowers and vegetables growing in Lizzie's and Mamma's gardens. Soon, though, Leah asked, "I'm still thinking 'bout that uncommon honey locust tree. . . . Remember?"

"Well, honey-girl, I 'spect we might be able to walk right to it, once we get home again."

Leah was delighted. Leaning back a bit, she settled into the front seat of the buggy, gazing at the now colorless sky, ever so glad to have talked openly with dear Lizzie. Now, if the days would just pass more quickly till Jonas returned to her.

Hannah chased after two nasty flies in the front room. Mamma had ordered her to go inside from the garden to escape the midday heat because she looked "sallow and all done in." Well, here she was, though not sitting down in the kitchen with a tall glass of ice water or fanning herself, but downright eager to slap the annoying insects with the flyswatter. Truly, she had been suffering a headache off and on all week, not telling anyone but her twin. And what had Mary Ruth gone and done? She'd told Mamma, "Hannah needs some lookin' after."

Aside from the fact she was gripped with worry over school opening soon, there wasn't much ailing Hannah. *If only summer could last all year,* she thought. She and her sisters always busied themselves from late spring on with the necessary tasks of planting and harvesting, cooking and cleaning, and on and on it went. There was little else to occupy one's mind during this season, and that was just how Hannah liked it.

Suddenly feeling too tired to stand, she went to the kitchen and sat in the large hickory rocker near the windows. She had been happy to keep up her supply of consignment handiwork, especially her array of embroidered handkerchiefs and pillowcases, thankful for the extra money she was earning at both the Strasburg gift shop and the family's own roadside stand.

Hannah put the swatter down on the floor and leaned her head against the rocker. Just as she was becoming droopy eyed, here came Sadie indoors. "You look all in, Hannah," she said, going to the sink for some water.

"Oh, don't fret over me."

"Here," Sadie said, offering her the tall glass. "Mamma said you had a headache. Two glasses straight down will ease it a bit."

Hannah accepted the glass and began to sip, watching

Sadie return to the sink, now splashing water on her forehead and cheeks. Sadie patted her face dry with her apron, then reached for another glass. When she'd poured a drink for herself, she went to the table and sat down, her face as red as Hannah had ever seen it.

They were still for a time; then Hannah got up the nerve to say, "I was wondering . . . did you ever happen to show off that birthday hankie I made you, the green-and-gold butterfly one?"

Sadie seemed to stiffen at the question, frowned, and shook her head. "Why, no, I didn't."

Hannah, taken aback by her sister's sudden unease, forced a smile. "Just wondered if someone else in the area might've seen it besides our own family . . . and started making some like it to sell."

Sadie said nothing for the longest time. Then she whispered, "That hankie's gone forever, I'm afraid."

"Gone?" Hannah was startled. "But I made it special for you. How could you lose it?"

Sadie shook her head slowly. "I didn't say I did." Her voice was weak now, as if she'd just returned home from the funeral of a close relative, the emotion of the day sapping her strength.

"Then what—"

"Oh, Hannah, please don't ask me any more. I loved your handkerchief, but it's gone and I won't be getting it back."

Hurt over Sadie's seeming disregard for her gift, Hannah pondered her sister's strange reply. *Why would she do such a thing?*

She began to wonder if the woman who'd inquired of the

cutwork hankie might, in all truth, be the new owner of Sadie's birthday handkerchief. *Is that possible?* she thought sadly but said not another word to her sister.

Leah waited in the buggy, hand loosely touching the reins, while Aunt Lizzie hurried to the front door of the Nolts' red-brick house. Lavender statice and pale peach dahlias decorated the front yard of the fancy *Englischers'* house, neat as a pin and as tidy and well kept as the Amish neighbors' yards nearby.

Leah looked forward to this evening, when Dat planned to read to her from the family Bible, translating the verses highlighting baptism. Today at the noon meal Dat had suggested they do this "the sooner the better."

Gladdened, she felt secure in his fatherly love, in spite of his evident disappointment toward her approaching marriage. She was determined to make him proud, even though he was not so happy with her at present. The fact Dat was eager to open the Word of God and discuss the Scriptures meant he was rejoicing at least in her upcoming baptism—a requirement for marriage. In spite of himself, he was making it possible for her to marry Jonas.

She heard footsteps and turned to see Aunt Lizzie coming down the walkway, swinging her arms and smiling. Once settled into the driver's seat, Lizzie shared with her that the Nolts' baby was "as cute as a button."

Leah listened with interest. "I should've gone in with you."

"Another time, maybe." Lizzie clucked her tongue, and the horse pulled the buggy away from the curb. "The missus says she could use a bit of paid help round the house a few afternoons a week. Maybe Sadie—what do you think of that?"

"Just so you know," Leah said, "I think you should steer clear of askin' Sadie at all."

"Might do her some gut, don't you think?"

"'Tween you and me, she's put off by our baby sister."

Lizzie nodded. "You think on it, honey-girl. Can you really expect she'd be any other way . . . considering everything?"

The notion was talked over till the horse made the turn off the road and pulled the carriage into Dat's long lane.

"So maybe Mary Ruth or Hannah, then?" Lizzie pulled back on the reins. "I'll clear it with your father first, though I doubt he'll be any too eager."

"Prob'ly he'll nix the whole idea . . . wouldn't surprise me."

Aunt Lizzie smiled, a twinkle in her eye. "You just leave that to me."

Leah was puzzled at Lizzie's confident response, but she said no more, hoping they'd take themselves off for a walk in the woods.

◆

In the midafternoon light, they moved quickly up the hillock. Leah and Lizzie stopped for a moment to take in the sounds—every little crack and rustle they might expect to hear—garter snakes seizing centipedes, and other tiny creatures stirring beneath layers of brushwood and leaves teeming with life.

Standing there in the midst of the woods, Leah was struck with a startling thought, one she spoke right out. "What do you s'pose would've happened if Sadie had delivered her baby full-term . . . if her infant son had lived?" she asked. "How would Dat and Mamma have reacted—Sadie not havin' a husband an' all?"

Lizzie paused for a moment. "Well, now, that's not so hard to say."

Surprised, Leah studied Lizzie. "Would Dat and Mamma have taken it in their stride?"

"I didn't say that . . . just that I think in time they would've come to accept the baby—their flesh-and-blood grandson, after all."

"Something we'll never know for sure, prob'ly."

"But when all's said and done, the Lord knew best. He saw fit to call the precious little babe home to Glory."

"Just think how torn Sadie would've been her whole life long over the baby's father bein' fancy and all . . . not having him by her side."

"I doubt the lad much cared," Lizzie broke in, moving up the hill again.

Leah suddenly wondered who the father of Sadie's baby might've been. All she'd ever known was his first name— Derry. Even that made her squirm; it sounded to her like someone who might double-dare you to do something you'd later regret.

She matched her stride to Lizzie's, pleased to see the locust tree not four yards ahead. "You found it. How on earth?"

Lizzie hurried to pat the thick, grand trunk. Such an

immense and powerful tree. "Well, there aren't so many like this one, ain't so?"

"It's mighty special . . . even scarce, I'd say." She turned to look from whence they'd come. "How hard would it be to find my way home from here, do you think?"

"I'll mark the way back." Aunt Lizzie reached down for a medium-sized stone to mark the trees.

"Then, you won't fret over me coming here alone?"

Lizzie's smile faded. "Oh, I'll never say *that*."

The sun broke through the uppermost canopy, causing a thin stream of light to illuminate the grassy patch near their feet. "Lookee there!" Leah felt more confident than ever. " 'Let there be light.' "

"Now, don't be thinkin' this is some heavenly sign or such nonsense."

At that Leah laughed along with Lizzie, yet she did wonder why the sunbeam had found them at that precise moment.

When the kitchen was redd up after supper and Mamma had gone to her room to nurse Lydiann, Dat and Leah sat together at the table, the large family Bible open between them. Sadie and Mary Ruth played a game of checkers on the floor while Hannah embroidered a bluebird on a white cotton handkerchief. Dawdi John, who had come to share the supper hour with the family, sat in a hickory rocker near the door leading to the back porch, a relaxed smile on his tanned and wrinkled face.

"We'll begin with the Lord Jesus being baptized by John," Dat said, his finger sliding down the page as he read. "'I indeed baptize you with water unto repentance. . . . '"

"Is that John the Baptist speaking?" Leah asked.

Dat nodded. "Our Lord set the example for us, even though He was the sinless Lamb of God."

Leah listened with rapt attention.

Dat continued. "Now, here's my favorite passage in this chapter. 'And Jesus, when he was baptized, went up straightway out of the water: and, lo, the heavens were opened unto him, and he saw the Spirit of God descending like a dove, and lighting upon him: And lo a voice from heaven, saying, This is my beloved Son, in whom I am well pleased.'"

Leah's ears perked up at the mention of a dove. Jehovah God had sent a gentle white bird, a symbol of peace, to rest on the Son of Man's head as a blessing.

"You must not take lightly this thing you're 'bout to do." Dat folded his callused hands on the Bible. "Membership in the church is a sign of repentance and complete commitment to the community of the People. It's also the doorway that leads to adulthood."

At this comment Leah noticed Sadie's head bob up as if she were listening, which was right fine. *'Specially now,* thought Leah, recalling their recent prickly exchange.

Dat began to quote Mark chapter sixteen, verse sixteen. "'He that believeth and is baptized shall be saved; but he that believeth not shall be damned.'"

"A divine pronouncement, and ever so frightening," Leah said, in awe of the Scripture.

At this Dat closed the Bible and reached for another

book, *Martyrs Mirror,* over eleven hundred pages in length. It was their recorded heritage of bloodshed and abuse—in all, seventeen hundred years of Christian martyrdom. "Obedience to God leads to a path of redemption, though it is exceedingly narrow . . . and few will ever find it," Dat said before beginning to read.

"We are a people set apart—we walk the narrow way, jah?"

Dat nodded reverently. " 'Tis our very life and breath."

"Without spot or blemish," Leah added, knowing the truth taught to her all the days of her life.

"Now I want to read to you about my mother's ancestor— a great-grandmother several times over." Dat turned the pages of *Martyrs Mirror* carefully, as if it were a holy book. He began to read the testimony of Catharina Meylin, who was fire branded on her fair cheek for her beliefs. " 'She held tenaciously to the doctrine of adult baptism,' " he read.

Leah struggled with tears for the courageous and devout mother of eleven children, wondering if she herself had that kind of commitment. *Am I willing to die for the Lord God?* At the very least she wanted to strive for strength of faith and character.

"Did she . . . live on?" Leah asked softly.

" 'Her feet were bound hard, and she was carried off to the convent prison, where she was given only bread and water for many weeks,' " Dat read in response.

He sighed loudly, glancing up. "She was allowed to write only one time—a testimonial letter to her grown children."

Leah listened intently. "Read the rest of the account, will ya?"

Her father nodded and followed the words with his finger. "'Daily, Catharina was beaten, and when she would not deny her faith she was, in due time, delivered by the grace of God from her earthly bonds.'"

Starved and beaten to death? Leah wondered, though she felt too pained by what she had learned to ask. Truly, Dat's ancestor was a faithful servant of the Lord God.

Dat's voice wavered a bit. "She wrote this to her dear children: 'Henceforth there is laid up for me a crown of righteousness, which the Lord, the righteous judge, shall give me at that day: and not to me only, but unto all them also that love his appearing.'"

She gave up her life for what she believed. . . .

Leah felt ever so convicted. Was she worthy to present herself to the almighty One in baptism?

Dawdi John grunted out of the rocker, standing there all wobbly in the middle of the kitchen. Leah looked to Dat for a signal, and his brow crinkled slightly, letting her know the end of their study time had come.

"Come along, Leah," said Dawdi John at last, leaning hard on his cane.

She hurried to her grandfather's side, steadying him as they made their way to the front room and the connecting door to his little Dawdi Haus. Gladly she would ponder the Scriptures and Dat's great-grandmother's stalwart conviction, as well as the many important things Dat had said this night. For now she was thankful both Deacon Stoltzfus and Preacher Yoder had given consent for this discussion of the Scriptures. Something Sadie had never consulted Dat about, far as Leah knew.

Chapter Eight

The letters from Jonas continued to arrive in the Ebersol mailbox, and fast as she possibly could, Leah penned back a response. She still hadn't mentioned his father's visit to Dat. She tried not to ponder it too much, ignoring the gnawing nervousness that something might go awry.

Saturday, August 16
Dear Jonas,

Tomorrow we're having Preaching service here. Actually, Dat's thinking we ought to hold it in the barn, since it's a bit cooler out there. We've been having fairly regular afternoon showers now, which is nice for the ground but not so helpful for the workers—the third cutting of alfalfa is in full swing.

I've been spending several evenings a week with Dawdi John, who tells interesting stories of his youth. Might be nice for you to visit him when you return for baptism a month from now. We could go together, maybe.

I've agreed to be a bridesmaid in Naomi Kauffman's wedding, which is November 11. After observing her at baptismal instruction classes the past weeks, she seems to be ready to turn her full attention to serving the Lord God and the People. Maybe you and I will have some good fellowship with her and Luke once we're all settled in as young married couples.

Sometimes I worry about Sadie, with both Naomi and me being younger and soon to be married. It can't be easy for her.

I want to share something with you. Dat's allowing Mary Ruth to do some light housekeeping and cooking for our English neighbors, the Nolts—the new parents I wrote you about. It's puzzling to me because he was so steadfast about keeping us younger girls separate from the outside world after Sadie attended public high school. Do you think this is wise, letting one so young and innocent work for English folk?

As for me, I'm ready to follow the Lord in the ordinance of baptism and can hardly wait for that most holy of days when I will bow my knees before the bishop and the church membership.

Oh, Jonas, I can hardly wait to see you again! To think we'll be joining church together.

> All my love,
> Your faithful Leah

She folded the letter and slipped it into the envelope. In no hurry to leave the quiet woodland setting, she leaned her head against the locust tree and stared high into its leafy structure. Her life was about to change forever. No longer would she live under the protective covering of her father, though she would always love and respect him and Mamma both. Her place amongst the People would be that of Jonas's helpmeet and wife, and the mother of his children in due season.

Since Dat had read to her Catharina's final testimony of faith, Leah had been thinking constantly of the Anabaptist martyrs. She struggled with the thing that separated *her* from the dedicated church members right here in Gobbler's Knob—the terrible secret she kept locked away inside. She truly felt the Holy One of Israel was calling her to repent of the sisterly covenant made last year, though she dreaded what such a thing might do to her and Sadie's relationship.

In the end Dat would understand if she broke her vow to Sadie. With his concern about Sadie's rumschpringe, he would undoubtedly accept the dire revelation of his firstborn's misconduct as true, but would it cause him undue grief?

Mamma, though she would agree with Dat, would understand why Leah had made the covenant in the first place.

And what of Aunt Lizzie? Leah felt her cheeks burn, knowing Lizzie was unyielding when it came to the tie that binds. She'd made her promise to Sadie, as well.

The battle within Leah's heart between doing what she knew was the right thing and keeping her word to Sadie was causing her to lose her appetite. She found herself whispering rote but fervent prayers, not just at mealtime and bedtime, but all the day long.

Walking barefoot to the Nolts' house, Mary Ruth heard a pair of woodpeckers hidden in the trees that rimmed the road. Though she couldn't see them just now, she knew they were much larger than the bats Dat sometimes spotted in the barn rafters of a night. Their wedge-shaped tails steadied their black bodies as they flew from tree to tree, driving hard bills deep into tree bark in search of a succulent insect dinner.

She kept to the left side of the road, still baffled by her father's voluntarily allowing her to work for fancy folk. To be sure, Aunt Lizzie had played a part. Seemed most anything Lizzie wanted lately she got, especially if Dat had much to say about it.

Awful surprising, she thought as she headed off to her first day on the job with the nice Englishers and their infant son. When she'd gone to meet them with Aunt Lizzie yesterday after supper, she'd noticed right away the baby's dark hair, unlike his blond and blue-eyed parents, though neither of them seemed to pay any mind. Dottie Nolt had quietly shared with her that baby Carl was indeed adopted, not common knowledge. Now in their midthirties, the Nolts were pleased to have a little one to love as their own. Mary Ruth thought they must be churchgoers because Dottie had told her yesterday they were planning to have their baby dedicated to God in church soon. There was something awful special about knowing they wanted to raise their little one with the Lord God's blessings. It made her respect them, English or not, though she scarcely knew them.

"Hello again, Mary Ruth," Dottie greeted her at the front door.

"Hullo," she replied. Stepping into the thoroughly modern front room, Mary Ruth felt such gladness to be here again. She had an uncanny connection to the larger world here. It was just as some of her older girlfriends had described their first visit to downtown Lancaster—that unspeakable, somewhat delirious feeling of rumschpringe—being allowed to experience something other than the society of the People . . . truly the only thing she knew.

After she was offered a glass of lemonade, freshly squeezed just like Mamma's, Mary Ruth agreed to sweep and scrub both the entry hall and the kitchen floors. "I'll even get down on all fours like Mamma does at home," she told Dottie.

Her employer appeared somewhat surprised, eyebrows arching as she smiled. "I can see I'm going to become very spoiled with you around, Mary Ruth."

So she took extra care to reach far into all the corners and crevices, washing the floor by hand. When that chore was complete, she dusted the front room. Carefully removing knickknacks and magazines from the sofa tables, she hummed, enjoying herself far more than she'd ever dreamed possible—in a worldly home, of all things. Except she'd seen an open Bible in both the kitchen and now here, on what Dottie called the "coffee table." Interesting, to be sure.

Moving upstairs, she couldn't help but think of the extra money she was going to earn. What a good idea to put it away for future schooling needs. Dat would have a fit when he put two and two together and discovered what she was saving up for. Yet it wasn't as if she had sought out this work. The whole thing had fallen into her lap, thanks to Aunt Lizzie.

Hannah, on the other hand, had appeared startled about this opportunity. "How will ya keep up with your homework once school starts?" she had asked Mary Ruth in the privacy of their bedroom last night.

"Dottie Nolt wants me only two or three times a week. That's all."

"Twice oughta keep the house clean enough, seems to me," Hannah replied.

"Maybe so, but I want to please my first employer. I'll still have plenty of time to help Mamma at home."

So, after talking it over with Mamma, Mary Ruth agreed

that if the job interfered with schoolwork, she'd ask Sadie to fill in for a while. But she doubted that would work, what with Sadie seeming to recoil at the sight of her own baby sister. Mary Ruth truly wondered about that.

Just now, going into the darling nursery, she stopped to admire a framed wall painting above the dresser—a small boy with suntanned legs making chase after a lone orange-brown butterfly that appeared to be just out of reach. She'd seen bright-colored butterflies like that many times in the high meadow over near Blackbird Pond, out behind smithy Peachey's bank barn and blacksmith shop.

The painting made her smile, and she set to work dusting the dresser thoroughly before moving on to the oak rocker, cleaning the rungs beneath. A peek at the empty crib let her know baby Carl was either cradled in his new mother's arms or tucked away for a nap in the wicker bassinet near the kitchen. Such a wondrous thing, these folk opening their home and their joyful hearts to an orphaned baby.

Eager to complete her housekeeping chores in an acceptable manner, Mary Ruth attended to every detail. When the rocking chair was polished, she moved to the round lamp table nearby. To her surprise, there on the table lay yet another open Bible, same as the two downstairs. She saw that a verse from the Psalms was underlined in red—*As the hart panteth after the water brooks, so panteth my soul after thee, O God.*

Why so many copies of the Good Book in the house? she wondered. Was Dottie a follower of the Jehovah Lord? Were there Englishers who were also devout like the People? For sure and for certain, the idea of an open Bible in every room—and in a fancy home—was ever so curious.

◆

Distracted and restless, Abram worked up a sweat redding up the barn for the Lord's Day gathering and the young people's singing that was to follow tomorrow evening. He'd made the decision to have the church benches set up on the threshing floor, where an occasional breeze might do some good keeping folk awake instead of the way it had been two weeks ago, when he and everyone else had been helpless to fight off the heat-induced stupor. And with Ida still tending closely to their infant daughter, the housework of removing all the rugs and rearranging the furniture would have fallen to the girls and Lizzie. Truly, it was better to have church in the barn, where he would plan the seating arrangement and direct the People to their seats.

He was mighty glad to have a strong helping hand this afternoon with the heavier duties. Far as he was concerned, Smithy Gid could easily become a necessary right arm to him, what with John suffering a hip ailment clear out of the blue.

Working with Gid, he shoveled manure out of the stable area. Then they raked and swept clean the widest area of the threshing floor, where the People would sit as hearers of the Word.

" 'S'mighty gut of you to help," Abram said, pushing hard on the long-handled broom.

"Glad to do it."

"Ain't so certain how I'll manage here in a few weeks."

Gid nodded but kept working. "I wonder 'bout that, too,

Abram. But more and more Pop needs me to help him with some of the smithy work."

Abram knew that, all right. But there was no real need to address the event both men dreaded. The topic of Leah's impending marriage was something they avoided discussing altogether. Abram had witnessed firsthand Gid's feelings for Leah, saw the hopeless longing in the young man's eyes whenever she was anywhere near.

Abram's feeble attempt to get Jonas Mast out of town and off to Ohio had backfired. The time apart had served only to solidify their love, visible by the number of Ohio letters arriving each week. So Leah had fallen in love with the boy she believed was to be her life mate . . . although Abram would be surprised if she and Jonas ended up together.

He heard the sound of the horses and buggies now, the womenfolk arriving to help Ida make ready for the common meal tomorrow. Plenty of baking would take place in the Ebersol kitchen this day. *Will Leah and Lizzie be on hand to help Ida?* he wondered. The chummy twosome had gone to run an errand an hour or so ago.

Frankly, it was downright unnerving how Lizzie had inched her way deeper into their lives, all of them. First she'd gotten her grip on Sadie last year. Now Leah. Worst of all, Lizzie had pressed Abram to make a hasty decision over an English housekeeping job down the road a piece—giving him no breathing room. He had little choice but to do things Lizzie's way to keep her hushed up . . . for now. Alas, Lizzie Brenneman was railroading him down a path of her own choosing. Downright unbecoming of her.

Ida, on the other hand, wasn't much help, either. Seemed

his wife and her sister were out of check, and the bishop would tell him so if he sought out spiritual counsel. He was losing sway over his family in more ways than one, and growing weary before his time.

As for the upper hand, he also felt at a loss when it came to his father-in-law. It struck him as peculiar that John's bum hip, if real, had come on the heels of a fiery discussion concerning none other than Lizzie and her past blunders, though long ago confessed. Thus Ida's sister was causing strife at every hand. He'd have to put a stop to it before things spun completely out of control.

Turning his attention back to the barn cleanup, Abram knew he'd be tuckered out by this time tomorrow. No doubt he and Ida would rise early and dress for the Lord's Day right quick after Lydiann's early-morning feeding, around three-thirty. There was much to be organized before the membership began to arrive—two hundred thirty-eight strong, and many more wee ones on the way.

So he and the young man who he hoped might still become his son-in-law continued that most honorable and sacred task: making an acceptable place of worship in the sight of the Lord God and the People.

Chapter Nine

The morning mist took too long to burn off, revealing at last a cloudless, pure sky. By the time Dat and Leah had finished the milking, Sadie, Mamma, and the twins had cooked up a full breakfast of fried eggs and bacon, along with some fresh fruit, toast, jelly, and milk. "Best not dally," Mamma chided the girls, though they knew better than to linger on this Lord's Day. "There'll be folks arrivin' well before nine o'clock, to be sure."

Sadie didn't much care when the People came. They were all going to be sitting on the church benches in the smelly barn—the last place she'd like to be today. But go she must.

Her parents' closed-door conversation of four nights ago still rang in her ears. Pity's sake, she'd thought so long and hard about what she'd overheard she'd made herself sick. One thing was sure, she was convinced they knew *something* of her reckless year with Derry, that good-for-nothing boy who'd brought an everlasting stain on her life.

Thinking on all this, she decided then and there . . .

maybe she was just too ill to attend church today. She could take herself off to the high meadow and try to keep from being queasy. Dat might not believe her, but Mamma would—and so would Aunt Lizzie if it came to that.

Before the womenfolk were to file into the barn prior to Preaching, Leah was surprised to see Naomi come running over to join her and Adah Peachey, along with the twins and Mamma—babe in arms—and the Ebersol family cluster. The main thing on Leah's mind was Sadie, who wasn't where she was supposed to be just now. Boldly, her sister had gone up to the outhouse right quick before the service was close to beginning. *Never mind her*, thought Leah, dismissing her errant sister. *If she comes, she comes.*

Leah got herself into the line for church, behind the baptized single girls at the front. The earthy scent of cats and hay and cattle filled her nose. *Best smells on earth*, she thought, ever so glad to be alive as she shook hands with Preacher Yoder and the visiting minister from Ninepoints.

She noticed Ezra and Elias Stoltzfus turn their heads in unison when spotting Hannah and Mary Ruth, but the twins reverently walked toward the benches set up for the womenfolk and young children. Though Leah did not crack a smile, inwardly she was amused and gladly so. Someday her younger sisters might end up married to the deacon's boys. Who was to tell? But if so, her nieces and nephews, Hannah's and Mary Ruth's babies—the whole lot of them—now, wouldn't *they* resemble each other? Cousins, for sure, but even closer.

What a bright future they all had, including Sadie if she'd just get her tail feathers down here to settle in for the Preaching service. And not only did she need to hear the Word of the Lord ... but Leah had just this minute decided Sadie might benefit from another straight talk. Life was too short to take risks with eternity, and her own conscience weighed ever so heavily.

———————◆———————

The raucous come-hither trill of a group of blue jays cut the stillness at the end of the long, final prayer after the three-hour meeting. Once the People were seated again after kneeling, Deacon Stoltzfus rose and announced the location of the next Sunday Preaching, "in two weeks at smithy Peachey's place."

Then, when the meeting was opened up for any business to be conducted relating to church discipline, there was an issue involving "a reckless teenager," or so the member reported. That being the case, the closing hymn was sung and the youngsters began silently filing out of the barn, followed by the unbaptized, single young people. Another forty minutes or so of pointed discussion was to follow, including the humiliating possibility of the wayward youth having to confess before the People.

Leah shivered, wishing Sadie had been present at Preaching today. Aware of the secret members' meeting now going on, she felt sure it might have put the fear of God in her sister.

Mary Ruth hurried with Hannah to help Mamma, Leah, and Lizzie with a smorgasbord-style spread laid out on long tables in the sunny kitchen. Today being a perfect day for a picnic, the People would eat and fellowship on the grounds. Bread and homemade butter, sliced cheeses, dill and sweet pickles, strawberry jam, red beets, half-moon apple pies, and ice-cold lemonade—the standard light fare for a summer Sunday go-to-meeting. Not that a body could eat himself full on such a menu. It was merely intended to squelch growling stomachs till the People could ride horse and buggy back home.

"Has anybody seen Sadie?" Mary Ruth asked of Leah and Hannah.

"Sadie's sittin' up in the meadow, head between her knees like she's under the weather," Aunt Lizzie offered.

Mary Ruth joked, " 'Cept ain't it an awful *nice* day to—"

"Now, leave her be," Mamma spoke up.

At this Mary Ruth turned to Hannah and frowned.

"You heard Mamma," Hannah whispered.

Still, Mary Ruth wondered how Sadie could get by with skipping church, soaking up the sunshine instead. Unless she *was* ill. But if she was simply having a sulk, well, then it didn't make sense. Why would Sadie bring unnecessary shame to her parents on the day they hosted the church meeting?

After the noon meal, enjoyed on the rolling lawns, the young men gradually began to gather in the barnyard. There they congregated in one of two groups: the more pious teens—some baptized and some not—and the known rebels who typically ignored the rules of dress, conduct, and were all-round less serious minded.

Elias stood with the teens known for following the letter of the law, even though he was also *hipperdiglipp*—the type of fellow who rode his new pony cart to the limits of speed and daring.

On her way back from the outhouse, Mary Ruth stumbled upon Elias and had to swallow her nervousness. She'd never been this alone with him, except for that one time at the vegetable stand, nearly a year ago. Her resolve not to pay him any mind flew out the window. She was ever so eager to reply if he should happen to speak to her.

And speak he did, removing his straw hat. "Hullo, Mary Ruth. How *are* ya?"

Well, she might've thought the Lord God himself had descended and stood before her, she was that tongue-tied. "I . . . uh, hullo."

She wanted to say more, truly she did. Not lose her words in this hopeless stuttering, of all things. Should she try to talk again? She might not get a second chance today, and the next time to prove herself to be a bright and expressive young woman would be another two weeks away. *Be calm*, she told herself. *Breathe deep . . . stand tall.*

He scratched his tousled red hair and nodded. He was looking at her, sure as anything, and she tried ever so hard not to stare back. Yet his eyes drew her, pulled her like iron to a magnet. For what seemed like a full minute, he stood smiling down at her. "Awful nice seein' you again, Mary Ruth."

"*Denki*—thank you" was all she managed to say before he was on his way. Oh, she could just kick herself for being so jittery. Was this how it felt to be falling in love? She hoped not, because she absolutely must dismiss her feelings for Elias.

Her thoughts turned to the singing in the barn after nightfall. Of course she wasn't free to go. At just fourteen she longed to be older—an adult, to be sure. But she was too young for the true freedom she longed for and too old to be treated like a girl with hardly a care in the world. For truth, in spite of seeing Elias just now, she wasn't too sure she'd ever be happy living amongst the People forever, being treated the way the menfolk seemed to manage the womenfolk—under the thumb, so to speak.

Lately, though, she'd observed *one* woman whom she wouldn't mind imitating at all. Aunt Lizzie. Her aunt had a lip that wouldn't quit, and Mary Ruth knew it firsthand because she'd heard Lizzie talking mighty straight to Mamma just last night. "I'm telling you, time's running out for Abram," Lizzie said. "Put that in your work apron and mull it over, Ida. I'm fed up with him muzzling the ox." And with that Mary Ruth had darted back into the front room, hiding behind the doorjamb, changing her mind about heading straight for the kitchen. It wouldn't be wise to barge into such a squall.

For tonight she and Hannah would simply sit out on the back lawn, listening to the courting-age young people sing their "fast" songs, having themselves a good time.

Sadie wouldn't be going, either, not the way she'd kept herself away from the meeting today. No, Dat would see to it Sadie was nowhere near the barn singing. As for Leah, being engaged to Jonas would keep her away unless Adah Peachey or Naomi Kauffman talked her into going with them. Jah, tonight would be an interesting sight, with more than likely not a single one of Abram's daughters showing up at their own singing.

Dawdi John was a bit sluggish, but sharp as a nail. Tonight he wore his white "for good" shirt, tan suspenders, and black broadfall trousers, same as he'd worn all day. Because of the exceptionally warm evening, no coat was needed, and he'd left his black bowtie in his dresser drawer. His weak eyes, when he removed his glasses, were somewhat pained as he sat on a folding chair next to his granddaughters in the backyard.

"Nice to hear the young people lift their voices in song, ain't?" Leah was quick to say. Ever since she'd known of his hip problems, she'd gone out of her way to show extra kindness to Dawdi.

"They sing as heartily as the youth did back when I was a lad." He nodded, smiling.

Hannah and Mary Ruth were caught up in their own talk, sprawled out on a large green quilt, frayed round the edges. As for Sadie, she had been sent upstairs following the common meal to contemplate her irreverent behavior this morning. Dat had ordered her off to the hot and stuffy bedroom, called after her that she was "never, ever to feign sickness on the Lord's Day again!" and she was not allowed to leave the premises for a full week.

Leah couldn't blame Dat, really. Sadie had it coming, plain to see—although Mamma had actually winced when

Dat raised his voice. Even Hannah and Mary Ruth had put their heads down, squinting to beat the band. But Leah knew the punishment had come forth in such a fiery way due only to continual problems. Before supper tonight Sadie had refused to hold Lydiann, though their baby sister was as sweet as pudding. She wouldn't budge even when Mamma spoke directly to her. "Take your baby sister for me, please."

Sadie had actually backed away when Mamma held Lydiann out to her, shocking all of them. Mary Ruth came to Mamma's rescue, taking Lydiann in her own arms, and Sadie made a beeline to the back door, sobbing as she ran.

Leah, chagrined, had been sent out to fetch her sister, ordered to do so by Mamma, then Dat . . . then both her parents in chorus.

She hoped—and prayed often—that Sadie might snap out of her cantankerous mood. Unknowingly, Dat and Mamma were being pulled into the thick of it. *Won't Mamma, at least, put two and two together if Sadie keeps behaving in such a questionable manner?* she had wondered.

Just now she saw Adah Peachey running through the cornfield. Leah waved to her, noticing Gid was nowhere in sight.

"Won't ya come along with me?" Adah called to her.

"I'm keepin' Dawdi company," Leah replied.

"Aw, please come?"

Leah, wanting ever so much to accompany Adah, turned to ask Dawdi, "Will you be all right here for a bit?"

"Sure, go on, Leah. I'm just fine. Besides, Hannah and Mary Ruth will look after me, won'tcha, girls?"

The twins nodded, and Leah rose to meet Adah. Mary

Ruth hopped up from the quilt to claim Leah's vacant folding chair. "Have yourself a nice time," Mary Ruth said, plopping herself down.

Hurrying off with Adah, Leah realized suddenly that she hadn't bothered to dress for the singing, since she hadn't planned to attend. For sure and for certain, she would not impress any of the young men in attendance. No need to when she was engaged to marry Jonas in a few months. Adah, on the other hand, had combed her hair, taking care to wash her face, Leah noticed, because it was shiny from the scrubbing. "What're you thinking?" Leah asked as they stood in the gaping opening to the barn, peering in.

"Just that it's time you had yourself a bit of fun."

"Oh, I'm okay, really I am."

"You don't convince me." Adah smiled thoughtfully. "You look worried most of the time."

"I do?"

"Honestly, I've been wonderin' if you have second thoughts 'bout Jonas."

"What makes you think that?"

Adah fell silent suddenly as, one after another, the young folk made their way into the barn.

Leah waited for her friend to respond, but when she didn't, Leah added, "If I didn't know better, Adah, I'd think maybe it was *you* who's worried."

That got Adah talking again. "Whatever for?"

"I daresay you don't like the idea of us not bein' sisters-in-law, for one thing." As soon as Leah said it, she knew she'd been needlessly insensitive.

"Well, jah, 'tis ever so true. . . ."

Leah was deeply sorry. "What I meant to say was—"

"No . . . no, you should never have said such an unkind thing."

Beyond doubt she hated what had just happened; she'd had no intention of exchanging sarcastic words with her dearest friend. "I'm sorry, Adah, honest I am. I don't know what got into me."

"Well, I 'spect *I* do." Adah breathed in ever so deeply. "I think you're upset at Sadie. Naomi Kauffman told me the most revoltin' story the other day."

"You know I don't care to hear gossip," Leah replied.

"Ain't hearsay. Naomi says she knows what she's talkin' 'bout."

Leah panicked. Naomi probably *did* know something she oughtn't to be telling. Things concerning Sadie and their Friday-night adventures in the English world. "Is this so necessary to say?" she asked softly.

"Come with me." Adah led her away from the barn, up toward the mule road. "I'm not happy to be the one to tell you this, but . . ." She paused then, still walking hard. "I think you might already suspect as much. Could be the reason you're on edge."

"What's so important we have to walk clear away from the barn?"

"Your sister, that's what. Sadie took her baptism last year with an impure heart. If Bishop Bontrager knew of it, well, she'd be shunned for certain—at least the temporary *Bann*."

The words sprang to life in Leah, smarting her eyes. "Impure?"

"Sadie had herself an English boyfriend."

"I don't like what you're sayin'." She had to speak up. She couldn't just go along with Adah, yet she didn't want to let on she already knew.

"I'm only tellin' you in hopes you can talk sense to Sadie. Help her see the light before Naomi goes to Preacher with this."

Leah's heart sank. "What do you want me to do?"

"Talk openly, sister to sister. Let her know what Naomi's threatenin' to do."

Leah sighed loudly. "What if Sadie won't cooperate?"

"Just try, Leah. For the sake of your family . . . and to spare Sadie eternal punishment."

Leah looked now at Adah. She began to wonder if Adah wasn't actually relieved her precious brother was not romantically connected to the Ebersol family.

High above them, in trees silhouetted against a dark sky, whippoorwills called from unseen branches, and Leah felt sudden despair. The thing she had greatly feared had come to pass. Sadie had been found out. Just how much Naomi knew, she had no idea. But she intended to worm it out of her.

In a few minutes' time, she and Adah had walked all the way to the brink of the forest. Without speaking, they turned and stood there, looking down over the Ebersol Cottage, as Leah liked to call her father's house. In the near distance she spotted a single upstairs window aglow—Sadie's and her bedroom—where her bold and surly sister sat alone contemplating her Lord's Day misbehavior.

Meanwhile, their two-story bank barn was alive with light and music. Lightning bugs blinked yellow-white sparkles here and there over the field and beyond to the Peachey farm, making Leah think sadly of Smithy Gid. What a good thing he'd stayed at home and let his sister go it alone to singing this night. Indeed.

"Won'tcha come to the singing with me, *please?*" Adah asked.

"I'm not dressed for it," she said.

Adah looked her over, brushing Leah's apron off. "There, now."

Her dear friend's pleading eyes tugged at her heart. "S'pose I could go with you, but only for a little bit."

"Wonderful-gut!" Adah's face lit up and she reached for Leah's hand, and the two of them went running down the mule road toward the barn.

Gid caught himself breaking into a full grin, having just now spotted Leah Ebersol and his sister Adah come strolling into the barn, hand in hand. And just when he was starting to wish he'd stayed home to frisk with his new litter of German shepherd puppies. Soon he would be advertising again by word of mouth—the way he liked to, since it took nothing away from his growing savings account—letting folks know his full-bred pups were weaned and ready to purchase. His father had mentioned not two days before that he was well pleased with the amount of money Gid had saved over the past few years, thanks to the thriving side business. Gid would have liked to be looking to marry before too long, though the girl he really wanted to court was Abram's Leah, who was all caught up with a beau clear out in Ohio. Just what was Jonas Mast thinking, learning the carpentry trade? Gid wondered. But it wasn't his place to question. He knew there had been talk amongst the brethren—and this had come straight from his own pop—that Bishop Bontrager didn't take too kindly to young men who chose to make their way by doing something other than farming. Working the soil was the expected way in the eyes of the People. Anything else was "mighty English." Besides, there was ample farmland in Lancaster County.

Gid slowed his pace, hoping to appear relaxed as he approached Leah and Adah, who were talking off by themselves. Not wanting to barge in—he did and he didn't—he hoped to make Leah feel comfortable with his presence. Yet what was *she* doing here, where the singing activities were meant for coupling up? Surely Leah and Jonas Mast were secretly engaged by now. But that was anyone's guess . . . at least up until the second Sunday after fall communion, when the deacon named each couple in the district who planned to marry during the wedding season. After the publishing, Abram Ebersol would stand and invite everyone sixteen and older to the wedding, also announcing the day and month.

Gid had long thought he might have some reason for staying away from church that day. Wouldn't think of putting on like he was ill, though. Although, if he thought on it long enough, he *could* be. But he would try to put on a smile for the Ebersols, no matter what inner turmoil he would battle that day. Because wedding or not, Abram and his family were mighty special in his book.

"Hullo, Leah . . . and Adah." He stopped a few feet from them, forcing his gaze on his sister and away from Leah, who always seemed to draw his eyes to hers. How was it a girl could wear her sweet spirit on her face? It had always been that way with Leah.

"Oh, Gid, you're here!" Adah said, letting go of Leah's hand and gripping his arm.

He felt his face flush red. "I decided to come over at the last minute."

Adah turned to Leah. "Same as you did, Leah," his sister declared, eyes sparkling.

"Oh, Adah . . . for goodness' sake." Leah turned from Adah and looked at him, smiling pleasantly, not flirtatiously. "I came to keep your sister company, is all," she said.

" 'Twas my idea, for sure," Adah agreed.

"Well, I'm glad you're both here." Their talk quickly turned to King, Leah's dog, and it seemed she considered him a devoted pet.

"Dat likes having King round, too," Leah stated. "He's even said it might be nice to have one or two more dogs."

Adah brightened again. "Really?"

Leah was nodding. "Dat thinks havin' dogs on the property keeps outsiders honest."

"Not that he distrusts the English, I don't s'pose," Gid spoke up. He knew Abram well enough to know better.

Leah shrugged. "Dat sometimes worries over us girls . . . bein' there's only one man to do the protectin'." She must have suddenly caught herself, realizing what she'd said, because she looked quickly at Adah and turned too rosy in the cheeks.

Gid stepped closer and found himself forming a circle with the two of them. He thought he smelled a hint of homemade soap—probably Adah, who'd cleaned up right good for the evening. Still, there was a unique freshness about Leah, the way her eyes shone with joy, her surprising openness. She was as confident as any girl he knew; not shy at all, nor too frank like one of the girls here from the Grasshopper Level area. He hadn't seen her, but some of the fellows had said Jonas Mast's spunky sister Rebekah was in attendance, along with three other girls from that district. "Bold Becky" had shown up tonight to one of her first singings since she'd turned sixteen. He was careful not to concentrate too hard on Leah, dividing his attention between both her and Adah . . . though it was mighty difficult.

Chapter Ten

Monday morning after completing her milking duties, Leah hurried off on foot to pay a visit to Naomi Kauffman.

Arriving at Kauffmans' dairy farm, she hurried across the barnyard to the milk house. There she found Naomi looking mighty surprised to see her. "I hope you don't mind me comin' so early."

"Leah, what is it? Something happen over at your place?"

"Everything's just fine." She paused. "I have to talk to you." She went on to share in whispered tones what Adah had confided last night. "I'm worried sick 'bout Sadie—what might become of her if you . . . well, if you go to Preacher before she has a chance to repent on her own."

"She's had plenty of time, wouldn't you say? Nearly a year's passed since she started spendin' time with her worldly beau. And what's worse, she kept seein' him after she was baptized. I know she did 'cause Melvin Warner, Derry's English friend, told me so. 'Course, now, I was wild, too, 'cept not thinkin' on bein' baptized . . . not till recently." Naomi took

107

a deep breath. "I just don't understand how Sadie could tempt the Lord God thataway. And she never made things right with the church brethren, neither." Naomi looked at her with stony eyes. "Has she confessed these things to you?"

Leah couldn't lie . . . not before God and her fellow baptismal candidate. "It's a touchy subject, the rumschpringe . . . so private it is, you know."

"Which is why Dat's been talkin' to Preacher Yoder and others about doin' away with it. Goodness' sake, I nearly got myself in a fix. Sadie and I . . . we went together clear up to Strasburg, seekin' out fancy fellas. We were *narrisch*—crazy. Truly we were."

"You don't have to come clean to me, Naomi. You've repented to God and Preacher, as we all must."

"Then, will you urge Sadie to do the same? Plead with her to go to the brethren."

"Why, so you won't have to?"

"Ach no, but ain't it true if a person knows of sin and doesn't encourage the sinner to own up . . . well then, they may be found to be just as guilty?"

Leah hated to think she, as well as Aunt Lizzie, was at fault right along with Sadie. Oh, they'd made futile attempts to get Sadie to express regret, pushing for her to at least tell Mamma what she'd done. Jointly and separately they'd done so, till they were blue in the face. But Leah couldn't reveal any of this to Naomi. It would never do to let *her* in on the fact that Leah had known all this for a long time.

"Jah, I'll do my best talkin' to my sister," Leah promised. "I'll tell her what you said. Or you could tell her yourself. Might be a gut thing for her to witness how you've turned your back on the world and all."

Naomi nodded. "Still, if she isn't willin' to ask for forgiveness, then I won't have any choice but to—"

"Talk to your beau's grandfather?"

Naomi blushed. "Has nothin' to do with Luke and me."

"Well, I surely hope not."

Squaring her shoulders, Naomi continued. "Listen, Leah,
I'm bein' truthful with you. I couldn't live with my conscience
if I didn't speak to *someone*. Don't you see? I want to present
myself as a living sacrifice and follow the Lord Jesus in holy
baptism with a pure heart."

Leah agreed. "Just as I do."

So it was settled. *Sadie's my sister, after all*, she thought.

Sadie would have one short month to offer atonement to
her parents and, if she was willing, the church.

At half past ten in the morning, the postman delivered
the mail. Leah ran down the lane, eager to hear from Jonas.
Just as she expected, there was a new letter from Millersburg.
Tearing the envelope open, she began to read.

My dearest Leah,

 *You are constantly in my thoughts and prayers! Just think,
one month from now I'll hold you in my arms again. While
I'm there for baptism, let's you and I talk over where we plan
to live. We could have a look-see at the rental house you wrote
about earlier.*

Today as I worked in the carpentry shop, I had an interesting idea. I hope you might consider it. I realize there must have been an important reason for you to remain in Gobbler's Knob through the summer. But now, here we are in the middle of August, and I'd like for us to be in the same town together, at least for our final weeks as a betrothed couple. I want to court you in person, Leah. My heart longs for your smile, your sweet face . . . your dear, dear ways.

Let's think seriously about the possibility of you coming back to Ohio with me after we join church. My final weeks away from home will be much easier with you close by. If necessary, I will write to your father to get his blessing on the matter . . . or, better yet, I'll speak to him when I'm there.

By the way, David Mellinger's elderly mother, Edith, could benefit greatly from your help, if only for a short time. (They're inviting you through me.) You can stay in the Dawdi Haus with Edith. What do you think of this?

I'm also eager for you to meet the godly bishop here. The Scriptures have come alive for me—passages in the Bible I never knew existed. Here's one I must share with you today. Second Corinthians chapter three, verse eighteen: "But we all, with open face beholding as in a glass the glory of the Lord, are changed into the same image from glory to glory, even as by the Spirit of the Lord."

Leah, if you read this verse over again, the amazing truth will sink deep into your heart. To think our lives can be mirrors of God's goodness and grace, making it possible for others to see Christ Jesus reflected in us!

I should sign off and prepare for a long and busy day. I'm holding my breath to see you again!

All my love,
Jonas

She held the letter fondly, gladdened by his invitation. Jonas still wanted her to visit him in Ohio! She went to seek out Mamma with the news.

Mamma was far more understanding than Leah expected. "That's right nice of Jonas, but you'll have to see what Dat says, ya know," Mamma said, standing at the wood stove.

"Do you mean you could be in favor of it? If Dat is willin'?"

"Let's just see what he says"—Mamma's parting words on the matter.

She kissed her mother square on the cheek.

Obviously pleased, Mamma reminded her the "decision remains with Dat, ya must know."

"But still, I'm more hopeful 'cause of what you said."

This time it was Mamma who kissed *her*, high on the forehead, right where her middle part commenced.

Promptly Leah marched out to the barn, her heart in her throat, knowing full well what to predict from Dat. She found him caring for a nasty gash on the lower hindquarters of one of the mules. "Aw, the poor thing. You've got yourself some tendin' to do." She stood back a bit as Dat soothed the hurting animal.

"Jah, but never too busy for my girl. What's on your mind, Leah?"

That was just like Dat; he seemed to know her better than almost anyone. Now . . . how to say what was on her heart? Dare she risk Dat's temper after his recent flare-up with Sadie? "I guess I don't know where to start, really."

He looked up from his squatting position. "If this concerns

your aunt Lizzie, I'll be blunt with you—I have no time for it. That's all I best say."

"Aunt Lizzie? Why, no . . . it's about a letter from Jonas. Arrived just today." She pressed on, shaking inwardly as she told him what Jonas had in mind. "I really want to do this, Dat. I wouldn't risk annoying you if it didn't mean ever so much to me."

"You want to go an' visit Millersburg before you're married to Jonas?"

She explained she could stay with the master carpenter's mother to help with the widow's daily routine. "Jonas would reside where he is now, next door in the main farmhouse."

"A bit too familiar for my likin'."

"You know that would not be a concern." She was hoping to rule out all roadblocks. "This could be a special time for Jonas and me."

Abram turned away, lifting the mule's leg, manipulating it back and forth. "I don't see it that way," Dat said quickly.

She wanted to say, *I'm not like Sadie*, but bit her lip. Dat knew nothing of Sadie's past. And besides, it wasn't an issue of purity that seemed to irk him. He was just plain stubborn about preferring Gid Peachey.

"It's a closed subject," Dat added. "*Verschteh*—understand?"

She didn't dare argue with him. But she wanted to go to Ohio something awful. Breathing in hard, then exhaling, she turned and walked away, trying to keep still and not talk back. But she could hear Jonas's earnest plea in the words he'd written. Loving words—the compassion of her future husband. Jonas wanted to spend time with his bride-to-be. What was wrong with that? After all this time they'd been apart . . .

Suddenly she spun round and rushed back to the barn. "What if Jonas talks this over with you when he comes for baptism? Would that set better with you, Dat?" she entreated him, desperate for this one thing. "I scarcely ever ask for much, you know that. But this . . ."

Dat stood up just then and looked her full in the face. "My dear girl, how can you ever know what's in the deep of my heart? You are precious to me . . . since the first day I laid eyes on you. Tiny little thing, you were. A helpless infant, bawlin' your lungs out."

She was nearly embarrassed at his tender words. "Dat?"

"No, now listen to me, Leah. You're the light of my eyes, always have been."

For goodness' sake, Dat was being much too serious. She said, "I know you think of me more as a son than a—"

"No . . . no, you haven't any idea."

"Then, maybe . . . well, might you be willin' to change your mind? Could you reconsider . . . just this once?" All their years working the mules in the field, tending to a multitude of barn chores—always together—told her he might listen. After all, she *was* Abram's Leah, and she knew that, in his own stubborn way, he was attempting to save face. Known to be unyielding amongst the People, Dat wanted to give Leah what she most longed for. She was sure of it.

Sighing, Dat removed his straw hat and raked his thick fingers through his cropped hair. "For how long did you say?"

"A month or so is all."

"And you wouldn't ever think of marryin' anyone but this boy, your mamma's cousin's son?"

By now she couldn't begin to utter a response. How she loved the darling boy of her childhood! Dat knew this. *Why must he continually test me?* she wondered.

Dat gave her a long look before continuing. "If you love Jonas as much as you seem to, then can you find a way to get yourself out there? I won't be givin' you the money to ride a train or bus all the way to Ohio, just so you know."

Joyful tears sprang to her eyes. "Oh, I can't thank you enough!" Leah reached over and hugged his arm tightly. "I promise ya won't regret this."

Her father clasped her hand tight for a moment before they parted. Then, still grinning, Leah ran to tell Mamma the amazing news.

Chapter Eleven

At noon Mamma suggested the girls enjoy a long lunch break from their work. "We all need a bit of time off," she announced at the table.

Leah and the twins agreed, welcoming the idea with nods of the head. Sadie, however, went right back outside as if she hadn't heard.

Standing in the doorway, hand on the screen door, Leah watched Sadie work the soil. *She's punishing herself out in that sun. . . .*

Was now the time to approach Sadie? Such a ticklish position Naomi had put her in. Just how would Sadie react to Naomi's threat?

Sadie worked the hoe, all bent over, Leah noticed, making deep furrows in the vegetable rows to assist their hand-watering efforts. Some much-needed rain had come recently, but all through July and this far into August they'd supplemented by pumping well water up to the holding tank and using hoses in the garden. With constant care the girls had practically salvaged the entire celery crop. *A sign of gut things to come*, thought Leah.

Awful tired herself and wishing she could heed Mamma's suggestion to rest up, Leah opened the back door and stepped out. There was not a breath of wind to be felt, and the birds were silent. Uncanny, to be sure.

Taking a deep breath, she stepped past the narrow swath of red-and-white petunias lining the cement walkway on the right. Dat could be heard clear off in the cornfield, talking to either Gid or the smithy. The peculiar stillness gave Leah a sense of renewed courage, as if the earth were holding its breath along with her. *Best talk to Sadie right now*, she told herself, thinking again of Naomi's ominous warning.

Turning at the end of the whitewashed fence, she made her way to the family vegetable garden. Sadie was as pretty as ever, her golden hair shimmering in the sunlight through her white prayer bonnet. Leah was struck with the notion Sadie could pass for a heavenly messenger—an angel—so fragile and lovely she looked.

"Sister," she called softly, "why aren't you inside takin' a breather?"

"Don't need any time off" came the terse reply.

Leah didn't care to dispute that; no need starting another quarrel. "I saw you out here and thought maybe we could have us a quick chat."

"Seems you're the one who's most eager to talk."

Right away she felt put off by Sadie's remark, yet Leah rejected the urge to respond in kind. "I was hopin' we could discuss somethin' . . . without fussin' this time."

"All depends."

Leah reckoned if she brought up Naomi just now, Sadie might let out a holler. She wouldn't put it past Sadie, not the way her emotions had run unchecked lately. "Have you given any more thought to, well . . . what we talked 'bout before?"

"Don't mince words, Leah. Say what you mean."

"All right, then. Isn't it time . . . I mean, don't you feel you should unburden your heart to Mamma, at least?"

Sadie scowled.

Leah crouched down in the small irrigation ditch between the rows. "Honestly, Sadie, I'm scared someone else might know the truth—besides Aunt Lizzie and me—and report you to Preacher Yoder."

Sadie raised her voice, blue eyes glistening. "So . . . did you go an' tell?"

"Actually, Naomi told *me* a thing or two. She's decided to make a stand for virtue and hopes you'll repent. And mighty quick."

"Naomi has nothin' on me."

Leah whispered, "She didn't know you were in the family way?"

Sadie shook her head. "Only that I kept seein' Derry after my baptism, is all."

"Even so, I'm as worried for you as Naomi is. Unconfessed sin is treacherous." She remembered the Scripture Jonas had written in his last letter. *Beholding as in a glass the glory of the Lord . . .* If only she could share *that* just now, but her sister's heart was closed up; Leah knew by the hard look of frustration on Sadie's face.

Sadie rose and shoved the hoe deep into the ground. "I don't care anymore what happens to me."

"You're upset, that's all. You don't mean it."

"Oh, but I do."

"Sadie . . . sister, don't you want to obey the vows you made to the church . . . to God?"

"Don't fret over me. The covenant I made was false."

"I fear that's even worse."

"Let God be the judge of that."

Leah felt the breath go out of her. "I can't stand by and watch the brethren put the Bann on you. Oh, Sadie . . . I won't!"

"How are you goin' to stop them?"

"By pesterin' you till you agree to do what is right. Wouldn't you do the same if the tables were turned? Wouldn't you shake me but gut . . . help me see the error of my ways?"

"You're not me. Be ever so glad. . . ." She was quiet for a time, poking at the dirt with her toe. Then she said, "I'm countin' on you to keep your promise about my baby. Naomi thinks she has something to confess 'bout me, but it's you— and Aunt Lizzie—who know the worst of it."

Leah wished once more she'd never made her covenant with Sadie.

Again she opened her mouth and tried to explain her sense of urgency. "Naomi insists she wants to present herself to the Lord God without spot or blemish so she can partake in holy baptism."

"Am I s'posed to believe Naomi's motives are pure?" Sadie laughed bitterly. "You should've seen *her* with them English fellas."

"But Naomi's sins have been forgiven. She's put her wild days behind her."

"'Tis hard to believe."

"She hopes the same for you, sister," Leah whispered. "I know this for truth."

"Naomi can't save me . . . neither can Preacher. No one can. Don't you see? It's too late for me. . . ." Sadie began to cry.

Glancing at the house, Leah hoped Mamma or the twins weren't witnessing this exchange. Tears sprang to her own eyes and she reached a desperate hand toward Sadie. Tall and stiff, Sadie remained aloof. "If I could take away your sadness and pain—all of it—even repent and bend my knee in your stead, I surely would," Leah said soft and slow.

"The People would set me up as an example. I'd rather be dead . . . like my baby boy." Sadie covered her face with her slender white hands, her shoulders rising and falling with the sobs.

Her heart breaking for her sister, Leah pressed on. "Won'tcha please talk to Dat and Mamma? They'll help you sort things out, help make things right with the church. Otherwise, Naomi will go an' talk to Preacher and his wife . . . in one month."

Sadie's hands flew up. "I won't . . . I *can't*, don't you see?"

"The People will not withhold forgiveness. So . . . why not confess?"

"Because I . . . I can't forgive myself, that's why" came the sorrowful reply. Sadie wrapped her arms round her own slender waist.

"Oh, Sadie . . ."

"One thing I would ask of Jehovah God if I could . . . and that would be to turn back time."

"Before your rumschpringe?" She hoped that's what Sadie meant.

"You're mistaken. I wouldn't trade those weeks and months, even though at times I loathe Derry for what happened." Sadie's tears spilled over her silky cheeks. "What I want more than anything is to hold my baby again . . . to bring my precious little one back from the dead. I have no right to seek God's forgiveness, don't you see?" Sadie turned abruptly and picked up the hoe, sniffling.

Astonished and pained by Sadie's words, Leah grasped a greater depth of her sister's agony. Sadie both despised and adored her former beau, and the departed baby was the only significant result of the forbidden union. No wonder Sadie was so terribly distressed.

"I'm thinkin' only of you, dear sister," Leah said softly.

"Haven't you done enough? You gave up your summer in Ohio for me."

"Isn't that what sisters do? Even if the People should shun you, which won't happen—will it?—you and I are sisters for always. Nothing can break that bond."

Sadie's expression softened. She leaned on the hoe, nodding. "But you mustn't try to carry the sorrow; it's mine alone."

"You know I'd do anything for you. Ev'ry night I pray for the balm of Gilead to soothe your poor, sad soul." Leah went to Sadie then, and Sadie received her as both girls fell into each other's arms.

"I'll think on what you said," Sadie said through her tears. "I'll think hard about confessin'. Honest, I will."

The flood tide was released. Leah wept in Sadie's arms for at least this glimmer of hope.

On the way out to the cornfield, carrying a tall Thermos of iced tea, Hannah heard Sadie and Leah talking in the vegetable garden. And of all things, it sounded like someone was weeping! *Well, what the world?* She turned to look over her shoulder and saw Leah standing near Sadie there between the rows, looking as if she, too, might be crying.

The sound of her sisters' sadness faded as Hannah distanced herself from the family garden and walked barefoot toward Dat in the field. The corn should have been knee-high by early in July. Sadly, much of it was only a little more than that tall now because of the long dry spell. Though, situated in a lower section of the field, a two-acre clump was thriving due to underground springs.

She turned to glance back at Sadie and Leah once more and decided not to vex herself about her sisters. She had enough to think on. For one, the secret stash of money she'd hidden away. She had no idea what would happen if Dat discovered she was planning to assist Mary Ruth in her quest for education, in spite of her own misgivings. With all the books piled up under their bed, she'd have to make sure no one but Mary Ruth helped move it away from the wall during early fall housecleaning!

Soon she was within earshot of Dat and the smithy Peachey. "Short of talking again to Gid, I have no idea where to go from here," the smithy was saying.

"I've done all I can and then some," Dat replied. "But let's not give up just yet."

Hannah called to her father. What an awkward situation. She hoped he might hear her and cease his discussion with the smithy.

Dat's expression changed when he saw Hannah and the Thermos. "Hullo!" he greeted her, shielding his eyes with one hand and waving big as you please with the other.

"Mamma sent some nice, cold tea—honey sweetened and sun brewed," she said, feeling the need to explain why she'd intruded on them.

"Denki, Hannah." He reached for the Thermos, exchanging glances with smithy Peachey, and right away he offered the cold drink to his neighbor and lifetime friend.

She turned to hurry back toward the house. The hillside was draped in purple clover, and in the sunlight the hue was at once as deep as it was radiant. She and Mary Ruth had often gone and rolled in the clover as little girls. Truth was, they still did sometimes at dusk when no one could see they were, indeed, still youngsters inside. But this day they wouldn't relax that way. She and Mary Ruth had an over-abundance of chores to accomplish before supper, what with the garden bursting its vines with produce and the vegetable stand needing tending to. On top of that, Mamma had come to rely on both Hannah and Leah to spell her off with baby Lydiann. Mary Ruth wasn't much of a choice, though, since with someone *else's* house to look after, she wasn't around every day of the week. As for Sadie, she wasn't much of a sister *or* a nursemaid, neither one. Hannah had been writing down her thoughts about her surly sister on the lined pages of her diary, so perturbed she was at Sadie sometimes. And she wasn't the only one.

Just this morning when she was helping run the clothes through the wringer, Mamma had said she thought it might be wise for Sadie to go live with Aunt Lizzie for a spell, "till she gets herself straightened out some."

Hannah was stunned—such strong words falling from Mamma's lips. But when Mamma asked what she thought of that, the best Hannah could say was—"Ain't ever wanted any of my sisters livin' out from under Dat's roof. Not just yet."

"Well, I daresay none of them has ever had such a defiant streak." Mamma had frowned and shook her head. Clearly aggravated, she groaned a bit as she bent down to hoist the wicker hamper filled with damp clothing. She carried it out to the yard without even asking Hannah to lift a finger to help.

The two of them hung the clothes on the wash line, and all the while Hannah wished she might have had the wit to say something right quick—even important—like Mary Ruth would have for sure if *she'd* been there helping Mamma. Her twin was never shy about speaking her mind.

Sometimes Hannah was convinced Mary Ruth had gotten all the gumption. Come to think of it, maybe a problem ran in the family when it came to twins. After all, Cousin Fannie Mast had written Mamma recently saying one of *their* twins was behind the other in growth and development. But wasn't it a little silly to think just because you were a twin, one of you might have gotten greedy in the womb with the nourishment? Mary Ruth had never been a stingy sort of girl, in *or* out of their mother's belly. What's more, Mamma had always said they'd each weighed the same, and both had walked and talked on the exact same day.

Hannah decided that more than likely she was bashful by nature, not slow in her thinking, and her hesitancy wasn't the result of being a twin. And she felt she had at least one small gift from the Almighty. Though she would never think of boasting, she believed she had a right nice way of writing down words and phrases. Her diary was living proof.

Nearing the side yard, Hannah raised her head to look again toward the big garden, wondering if Sadie and Leah had talked out their problems. But her sisters were nowhere to be seen.

Chapter Twelve

Later that afternoon Leah hitched the slow horse to the family buggy, then returned to the house and helped Dawdi John limp across the walk. She still couldn't get over Dat having given her the go-ahead to spend a full month in Ohio, however reluctantly. Jonas would be mighty surprised and pleased, and this could go a long way toward bettering the relationship between her future husband and Dat. Now if she could just get together the money for her train ticket.

The sun hid behind a cloud as she and Dawdi rode toward the small medical clinic. Dawdi had complained all last week of his worsening hip, so Mamma had stopped in at Dr. Schwartz's last Friday on her way back from Strasburg and made an appointment.

More than happy to take her grandfather to see the doctor, Leah was equally glad for a bit of quietude—Dawdi being a peaceable man even when seriously ailing. Goodness knew, she needed a breather, and she felt herself relax some while she held the reins, letting the horse do the hard work. Such troubling things Sadie had blurted to her out in the garden.

Seemed, though, there might be a ray of hope for Sadie to confess. Truly, her sister's heart was broken and bleeding.

After their private talk Sadie had gone inside and created a fuss, all because Mamma had suggested Sadie take herself upstairs and lie down. "You look so hot in the face," Mamma had said sweetly, offering a concerned smile, no doubt noticing Sadie's swollen eyes.

"I'm all right, really," Sadie replied.

"Just thought a rest might do you good."

Then Sadie burst out crying. "I'll go out to the pasture if you say to—coax all the cows home for milkin'—do Leah's chores, but I *won't* be resting!"

Both Hannah and Mamma gasped, though Mamma the louder. "Such foolish words, Sadie dear. Time you behave like a baptized church member . . . and bite your tongue."

Sadie brushed her tears away, standing there silent now.

"You best go to your room," Mamma insisted. " 'Tis not becomin' of you to disobey."

Suddenly Sadie brushed past Mamma and Leah, breaking into an all-out run. Out the back door and down the steps she went, toward the barnyard.

"Go now an' talk to Dat!" Mamma called after her, her face boiling red. She probably wanted to holler out in the worst way that Sadie best get inside this minute and do as she said.

But Sadie was already past the milk house and heading for the outhouse; Leah guessed she was flying off to Aunt Lizzie's—a good place for her, in Leah's opinion. Lizzie was the best one to calm down a distraught girl like Sadie, although Mamma might not think so.

For sure and for certain, just now Leah relished this peaceful time with Dawdi John. She looked over at him, hoping Dr. Schwartz could alleviate the severe pain, though at the moment Dawdi looked as relaxed as a sleeping baby, his head bobbing as the horse pulled them gentle and slow down the road.

"I hate Gobbler's Knob!" Sadie cried as she rushed into Aunt Lizzie's kitchen. "Mamma has it in for me. I know she does!"

Lizzie went to her. "Ach, your mamma loves you more than you know, Sadie dear." She led her to the front room and sat her down, loosening Sadie's prayer bonnet to stroke the top of her head. "You just listen here to your aunt Lizzie," she whispered low, beginning to hum a slow church song from the *Ausbund*.

Sadie felt an awful tightness in her neck and shoulders and thought she might burst apart, so distressed she was. Now that she was here, safe and secure in Aunt Lizzie's cozy house, she quite liked all this cooing and whatnot. Lizzie's soft arms and gentle touch made her feel as if, just maybe, the whole world wasn't going to fall apart.

After a time, when her sobbing slowed to a whimper, Sadie lay quietly with her head on Lizzie's lap, soaking up all the love, the soft humming, and an occasional "now there." At this moment she secretly wished Lizzie were her mother instead of merely her aunt. She could only wonder what life might be like living up here in the woods with Aunt Lizzie, not being the eldest sister to three, no, *four* girls, but rather a cousin-sister to Leah, the twins, and Lydiann. Goodness' sake, it was a trial putting up with Mamma's colicky baby crying all hours of the night. "Every time Lydiann wails, I feel like crying, too. 'Cept I do it inside."

"No wonder you weep," Aunt Lizzie said. "You have strong ties to the babe you carried close to your heart—right or wrong—and nothin' can take away the emptiness, now that he's not in your arms."

Sadie raised her head and looked into Lizzie's pretty hazel eyes. "So there's nothin' wrong with me?"

Lizzie smiled faintly. "No, my lamb. Don't be thinkin' thataway."

"Oh, Aunt Lizzie, what would I do without you to talk to?"

"Well, now . . . you'd prob'ly do like we all do, sooner or later, and be talkin' to the Good Lord about your trials."

"What's the point of prayin'?" Sadie asked. "I doubt the Lord would hear me, anyway."

"You may be thinkin' that, but believe me, there ain't a shred of truth to it."

She sat up, wiping away her tears. "Why's it seem so, then?"

"Your spirit's all closed up—like a rock-hard honeycomb. Back when you gave up your innocence, you hardened your heart to the gift of purity that's meant for your husband. You're altogether different now that you've been awakened to fleshly desires, the longings a wife has for her husband."

Sadie felt her pulse pounding in her stomach. She did yearn for Derry every day of her life. "You seem to know what I'm feelin', Auntie."

Lizzie turned to look out the window for a moment. Her

lip quivered slightly. "I'm guessin' it's about time I own up to you. You're plenty old enough now. . . ." She sighed. "Indeed, I do know what you're feelin'. Know it as sure as you sittin' here next to me."

"Whatever do you mean?"

Aunt Lizzie faltered, and if Sadie wasn't mistaken, there was a sad glint in her eyes. "As a young woman I committed a grievous sin against the Lord God, one of the reasons my father, Dawdi John, sent me here to Gobbler's Knob—to escape the shame that was sure to come in Hickory Hollow."

"Are you sayin' what I think?" Sadie asked, nervous to hear more.

"You must keep this between just us. Abram would not want me speakin' of this, not without his say-so."

"*Dat* wouldn't?" She was truly perplexed, yet the urgent look on Aunt Lizzie's face was nearly irresistible.

"He's an honorable man, Abram. Still, he is tight-lipped, and with all gut reason."

Sadie purposely turned to face Lizzie as they sat on the couch. She felt ever so drawn to her aunt now, desperately needing to concentrate on her gentle face, witness the haunting sadness and the truth-light in her eyes as Lizzie whispered tenderly, if hesitantly, of "the darlin' baby girl born to me when I was but a teen." Lizzie's eyes spilled over with tears, but she kept them fixed on Sadie.

"A *baby?*"

Lizzie nodded her head slowly.

"I never would've guessed. Not now, not ever," Sadie whispered, unable to speak in her normal tone, so stunned she was. Had Aunt Lizzie been required to live as a maidel for this reason?

"I've borne this secret these many years."

"Oh, Aunt Lizzie . . ."

"My dear girl, I've suffered the terrible consequence of my sin by not bein' able to raise my child as my own. But long ago I purposed in my heart to follow God in spite of what had happened to me."

"So . . . I'm not the only one to lose a child. . . ." She was aware of Aunt Lizzie's steady breathing. *No wonder I feel so close to you,* she thought, leaning her head against her aunt's shoulder.

Lizzie caressed Sadie's head, and for a moment they sat there, not speaking, scarcely moving.

After a time Sadie opened her eyes. Her heart was bursting with love and sympathy both, and she wondered just where Lizzie's daughter was now, all grown-up. Had one of Dat's or Mamma's many siblings stepped in to raise the little one? She didn't have the heart to ask just now, though she was dying to know.

———◆———

Leah sat in the waiting room, hoping the doctor could help ease Dawdi's pain, his being the last patient of the day. Dat had said the strangest thing about the sudden onset of Dawdi's health problems the other day. He'd indicated Dawdi surely had something "all bottled up inside," and when she had asked just what that could be, Dat had brushed it off like it was nothing to worry over. Well, far as she was concerned, Dawdi wasn't putting on. She'd seen him shuffle along, nearly lame. She'd seen him wince as he stepped in and out of the buggy, too.

Reaching for a magazine on the lamp table, she opened to a full-page advertisement. A sense of guilt swept over her as she read the caption: *Which Twin Has the Toni?* She stared at the smiling faces of identical twin girls with matching home waves and bare necks. Englishers seemed bent on short hair, lots of curls, and too much skin, along with the many things their money could buy. She had come to this conclusion the few times she'd allowed herself a glance at the magazines displayed here in Dr. Schwartz's office. Convicted, she returned the magazine to the table.

Thinking now of Sadie, she hoped maybe her sister *had* run off to see Aunt Lizzie this afternoon after the spat with Mamma. Surely their aunt could help focus Sadie's mind on holy living—on obedience, too.

Getting up, Leah went to the window and stared out. The lone horse and buggy looked nearly out of place in the empty parking area, yet she was glad for Dr. Schwartz's willingness to see patients besides his English clients.

She pondered again the frightening night Sadie had given birth. She alone had been the reason the doctor had come to help Sadie, having ridden bareback on one of Dat's horses—a phantom ride through the midnight darkness, up the narrow road to the clinic. She recalled how reluctant she had been to travel back to the Ebersol Cottage and up the mule road with Dr. Schwartz in his fast automobile . . . yet she had. Gripping the door handle, she'd worried herself nearly sick at what might await them in Aunt Lizzie's log house.

Moving away from the window, she walked slowly about the room, noticing the many framed photographs on the light-colored walls. Pictures of people intrigued her, perhaps because she had been warned to avoid cameras, ever present in the summer when English tourists came calling. It was all right to display pastoral scenes on the walls, along with cross-stitched designs and floral or nature-related calendars. Bishop Bontrager permitted such things, but photographs of people were downright prohibited.

But here she was met by one smiling face after another, each framed in wood, all English folk. Nearly a whole wall of people dressed in fancy clothes, especially a woman with cropped and curled hair, seated on a white-wicker bench. Two young boys and a man encircled her, all smiling at someone's camera.

Looking closer, she recognized the man to be Dr. Henry Schwartz. *Is that his wife?* she wondered.

Several more photographs featured the foursome, no doubt posing at the photography studio she'd seen in downtown Lancaster, though of course she had never dared darken the door. The last in the lineup was a portrait of a boy with thick brown hair and exceptionally dark eyes, wearing what she guessed was a baseball team uniform, since there was a baseball bat in the youngster's hand.

She was drawn to the smiling face and saw the words: *Thanks, Dad . . . Love, Derry* in the bottom corner.

How peculiar to think someone would actually write on a photograph. But then she guessed that this, too, was another one of the strange customs of the English.

Derry . . .

Suddenly she began to shiver uncontrollably. Her scalp felt prickly as she stared at the boyish scrawl. She'd heard of only one such Englisher by that name in her life.

Her mind was spinning now. But no! This couldn't be Sadie's Derry, could it? *Did Sadie go and fall in love with one of Dr. Schwartz's sons?* she wondered.

Rejecting the notion, she went back and studied each of the framed pictures yet again, discovering one that was surely the same boy, only much older, possibly a graduating high-school senior. She moved back and forth between the two pictures, double-checking the young man's features against those of the child. She was desperate for something more to go on.

At last she spied gold lettering in the far corner and the name of the photo studio. *Gold Tone, 1946.*

Could this be the boy Sadie still wept for . . . the father of her dead baby? Going to sit on one of the several wooden chairs that lined the wall, she felt truly bewildered. If what she suspected was true, then Dr. Schwartz had delivered his own grandson last April.

Her heart was pounding. Her sister had been defiled by the good doctor's son!

She bit her lip, refusing the anger that threatened to overflow. She felt like running out the door and all the way home; she wanted to ease her exasperation but was ever so mindful of her surroundings. *I'll wait right here for Dawdi . . . I must hold my peace. . . .*

To stave off her fury, she turned and looked out the window yet again, across the yard to the road and the forested hillock beyond. She wanted to hurry home and ask Sadie if Derry Schwartz was, in fact, the father. On further reflection, she determined not to. She must not question her sister because it would be one more irritation between them. She was unwilling to further jeopardize their sisterhood.

When Dawdi emerged on the doctor's arm, still rubbing his thigh from the sting of a shot, she felt her head spin a bit. Carefully she rose and helped Dawdi John out the door and down to the horse and carriage. "Ach, I forgot to pay the doctor bill," Dawdi said once she had him settled.

"Not to worry, I'll return tomorrow," she replied, her thoughts in a flurry.

"Denki, Leah. You're such a gut girl."

Gut girl . . .

If only Sadie had been so. If only Sadie had refused the affections of an English boy.

Purposely Leah directed her attention to dear Dawdi, engaging him in slow conversation, attempting to soothe him, as well as to drive away the anger within herself.

Chapter Thirteen

After breakfast Mamma said she would be the one to go to Dr. Schwartz's clinic to pay Dawdi's bill from the day before. "I won't be but a minute," she announced before stepping out the back door.

Sadie was aware of Leah scurrying out to the chicken coop to feed the hens and the lone rooster while the twins kneaded two mounds of bread dough. It was Sadie's morning to tend the roadside stand, but instead of heading there she stood in the window and watched Mamma leave in the carriage. Aunt Lizzie's heartrending confession continued to fill her mind. To think both Lizzie and she had done the selfsame evil in the sight of God. During that troubling time, Mamma and Dat had taken Lizzie under their united wing, helping her through the pregnancy and delivery of a baby girl. But Lizzie had stopped short of telling the whole story, saying, when Sadie had asked at long last what happened to her baby, that the bishop decided the child should be given away. "To be adopted?" Sadie had said, horrified. Lizzie indicated it had been so with a solemn nod of her head. When Sadie pressed for more details, Lizzie assured her "'twas best for the baby, indeed."

Befuddled, Sadie hadn't even thought to ask how old Lizzie's daughter would be by now. She was astounded at the account Lizzie had given of her wild and youthful days. It wasn't any wonder why her wounded aunt was so understanding and kind toward her. Toward everyone whose life she touched, really.

Sadie went and asked Mary Ruth to cover for her out front at the roadside stand. "Just for a few minutes, would ya?" And Mary Ruth reluctantly agreed, washed the flour off her hands, and headed out the back door.

Sadie then crept up the stairs to the biggest bedroom, Dat and Mamma's room. There in the corner, snug in an oversized cherrywood cradle, Lydiann slept soundly. Last night had been a ruckus of sorts, a difficult one for the whole household. Lydiann's crying had kept Mamma and Dat from having much rest at all. Both Sadie and Leah had awakened to Dat's voice, then to his footsteps on the stairs as he headed outside for a spell, probably needing a bit of repose. Mamma had been the one to stay with Lydiann, humming and cajoling, finally getting her settled down again in the wee hours.

Standing over the pink-cheeked bundle, Sadie peered into the cradle. Lydiann's facial features, even her little head, were changing ever so quickly. Maybe all that crying and fussing made her grow faster. In no time at all she'd be sitting up, even crawling, talking . . . and before they knew it, she'd be off to singings, married, and a mamma herself; so the life cycle went. Goodness, Sadie had observed enough babies and toddlers growing up just that quickly in the church and at home, too, right under her nose.

She knelt beside the cradle, touching the side ever so lightly . . . rocking, rocking. She stroked the precious, dimpled hands, soft as cotton. "You're a perty baby girl," she whispered. "But you cry every night like your heart's a-breakin'. What an awful sad time it is round here. But you . . . just look at you. You're all right, Lydiann. You're alive . . . breathin' and growin'. . . ."

She leaned down and lifted the sweet-smelling bundle out of the cradle. Pacing the wide-plank floor in her bare feet, she gazed at the sleeping angel in her arms. *You . . . you're as sweet as a flower, but* my *baby's dead. You came to us just as I lost my own little one.*

She went and sat in the big rocker, across from the dresser, her arms warm with Lydiann's body so close to her. "A sorry excuse I am for a big sister," she whispered. "It's not that I don't love you, Lydiann . . . I do."

She began humming a mournful tune, something Gideon Peachey had played on his harmonica years ago. Back when they, all the girls and Dat and Mamma, had been invited by the smithy and his wife for a family picnic. And Gid, surrounded by his two younger sisters and the four Ebersol girls, had played the sad melody. Maybe he was outnumbered by girls and miserable, or he was secretly longing for a girlfriend, but Sadie had never forgotten the song. Nor the light in Gid's eyes for young Leah, who seemed oblivious to him, except that she nodded her head slowly to his melancholy music.

So Sadie hummed for Lydiann, thinking back over the years . . . all the happy days growing up here in Gobbler's

Knob, playing both in and near Blackbird Pond, swinging on the haymow rope, making grape jelly with Adah and Dorcas, watching Gid with his newest batch of German shepherd pups. . . .

Unexpectedly, the baby stirred, and lest the melody awaken her, Sadie stopped humming and began to rock more steadily. Then, once Lydiann had relaxed again and drifted back to sleep, Sadie talked to her, oh, so softly, scarcely able to stop. "I wish it weren't true, but you'll never, ever know your tiny nephew, my dead little baby. Not this side of the Jordan. You see, the Lord God took him away . . . before he ever had a chance to breathe or live or know how dearly loved he was."

She struggled, trying to hold back the tears lest they fall unchecked onto the tiny cotton nightgown. Besides, if she gave in to her urgent need to cry, she might not stop for a long time, like Lydiann did each and every night. But no, Sadie didn't want Mary Ruth and Hannah aware she was up here confessing her sins to a sleeping baby, of all things.

Confessing . . .

She sat there, rocking and sniffling. Leah's and Aunt Lizzie's constant urging echoed in her ears—and now Naomi threatening to tell if she didn't. . . .

She pondered what it might be like to tell the sorry truth of her sins to her parents and, eventually, to the church brethren . . . how she would kneel low on bended knee in front of the entire membership of the People. Such a hushed silence there would be in the house of worship, with the newly baptized young people staring at her, including the young men.

Awful difficult it was to imagine, yet she persisted. She would be required to speak up enough to be heard not only by the deacon and the preachers, but *all* the People must be able to hear what she and Derry had done in the private haven of the hunter's shack, in the name of love.

She felt the heat of her shame and reproach like the fires of hell licking at her feet. Sadie shuddered at the mental images—the sadness and shock on Mamma's face, the tense set of Dat's jaw, the accusing eyes of the People boring into her, the ministers asking repeated questions.

How could she go through it? How could she repent of loving her child? Repent of her anger toward God, who had *taken* her child, had killed him?

She looked down at Lydiann. The sweet peace of sleep on her wee face gave Sadie a sudden and terrible panic. She realized anew that repentance would mean the loss of everything she'd ever wanted. No boy in Gobbler's Knob would give her a second look, pretty as she knew she was. And worst of all . . . having a dear, precious baby of her own, one just like Lydiann, would be forever impossible.

Hannah felt uneasy standing there in the hallway. She had come upstairs to inform Sadie that Mary Ruth was getting more customers than she alone could handle at the vegetable stand. She preferred not to run out front herself but wanted Sadie to go instead, since it was Sadie's responsibility, anyway.

When she finally found her oldest sister, she almost called to her. But she was taken aback seeing Sadie sitting in Mamma's rocking chair, talking to Lydiann, who was sleeping right through it.

Listening, she overheard the most startling words. *Could it be? Ach no.* Sadie was surely making up a story—a sordid one at that—just talking slow and soft to soothe Lydiann. To be sure, their baby sister had been awful fussy since she came into the world. A person might whisper most anything to quiet down a tot like that. Still, Hannah had not heard Lydiann cry out or fuss at all this morning, not since Mamma left. *So what's Sadie doing up here?* she wondered.

Having listened in this long, she decided it wouldn't hurt to stand here a bit more. The English customers out front would just have to wait their turn with Mary Ruth. She locked her knees and leaned her ear, but what came next shocked Hannah no end. Sadie was cooing to Lydiann, her voice trembling as she spoke of another infant, though dead. "He was my own baby boy. The result of the worst sin I ever committed, yet I loved him so."

Hannah began to wonder just when on earth was it Sadie had been in the family way? If any of what she was babbling was even true.

But Hannah had heard enough. More than she cared to, really, yet she stood there nearly frozen in place, contemplating the meaning of Sadie's confession. Were Mamma and Aunt Lizzie privy to any of this? And what would Dat say or do if he knew? She could scarcely breathe at the thought.

Leah finished up with the chickens, gathering in the eggs before closing the door on their squawking. She hurried to the house as Mary Ruth came flying across the side yard. "It's Sadie's turn at the vegetable stand now," Mary Ruth said hastily. "I'm plumb wore out."

"Oh? What's Sadie doing?"

"I thought *you* knew where she was," Mary Ruth replied.

Leah had no desire to look for or exchange words with Sadie this morning. They'd said not a word to each other last evening as they undressed for bed. She must simply wait and pray Sadie would do the right thing.

She must not borrow trouble and worry over what might be. She turned her thoughts to Jonas. Time at last to write and tell him of her surprising chat with Dat, that her father's heart had softened. She would head up to the woods, to her favorite spot in the sun. No need telling anyone where she was going, not with the day so bright and blue and not a cloud in the sky.

Hurrying upstairs, she bumped into Hannah, who looked rather pale in the face. "Are you ill?" Leah asked.

Hannah shook her head no.

"Is Sadie around?"

Hannah pointed meekly toward Mamma's bedroom. "In there."

Leah turned to look just in time to see Sadie putting Lydiann down in the cradle. "What's she doin'?" she whispered.

"I wondered the same" came Hannah's reply.

Well, wasn't this an interesting turn of events? Sadie was tending to Lydiann without being asked. *What does it mean?* Leah wondered.

Leah turned to Hannah. "I'd like to talk with Sadie . . . alone."

Hannah nodded and headed down the steps.

Without delay, Leah went to Sadie, who was still staring

down at Lydiann. "Sister?" she said, standing near.

Sadie's cheeks were wet with tears.

"What's wrong?" Leah asked, touching her sister's elbow.

Sadie sighed, casting her sad gaze downward. Soon she looked up, her lower lip trembling uncontrollably. "I've been trying, Leah. Honestly, I've been thinking through my kneeling confession, and I can't do it."

For a moment Leah was at a loss for words. Sadie seemed unwavering in her decision. "Maybe later, then. Won't you give yourself a bit more time?"

"I'm simply markin' time now, waitin' with no purpose," Sadie replied. "Don't you see? There's no hope of a normal life for me here. Not anymore . . ."

"Oh, Sadie, that's not true. You're still grievin' for your baby. Things will certainly get better. Won't you reconsider?"

"Jah, things *will* be better, and soon, because I'm leavin' home."

Such unexpected words made Leah feel queasy. "Leavin'? But . . . I'm gettin' married soon. Won't you be here for that special day?"

"I'm awful sorry, Leah . . . truly I am." Sadie's eyes glistened with more tears.

"Where are you thinkin' of going?"

Sadie shrugged sadly. "Doesn't matter really. Anywhere. Maybe I'll set out on foot, then hitch a ride on the road."

Leah was horrified. "That's too dangerous."

"I just can't wait anymore." Sadie shook her head. "I thought I could stay put, but I can't. Once Naomi goes to the preacher 'bout me, the ministers will demand penitence . . .

and when I refuse, I'll be shunned. What's the point in stayin' any longer?"

Leah felt her throat close up. Yet she managed to ask, "Can't you talk to our parents, at least?"

"And tell them what? *Why* I'm leavin'? That I had a baby out of wedlock and I can't apologize to God?" Sadie looked over at Mamma's pretty blue go-to-meeting dress, hanging on the wooden peg. "'Tis best I disappear."

Leah slipped her arm around her sister's waist. "Would you wait at least another day or so?"

Sadie looked pained. "Why? So you can tell everyone I'm goin'?"

Leah shook her head. "I promise not to, truthfully."

Sadie seemed to give it some thought. "All right." She sighed, her shoulders falling. "For you, I'll wait a bit. I can trust you, Leah. You and Aunt Lizzie."

"What about Dat and Mamma—you can trust them, too, ain't?"

"Maybe, 'cept they hold fast to the Old Ways. They'll never understand what's in my heart."

Leah breathed deeply, still vexed. "You won't just up and leave, then, not until we talk again?"

Sadie consented. "I'll say good-bye to you, *jah*. I promise."

Leah reached for her sister, who trembled in her arms. They clung to each other as Sadie quietly wept. *How much time do I have left with her?* she worried. *If Sadie leaves, the Bann will separate us . . . possibly forever.*

Sadie brushed away her tears and kissed Leah's face. Then she headed out to help mind the vegetable stand.

Watching Sadie go, Leah recalled her plans to write to

Jonas. Here, just a few moments before, she had been rejoic-ing with the good news she couldn't wait to share with him, that she would see him soon. And now? Everything had been colored by her dismal conversation with Sadie.

But wasn't her first responsibility to her beau? She had pledged her love and life to Jonas Mast. Sadie, on the other hand, was bent on making wrong choices, as seemed more evident with each day that passed.

Leah felt frustration toward her sister . . . yet at the same time, she felt ever so guilty for feeling so. Sadie had promised to stay for a few days longer, so perhaps Leah might have time to talk her out of running away. And if *she* couldn't reason with Sadie, maybe, just maybe, Aunt Lizzie could. Although the determined look in Sadie's eyes had frightened Leah no end.

Heaving a sigh, she headed down the hall to their bed-room, taking her best stationery pad and pen from her bureau drawer. Then she hurried back downstairs to the kitchen, where Hannah and Mary Ruth were busy scrubbing the floor on their hands and knees. "I'm goin' for a quick walk," Leah told them.

She dashed outside, looking toward the road as she went. She could now see that Sadie was busy with a customer. *'Tis gut,* she thought, glad everyone was accounted for, especially Sadie.

She spied Aunt Lizzie near the barn, hitching a horse to the carriage. "Are you headed somewhere?" she called to her.

"Over to Mattie Sue Byler's for a canning frolic," Lizzie said, smiling. "You?"

She remembered her promise to Sadie and decided not to

breathe a word. *How many more times must I make such promises to that sister?* Leah thought.

"My morning chores are done, so I'm off to write a letter," she said, hoping her voice didn't betray her stirred-up emotions.

Lizzie seemed to be in a hurry, but her eyes registered concern. "Watch closely for my tree markings, hear?"

"I know my way there and back."

"For certain?"

"No need to fret over me," she insisted. "I'll return well before the noon meal."

"All right, then." Lizzie waved and tore down the lane, the horse going too fast for Leah's liking.

Leah hiked up to the edge of the woods, eager to think about other things. This close to the end of August, she noticed the mornings felt cooler than even last week. Mary Ruth and Hannah would be starting school next Monday, the twenty-fifth. But today they would tidy up around the house, help weed the gardens, and maybe bake an apple dapple cake for supper. And they'd all be helping Mamma can plenty of pears and peaches this afternoon. Once she returned from writing her letter, she'd help Dat some, too, though it looked like Gid was already in the barn pitching hay to the mules.

Aunt Lizzie was right about these woods being daunting. The minute she stepped past the clearing and onto the densely treed hillock, she felt a foreboding, although it was

145

probably just her distressed state of mind.

She looked for the first marked tree . . . there it was. The path led across furrows and hollows through the deepest brushwood. Then, when she reached a rather low summit, she caught glimpses of the horizon to the north, the blue of the sky like a wide ribbon woven through the trees.

She was alone. Not a single soul was within calling distance. Now she could sit beneath the honey locust tree and put aside her fear for Sadie. It was time to dwell on the fact Dat had said she could go to Ohio. Who would have thought it?

In this vast forest, she felt herself equal in smallness to the tiniest woodland creatures scurrying here and there as they sensed her presence. In the sight of the Lord God, was she like a little bird? A robin, a jay, a common wren? She understood from Dat's big Bible that the Lord was in all places at once—everywhere present—and all-knowing and wise, too. Could He see into her heart and know the things that concerned her? Did He see Sadie's sorrow, too?

She watched eagerly for the next tree marking, and the next, each put there so kindly by Aunt Lizzie. Walking quickly, she was eager to get to her spot, not taking time this day to pick up a pretty stone or a wild flower as she went.

At last she laid eyes on the enormous tree, a hint of yellow in the leaves welcoming her to the verdant place. Getting situated, she took a moment to orient herself, breathing in the rich, lovely scent of the forest. High in the canopy, squirrels leaped back and forth overhead and bees collected nectar.

She thought of Jonas's descriptions of Millersburg and longed to see it for herself. He had written of Killbuck Creek and its wide creek bed and clear waters, scurrying over rock and limb until it ran smack-dab through town. All the familiar trappings of the area came alive for her in his words, including the Swiss cheese factory near Berlin and the old Victorian house in Millersburg, considered a mansion in every way. An old general store was situated across from the majestic courthouse, Jonas had said, with its ornate stone exterior and unusual clock at the top of a tall turret. The historic building was surrounded on all sides by formal, well-manicured lawns, where courting couples liked to go and sit at dusk, ice-cream cones in hand. She assumed Jonas would take her there, too, when she went to visit him. Oh, if only the days till then would pass more quickly!

She began to write her letter, pouring out her heart to her darling, sharing all of her hope for the future—theirs together—putting it down on the page. She wrote how truly happy she would be to go to Ohio and meet David Mellinger, the man who had made Jonas's long-time dream come true, as well as the master carpenter's wife and family. She told Jonas she was beholden to them for the invitation to stay with their widowed mother, Edith, in the Dawdi Haus, and she kindly offered any help she might give to the ailing woman.

Such a pleasant time we'll have together, Jonas, in the days before our wedding. I'm also curious to learn more about the bishop there—the one you spoke so fondly of—and his teachings.

Referring to the Scripture Jonas had shared in his last letter, she couldn't help but think again of Sadie. Did her sister honestly think leaving Gobbler's Knob would make things better for her?

Suddenly a most unsettling notion came to her. Leah

sighed so loudly in response, she frightened a chipmunk nearby. Would sitting under the teaching of the Ohio bishop be of some benefit to distraught Sadie? According to Jonas, the man was well versed in New Testament Scripture, a rare thing amongst the Old Order.

Leah agonized, thinking of Sadie's delicate emotional state. She doubted her sister could survive on her own away from home. Even though Sadie might fancy herself a confident woman, Leah feared she might be harmed or taken advantage of—or worse yet, be pulled deeply into the English world, never, ever to return.

Placing her trembling hand on her heart, she breathed slowly. *Should I offer Sadie the chance to go to Ohio?*

Tears sprang to her eyes. This idea brewing in her heart— had it been put there by the Lord God? She wondered if she had any right to think like that. *What shall I do?*

She went back and forth in her mind, torn between what she desired for herself and Jonas, and what might possibly be best for Sadie. Yet another hurdle would be to convince her parents—for the sake of Sadie's right standing in the eyes of God and the church. Perhaps, too, Jonas could befriend Sadie without having to know the details of her sins, nor her persistent rebellion. He need only know she was desperate for a change of scenery, at least for a time. Then, when Jonas returned for the harvest, he could simply accompany Sadie back home. Surely by then she'd be ready to offer her repentance. The short time away would also spare Sadie from suffering even a temporary shunning, most likely.

The biggest obstacle was dear Mamma. She would grieve Sadie's leaving, no question. On the other hand, Dat would be relieved to have Leah's help for a while longer than he expected, but he'd certainly want to know why Sadie must go away. Therein was another knotty problem. But she knew enough to trust God, and the more she thought on it, the more she believed the idea *had* been planted in her heart by the almighty One. The crooked way would be made straight, and the rough places made plain.

Unwavering in her resolve, Leah began to tear her letter to Jonas in half, then in fourths, till she had a dozen or more pieces. They lay in the lush grass beside her, and she touched them gently as she wept. A second refusal from her to Jonas. *Will he have an understanding heart?* she wondered. Somehow . . . someway, she hoped he might.

A breeze came up and scattered the pieces out of reach before she could attempt to rescue them. She felt nearly helpless, watching them flutter through the trees as they came to light on moss and twig, like the haphazard markings of a lost soul.

Chapter Fourteen

Around eleven-thirty in the morning, Ida's dinner of veal loaf, baked macaroni and cheese, buttered lima beans, and fresh-tossed greens was ready to serve. She wanted Abram and the girls to come and sit down right away while the main course was still nice and hot. Since Sadie was tending the roadside stand and Ida hadn't seen Leah around all morning, she suggested Mary Ruth ring the dinner bell to alert the family.

The loud *dong-dong* brought Abram in promptly, and he headed for the sink.

"Is Leah on her way in?" asked Ida.

"You mean she's not in the house with you?" Abram glanced over his shoulder, rubbing soap over his big, callused hands.

"I thought she was outdoors. Have *you* seen her, Hannah?"

"She was standin' right here last I saw her," Hannah said, holding wide-eyed Lydiann, awake from a long morning nap.

"But that was hours ago. She said she was goin' for a walk somewhere."

Mary Ruth spoke up. "She and Aunt Lizzie were out talkin' together earlier."

"Before Lizzie left for Bylers'?"

"Jah, 'bout then." Mary Ruth placed hot pads on the green-checked oilcloth. "I daresay she might've hopped in the buggy with Aunt Lizzie, come to think of it."

Ida dismissed that comment; Lizzie had better sense than to allow that. Besides, Ida didn't think Leah would be interested in a canning frolic at Gideon Peachey's grandparents' place. For that reason alone, she was sure Leah had not gone with Lizzie.

She *had* noticed Leah picking at her food here lately and wondered if something was troubling her. *Is that why Leah isn't home for dinner?* she wondered.

"Ain't like her not to tell someone," Hannah said, handing Lydiann to Mamma.

Abram added, "Oh, she'll be along soon enough, I 'spect."

But by dinner's end, Leah still had not come. "Shouldn't one of the girls go lookin' for her?" Ida suggested, beginning to worry.

Abram pulled on his beard, squinting his eyes. "Maybe she got to talkin' to Adah over at the smithy's . . . and just stayed round there for lunch."

But Ida doubted that. Leah was being real careful not to run into Gideon Peachey too often these days. Abram's remark was downright silly, and he knew it.

They bowed their heads for the after-mealtime prayer, but Ida beseeched the Lord God heavenly Father for Leah's protection, especially if she'd taken herself off to the woods. Heaven knew, Leah ought not to be up there alone.

Completely off course, Leah pursued yet another direction. This time the way was even more densely overgrown with hedge and briar, leading to an outcrop of rocks and the sudden smell of animal carcass below. She shook her head, frustrated she'd gotten herself so disoriented after telling Aunt Lizzie she felt right confident. *What would Dat say if he knew?* But Dat hadn't any idea of her dilemma or that she'd even set off for the woods. None of the family did.

Why didn't I think to tell someone besides Aunt Lizzie? she thought.

The farther she went, the less visible the sun became, its light blocked by thick clusters of branches overhead, webbed and interlocked like an enormous barrier between heaven and earth.

———◆———

By late afternoon Ida was beside herself with concern. Abram was out running errands, and she didn't dare try to set off looking for Leah on her own. She wouldn't consider sending her frail father to search, not with his bad hip, nor the twins. With Lizzie gone, the only other option was Sadie, but Ida didn't feel comfortable sending her eldest off to the dark woods. Until her rumschpringe Sadie had always been a home-body, and Ida hoped to nurture that in her again. Besides, it would never do if *two* of their girls got themselves lost up there.

Pacing back and forth between the barnyard and the kitchen door, she spied Gid strolling through the cornfield big as you please. "Say, Gideon!" she called to him, and the smithy's son came running. When she explained Leah had been gone since morning, "didn't even come home for the noon meal," Gid's face dropped and turned nearly ashen.

The young man sprang to life. "I'll take King along for some company," Gid said, calling to the German shepherd.

Ida was ever so glad; she felt she could rely on Gid to bring their girl home safe and sound. If anyone could, he could. She hoped and prayed it would be so.

The first signs of Leah were a few snippets of cream-colored stationery, torn to shreds. Gid picked up several, noticing the words *Dear Jonas* in Leah's own hand. Having attended school with her through eighth grade, he could have recognized her handwriting most anywhere. Truth be known, he was more than impressed with her neat writing, not to mention everything else about her, from as early as preschool days on. But lately he'd become more cautious, guarding his heart. He wouldn't allow himself to picture the day Abram's Leah tied the knot with someone other than himself because in his opinion she was the sweetest girl in the Gobbler's Knob church district. Sometimes he thought he might explore another district just once to see what other girls were available, but he hadn't been able to bring himself to do it, not yet. He couldn't imagine another as pretty and sweet as Leah, nor as kind.

Leah's dog sniffed the ground, as if trying to pick up her scent in the depth of the woods. The dog, though intelligent, had not been trained for tracking. Still, Gid was mighty glad for King's company today.

He glanced at the torn pieces of Leah's letter, feeling awkward with them in his hand. Had she changed her mind about something important, tearing up the letter this way? Gid pushed the idea aside. After all, Leah was a girl who knew what she wanted, always had. Just as he and Leah had been friendly since childhood, Leah and Jonas Mast had also been chummy, though even closer, evidently, or so the grapevine had it. Who was he to think otherwise?

Except now, with this torn letter . . .

Cupping his hands around his mouth, he began to call Leah's name loudly. He hoped she was safe, not hurt or frightened in any way. There were enough chilling tales associated with this forest; it wouldn't do for a young woman to come wandering up here alone, especially at night. And, best as he could estimate, dusk was less than three hours away.

He'd heard tell by his father—Abram's closest friend—that something terrible had happened to Lizzie Brenneman one night in the midst of her rumschpringe in these very woods. As a result, Lizzie had ended up with child, or so he thought the story went. Providentially, only a handful of folk had been aware of the circumstances at the time, and Bishop Bontrager had promptly ordered the whole thing hushed up.

But now, in the midst of his own "running-around years," Gid was surprised to discover more than a few young people held an alarmed apprehension of the enormous, dark Gobbler's Knob forest—especially the girls. It was as if Lizzie

Brenneman's secret had slowly trickled out over the years.

Leah, however, must not have heard the warnings, though he didn't see how, being Lizzie's niece and all. How was it possible for the Ebersol girls not to be privy to at least some of the dark rumors? For Lizzie's sake, he certainly hoped Abram's daughters *had* been protected from the truth. It wouldn't do to harp away on a close relative's painful past, even a shameful sin—though thoroughly repented of, to be sure.

When Gid finally found Leah, he had been tramping through the wilds for a good forty minutes or longer. There she was, perched forlornly on a fallen oak tree, a mystified frown on her pretty face. "Did you hear me callin' back to you?" she asked when she saw him. "I heard you a-hollerin' . . . heard King's barkin', too. Oh, I'm so glad you found me!"

He hurried to her side. "I heard you, all right. I'm glad you're safe."

"I'm just tuckered out, is all. I've been wanderin' round and round in these woods—for hours, seems to me."

"Do you know what time it is?" he asked, kneeling in the leaves.

"Past dinnertime, I'm sure."

Knowing Leah as he did, he was fairly certain she was being plucky for his sake. She must have been awful concerned . . . and hungry. Then he saw tears well up in her eyes. At once gone were his former intentions, his determined stand against getting too close. Where Abram's Leah was concerned, his heart was still tender, though he would have liked to think otherwise. "I could carry you home if . . . well, that is, if you're too wore out to walk."

"Oh, I think I'll manage." She looked at him and smiled, then glanced at her stationery pad in her lap.

"Your family is awful worried, Leah. We daresn't delay," he said, enjoying these stolen minutes more than he cared to admit.

"When I got lost this morning, I realized I'd mistakenly told only one person where I was goin' . . . Aunt Lizzie." She paused, looking at him with inquisitive eyes. "She must not be back from Grasshopper Level yet."

"Far as I know, she wasn't." He nuzzled King, too aware of the awkward silence between them. To break it, he said, "Your dog here is a mighty gut companion. And even though he ain't a trained hunter, he sure seemed to know where you were."

"He prob'ly followed the smell of the barn on me," she replied.

This brought a peal of laughter, and his heart was singing. Was there any chance for them? Any at all?

King went and licked Leah's face, and she put her head down and talked to him like he was one of the family. Then she looked up at Gid. "I'm so grateful to you," she said, still smiling. "And to your dog."

"He's *yours*, don't forget." He watched her face, the brightness in her eyes. *No*, he thought, groaning inwardly. *I must deny my affection for her. Soon she'll be married to another.*

For now it was enough to see Leah smiling, knowing she'd been found.

Sadie watched as Dat, Mamma, Dawdi John, and the twins all stood out in the backyard, eyes trained in anticipation on the woods beyond the barn. She had to wonder if such a fuss would be made over her once *she* turned up missing. The look of dire consternation in Dat's eyes just now was ever so telling.

"How long ago did you send Gid to search?" Dat asked Mamma, his right hand resting firmly on his lower back, as if in pain.

"More than an hour ago." Mamma shifted Lydiann in her arms.

"Why'd she have to go and get herself lost?" Sadie spoke up.

"Now, daughter . . ." Dat came walking toward her. He lowered his hat and his voice both at the same time. "You've done things twice as dumb as this," he said so only she could hear.

His remark took the breath clean from her.

She had nothing to say in response and wished she could run fast away. But she waited till they, one by one, headed inside for some cold drinks, Dat declaring up and down for her to holler right quick if she saw Leah or Gid, either one. She stared at the back door, her bare feet planted firmly in the grass as she peered past the screened-in porch and into Mamma's big kitchen beyond.

Once she was sure they were all preoccupied with ice-cold tea and whatnot, she stole away to the outhouse. Stopping to look back from that vantage point, she checked to see if they'd even noticed she was gone, then hurried on up the mule road, fast as she could go, to the woods herself.

Out of breath, she stopped for a moment near the old stone wall that surrounded Aunt Lizzie's vegetable and flower gardens. From far in the distance she heard the music of a harmonica and spirited laughter, and she caught a glimpse of Gid and Leah, the dog on their heels. Carefree-like, they made their way down the long rise together.

Sadie stared at the smithy's son and her own sister with unbelieving eyes. She never would've expected to see them like this. Not with Leah planning to marry Jonas here in a few months, if not weeks.

Yet there they were, Gid and Leah, holding hands and laughing and talking, looking like they felt awful cozy together.

She crouched behind the ivy-strewn barrier, making sure neither one could spot her.

Chapter Fifteen

The family gathered around Leah and Gid, making over Leah.

"The lost is found," Dat said, eyes shining. Mamma nodded, hovering near.

Hannah glanced around and noticed yet another sister missing. "Well, now, where's *Sadie?*" she asked Mary Ruth, who stood close by.

"I just saw her here. But maybe she's up there." Mary Ruth looked toward the outhouse.

Hannah didn't think so, but she kept silent. Instead, she continued to stew over Leah having disappeared for so long as all of them thanked Gid repeatedly for bringing her home safely.

Dat followed close beside Leah as they headed toward the house, his arm out slightly as if he might scoop her up and carry her inside. Once indoors, Mamma insisted on sitting Leah down in Dat's hickory rocker in the kitchen and giving her some fresh-squeezed lemonade. Then she poured some for everyone.

All the while, Gid's face kept changing colors from pink to red and back again, and Hannah wondered what *that* meant. She kept her eyes wide open, noting how he spoke ever so kindly, if not tenderly, to Leah. And she knew, right then and there, why Dat had set his sights on Gid Peachey for Leah. Such a thoughtful young man he was. *What's kept Leah from losing her heart to Gid?* she pondered. *Did Jonas simply catch her attention first?*

Just then Gid began to recount how he'd found Leah in the woods. "King, here, sniffed his way to her, just like a trackin' dog."

"But we know he ain't that!" Dat said, having himself a hearty laugh, surely aware even the dog was fond of Leah, just as they all were.

Especially Gid, Hannah noticed again.

Except for Sadie now being the absent one, it looked as if things might return to normal this evening. She hoped so because she didn't ever want to endure another day like this. She wanted her family, each one, to remain sheltered and altogether free from care. It wasn't good for a body to get as worked up as they all had been.

◆

A few hours after Leah's return, Aunt Lizzie and Sadie came wandering into the kitchen together. Smithy Gid had been gone for quite some time, and the rhythm and routine of the family was as expected, even though supper was to be served much later than usual.

Leah was relieved to be home. Gladly, she helped Mamma and the twins with the cooking and took turns keeping Lydiann occupied and happy.

Due to her own difficult decision made while in the woods, Leah felt her joy had evaporated—her month-long visit to Ohio was not to be. Yet she believed her idea was Sadie's best and only hope.

The minute she and Sadie were alone in their room, she revealed Jonas's written invitation and their father's un-expected decision. "Dat gave me his blessin'," she said, then paused. "But now . . . I'm startin' to think it might be best if I don't go at all. Why don't you go instead?"

Sadie, suddenly wide-eyed, stared at her. "You want *me* to?"

"Jah, and stay with the Mellingers' elderly mother—you'd have a right nice visit."

"You're giving up your time with Jonas?"

Slowly at first, Leah opened her heart to her sister, sharing what she felt was of the greatest importance. "The bishop there might help you, Sadie."

"You really think this is a gut idea?" Sadie rose and walked the length of the room and then turned to face her sister. "Do you honestly think Dat might agree to this—me tradin' places with you?"

Leah's heart sank. "It would keep me on here longer—helpin' him outdoors and all."

"I wasn't goin' to tell you this, but I had once thought of headin' to Ohio." Sadie paused a moment before continuing. "Aunt Lizzie got me thinkin' that way last spring, said she'd give me money for a bus ticket. . . ." Her voice trailed off.

Leah remembered her conversation with Lizzie in the hunter's shack. "But this is better; it's the perfect situation," she said. "And you'll be back before too long."

Leah spoke up again quickly, sharing what Jonas had said of his bishop being so knowledgeable about the Scriptures. "Now, what do you think of that?"

To this Sadie nodded. "I wouldn't mind attendin' the Mellingers' church."

Leah was startled, really, at how easy it had been for the light to dawn in Sadie's heart. But wouldn't Dat and Mamma nix the idea? Unless they didn't have a chance to. . . .

Why not help Sadie leave secretly . . . not tell a soul? she thought. But how could that happen, and with what money?

"How soon can you be ready to leave?" she asked Sadie.

"By tomorrow if need be." Sadie's reply was not only swift but certain.

"That quick?" Leah asked, quite startled. Seemed her sister would be gone before Leah even got accustomed to the idea.

After milking the next morning, Leah returned to the house from having used the telephone at Dr. Schwartz's clinic to call Jonas. Right quick she sought out Mary Ruth, knocking on the twins' bedroom door.

"Hannah, is it you?" asked Mary Ruth.

When Leah opened the door, she found Mary Ruth dressed, all but her long apron. Her face registered surprise.

"Oh, it's you, Leah. I thought maybe Hannah forgot somethin'," she said.

Leah got to the point. "I need to borrow some money. I could pay you back in a few months. Is that agreeable?"

Promptly Mary Ruth went to the bureau, opened the second drawer, and pulled out her pay for the past several days. "Here, take what you need."

Leah was both stunned and grateful that the way for Sadie's leaving seemed to be ever so smooth. Thus far.

If Sadie *had* to go, at least she'd be safe with the Mellingers. And perhaps she'd have a change of heart while there in Millersburg. Leah could only pray so, because nothing changed the fact that if Sadie didn't return, the People here would shun her—for sure and for certain. Leah hung on to the hope that a short time away from Gobbler's Knob, with Jonas and his minister, was the best thing for her troubled sister. After all, she believed the whole idea had been given her by the Lord God.

Chapter Sixteen

At this time of year—less than a week before the school year resumed—everyone was so keen on cooler weather they wanted to taste it in the form of Strasburg Bakery's famous and exceptionally delicious sweet rolls. "Sticky buns," as they were commonly referred to, were always added to the specials board every year just before September, and at a discount. Any number of Sadie's relatives and neighbors might have easily made up a batch of them, but there was something special about going to the cheerful shop to eat them.

But this Thursday was not a typical day for either Sadie or Leah. Long before Dat or Mamma had awakened, Sadie had taken her suitcase out to the buggy, and shortly afterward, she and Leah had slipped away to the quaint village of Strasburg, which was a good, long ride in the dark.

By the time they arrived, the sun had begun to peek over the eastern hills. The window shades on the bakery shop had been raised, inviting early risers inside to enjoy the freshly brewed coffee and a variety of pastries.

Entering the bakery, Sadie noticed the place was already

buzzing with folk. Word of mouth was always the best advertisement for both English bakeries and Amish roadside stands. She and Leah stood in the line and waited their turn, knowing full well they had plenty of time before the Strasburg trolley left for Lancaster.

She eyed a large wall poster. *Annie Get Your Gun, an Irving Berlin musical* were the words most prominent. "Annie," who must be Ethel Merman, the woman named on the poster, was all decked out in glittering western attire, staring back at her from the wall as the line to the counter inched ahead.

Once their purchase was made, they found a vacant table, talking softly all the while in their common language, Pennsylvania Dutch, to guarantee the privacy of their conversation—precisely how Sadie preferred it this day. While she and Leah wondered aloud about Mamma's and Dat's ultimate reaction to her unexpected leaving, not to mention Leah's assistance, other customers around them had their own concerns.

At a nearby table there was hushed, somber talk of war casualties, even this long after America's boys had returned to the homeland. The enormous loss of life continued to be on the minds of those whose families had been ravaged by war's calamity, though the community of the People in Gobbler's Knob had scarcely been touched by the horror. At another table, plans for building a new shed were being discussed, and at yet another, women spoke of sewing new Girl Scout uniforms.

Sadie briefly considered asking Leah about Gid Peachey and seeing them in the forest the day before, but she quickly dismissed the idea. This wasn't the time or the place to ask

Leah such a question. Surely she and Gid were simply friends, as Leah had always declared.

After sipping coffee and relishing their sweet rolls, the sisters sat without speaking for a moment. Then Leah licked her fingers before reaching into her pocket to hand a wad of bills to Sadie. "You'll need part of this for your trolley fare and again in Lancaster when you purchase your ticket at the train depot. Be sure to save the rest for your return trip in October."

I won't be comin' back, Sadie thought, a lump in her throat. She mustn't let on, though. She must keep her chin from quivering when they said good-bye.

Sadie felt thankful for her younger sister's unmistakable gentleness, noticing for the first time the beauty that radiated from her smile and the way she sat tall and slender in the chair. Her hazel eyes shone with tenderness. Strong both in body and spirit, Leah was the kind of young woman a person could entrust her life to. Sadie felt she was doing just that by allowing herself to be secretly whisked off to Ohio.

◆

Sadie and Leah sat together in the family buggy on Main Street, waiting for the trolley. "I guess this is *Hatyee*—so long—for a little while," Leah said, smiling sadly. "'Tis hard to believe you're goin'."

Sadie thought of the many miles that would eventually separate them. "My head's still spinnin', so quick you were to arrange things. I don't know how I'll ever thank you."

"Jonas was a big help with the plannin' . . . though he

knows nothin' at all about what you did during rumsch-pringe." Leah looked downright glum. "He'll be the one to meet you in Millersburg. Stay alert when you change trains in Pittsburgh, jah? Don't be shy about askin' for directions. It'll be wonderful-gut for you to get away."

They embraced ever so tightly. Sadie hung on to her sister longer than she might have under different circumstances. It was next to impossible to think of saying good-bye forever. "Oh, Leah, thank you for keepin' my awful secret—you and Aunt Lizzie both. You're a dear sister."

Leah's face turned ashen just then. She seemed at a loss for words.

"You'll tell Mamma and Aunt Lizzie I love 'em, won't you? After they realize I'm gone and all. Same for Hannah and Mary Ruth . . . and Dat, too."

"I'll be sure and tell everyone."

Sadie reached for her suitcase. "Don't worry 'bout me, hear?"

Leah nodded. "I've been wantin' to ask you somethin', Sadie. Will you still consider bein' one of my bridesmaids, come November?"

"Well, I—" She fought hard the tears. Truth was, long before then Naomi would have gone to the brethren with her revelation of Sadie's sins. And if so, Sadie could be in Leah's wedding only if she was willing to confess, and they both knew it. Still, she couldn't blame Leah for asking. "It'll be a wonderful-gut day for you and Jonas."

"I really want you to stand up with me," Leah persisted. "Will you think on it?"

"I'll send you a letter in due time." They hugged again.

"I'll be missin' your baptism, too," Sadie said, torn with emotion.

" 'Tis all right."

This was torture, now that she was this far into her flight away from home. To think she might never lay eyes on Leah—on any of her family—ever again.

Sadie did not delay. Climbing down from the carriage, she waved one last time, tears threatening to spill down her cheeks.

"Safe trip!" she heard Leah call.

Turning to look once more, she saw her sister stand, waving to her from the buggy. The horse started a bit, and Leah sat down quickly, still holding the reins tightly in her hands.

The image of Leah, looking so forlorn, even anxious, remained with Sadie during the trolley ride past the Strasburg Mennonite Church and cemetery and down Route 222 to Lancaster.

Once she was settled on the train, she kept to herself, not once speaking to the passenger next to her. She warded off the ever-present stares of the English while covertly looking around herself. Two women with bobbed hair wore interesting dark suits with collared jackets that hugged the bodice, then flared slightly below the waistline. One woman powdered her nose and applied bright red lipstick before opening her book, *The Egg and I* by Betty MacDonald. Sadie wondered how the author had come up with such a peculiar title.

The passenger across the aisle and up one seat was reading a page from *The New York Times*. A half-page advertisement for something called *A Streetcar Named Desire* caught Sadie's attention, but she had no idea what such a thing as Broadway was.

Turning toward the window where she sat, she realized just how excited she was to be on a train for the first time—going *anywhere*, really—as the rhythmic sway of the passenger car lulled her into thinking she was indeed doing the right thing. To think it was Leah, of all people, who had made it possible for her to take the train, which ran from Pittsburgh west to Orrville, Ohio, before heading south to Millersburg.

Already, Sadie was missing home. Dear Mamma and Dat, her sisters, and Aunt Lizzie, along with the deceased baby she'd birthed—missing *him* every day she lived. She must dry her endless tears and attempt to make a new life for herself, leaving the old behind, including her constant thoughts of the love she'd shared with Derek Schwartz. Hard as it was to forsake the only folk she'd ever known, she must set her mind on meeting a good Amish boy and becoming his wife some-day. Nothing else would do.

◆

The more Mary Ruth read from the book *Uncle Tom's Cabin*, the more outraged she became. She thought con-stantly about the enslavement of helpless black folk—during her chores, on the way to house church, and while she prayed silent prayers at night. *What a torturous life poor Tom led in the south!* she thought sadly.

Sometimes her imagination ran unchecked, and she won-dered if somewhere in the world there were other men as cruel as plantation owner Simon Legree. *Never in Pennsylvania Amish country*, she assumed. Her world was far different; she was safe here.

She would not think of breathing a word of this book, or any like it, to her family. Not even to Hannah, though she had heard last year from several students at the Georgetown School that the book was required study in high school. That being the case, she'd done herself a favor by devouring it ahead of time.

When she scurried downstairs to help Mamma with breakfast, she was startled to find Sadie nowhere around. To top it off, Dat was just now coming in from the barn, asking, "Ida, have ya seen Leah?"

Mamma's red and swollen eyes told a sad story.

◆

Abram locked his legs deliberately where he stood, there in the lower portion of the barn where he milked, fed, and watered his cows daily. He listened with ears to hear, but he did not comprehend—not immediately—the things Leah was telling his weeping Ida and him. "What do you mean, you helped Sadie leave home?" Bewildered, he took off his hat. "Why would you do such an impulsive thing, daughter?"

Leah hung her head.

"Ain't like you, Leah," Ida spoke up.

At last Leah raised her head. "Sadie was . . . well, afraid you wouldn't give her your blessin' to go away."

Ida was rocking back and forth as she sat on a milk stool.

"Your sister's wants and wishes haven't influenced you before. How could you act on your own judgment, without your father's say-so?"

"Truth be told, Sadie was plannin' to sneak away on her own."

"And you felt you ought to help her?" Abram felt the ire rising in him and struggled to keep his temper in check. Then, before Leah could respond, he added, "I thought it was you who was lookin' to go out to Millersburg."

"I was, but I honestly thought it wiser for Sadie to be the one. There she'll be welcomed by shirttail cousins—looked after, too. I guess you could say she and I traded spots."

"Just a short trade, I hope," Ida said, her jaw set as she leaned against a bale of hay. Her blue eyes looked faded, as if her tears had washed away some of the color.

"Jah, 'tis what both Sadie and I thought she needed—a new outlook on life for a little while," Leah replied, looking as sheepish as Abram had ever seen her.

"And was this turn of events disappointin' to Jonas? Sadie goin', 'stead of you?" he couldn't help asking.

"Jonas seemed to understand when I called from Dr. Schwartz's office."

"You used Dr. Schwartz's telephone?" Ida was obviously disappointed.

"I left money beside the phone," Leah said. "I know it sounds awful forward, Mamma, but there was no other way to make plans quickly. And since Jonas took the train out there, I knew he could give me advice for Sadie's trip."

"Why on earth was it necessary to do all this so quick-like?" Ida folded her arms over her ample bosom.

Looking up at him, Leah captured Abram's heart anew. "I wonder, Dat . . . and Mamma, did you ever happen to hear Sadie weepin' in the night?"

Ida's sad eyes gleamed and she nodded her head.

Abram didn't own up to having heard any such goings-on. He was more interested in knowing the real reason for Sadie's wanting to up and leave . . . and where on earth she'd gotten the money.

"I believe gettin' away for a bit will help my sister." Leah turned her head and stared at the hayloft.

Scant as it was, that was all the explanation she appeared willing to give for now. Yet he was almost sure Leah knew more than she was letting on. "You must go to Preacher Yoder with whatever you're not tellin' us," he said. "Tell *him* why Sadie's in Ohio."

"But . . . Dat, I love my sister" came the soft protest.

Abram felt he might burst, so frustrated was he. " 'Tis best you confide in Preacher if you care 'bout her at all."

"Sisters may come before a beau," Ida added, "but not before the Lord God or the church." She was growing tearful again. "Oh, what'll we do round here without Sadie?" she whimpered.

He felt right sad for his wife, surely he did. He understood how she felt because he felt the selfsame way toward Leah. Going over, he placed a gentle hand on Ida's shoulder. "Might be this is gut timin', seein' how rebellious Sadie's been lately." It was mighty hard to erase from his mind Sadie's repeatedly unruly ways.

"Maybe she'll appreciate home more once she returns," Leah offered.

Ida wiped her eyes. "Meanwhile, what'll we tell the twins?"

"Best let me think on this and discuss it tonight at supper," Abram spoke up.

Ida nodded in agreement. So it was settled. Hannah and Mary Ruth would be told something—just what, he didn't know yet. He was thankful to have Leah still here living under his roof, that much was certain. Could it mean her affection for Jonas was beginning to fade? He would continue to hold out hope to that end.

"Sadie's visiting some of Fannie Mast's cousins in Ohio for a few weeks," Abram said when they'd all gathered at the table. The twins had begun eating Ida's Swiss steak and rich gravy, but when realization set in, their fair faces drooped identically, as if they'd each lost their best friend.

"This surely is awful sudden, ain't so?" Mary Ruth spoke up. "But Sadie did seem dreadful sad, I daresay. Maybe she'll be happier there."

"Will Sadie be looked after . . . out there, so far away?" Hannah asked shyly.

Abram was glad to reassure his gentle Hannah. So much like Leah, this twin was. Mary Ruth, on the other hand, reminded him of Sadie—a troubling thought, to be sure. "Sadie will be just fine, and you'll hear of Millersburg in her letters."

Leah was nodding at that. "Sadie said she'd write. I 'spect

we'll be hearin' something in a few days."

Mary Ruth looked up from her plate and gazed at Leah just then. Abram noticed the knowing glance exchanged between the two. *Just as I guessed,* he thought. *Mary Ruth provided the money for the train ticket.*

Later, during Bible reading, he read from the Ninety-first Psalm to comfort his family. " 'He that dwelleth in the secret place of the most High shall abide under the shadow of the Almighty. I will say of the Lord, He is my refuge and my fortress: my God; in him will I trust.' "

Besides him, Mary Ruth was the only one not sniffling as he finished up the chapter.

Lizzie paced back and forth in her kitchen, wishing she'd had a chance to stop Leah from doing what she'd gone and done. She was downright annoyed to hear the news from Abram of Sadie's leaving, much preferring Leah or Sadie to have told of their plans.

Sighing, she was awful sure they'd never see hide nor hair of their pretty Sadie again. *Ach, the pain of it all,* she thought. She stepped out onto her back porch and went to lean on the banister, taking comfort in her colorful garden flowers, nearly too many to count. It was as she leaned hard against the railing that she was struck anew how this whole terrible idea of Sadie's—to forever keep such a secret—was so wrong. She, of all people, knew what it was like to have a secret burning a hole in your heart. And with the knowing came the heartbreak . . . and the praying.

Chapter Seventeen

The day after Sadie's departure, Ida carried sleeping Lydiann to the wooden crib, recently passed down from her sister-in-law Nancy Ebersol, Abram's younger brother's wife. "Sleep tight, little one." She kissed the sweet face, then gently lowered the tiny girl onto the small mattress.

With Lydiann snug for her first long nap of the day, Ida had the idea to get a head start on some fall cleaning. She had to do something with herself to get her mind off her eldest slipping away without thinking enough of them to say something ahead of time. Ever so sneaky, it was. And Abram's Leah . . . goodness' sake, what was *she* thinking by helping Sadie do such a thing?

It wasn't enough for Leah to tell her side of the story hours after Sadie had already left Lancaster by train; Sadie should have spoken for herself. Leah revealed she had gone so far as to contact Jonas Mast to make plans by ringing the telephone David Mellinger kept out in the woodworking shop—ever so surprising *that* was. So . . . the Mellingers were much less conservative folk, it seemed, if they were allowed a telephone on

179

the property. She did know of a family who had urgent need of a phone for emergencies—a child allergic to beestings, she recalled. So maybe David had gotten permission from his bishop for some such reason. A rare thing, indeed. Whatever the circumstances were, the ministers *here* felt strongly that telephones were not to be had by "a holy generation." Let the Mennonites have their telephones, electricity, and automobiles.

Ida much preferred the strict teachings of *their* church district, where the People were encouraged to carry the truth within them, hour by hour, and simply write letters or go visiting whenever they could. After all, they were working toward the highest goal: to get to heaven some sweet day.

Most disturbing was that both Sadie and Leah had taken matters into their own hands. Such behavior was typical of the teen years, though Sadie had already joined church and wasn't considered to be running around any longer. Ida would be ever so glad once all her girls had joined church, safely within the Fold . . . and settled down as young wives. So surprising it was that her pretty eldest daughter hadn't yet chosen a life mate. If only Sadie could be married first, before her younger sister.

She sighed and got to thinking about making ready for heavy-duty housecleaning. *With Hannah and Mary Ruth going off to school next Monday, why not have all the girls pitch in and help?* she thought. Standing at the top of the stairs, she called down to the twins. "Hannah . . . Mary Ruth . . . can you hear me?"

When she received no answer, she assumed they were outdoors, so she headed downstairs herself, to the utility room where she kept her many mops. Back upstairs, she hurried to the twins' bedroom, eager to eliminate any and all cobwebs that might be hiding from view. Though she could not move the heavy double bed herself, she got down on the floor and lifted up the quilt, peering beneath. Pushing the dry mop as far back against the wall as she could, she felt satisfied. Then she rose and went to do the same on Mary Ruth's side of the bed.

This time the dry mop bumped into something, and she raised the quilt even farther. Getting down to look, she was surprised to see books—a good many of them. "Well, what's this?" she whispered, stretching to reach them.

———◆———

Mary Ruth knew right away she was in hot water when Mamma singled her out upstairs following the noon meal. "I need to ask you something," her mother said.

Gesturing for her to go into the big bedroom, Mamma went and pulled out the bottom drawer of her wide dresser and brought out Mary Ruth's library books. "I dust mopped your room," she said, waving *Uncle Tom's Cabin* at her, "and I found these under your side of the bed. I s'pose they belong to you?"

By the way Mamma's brow knit into a frustrated frown, Mary Ruth knew she was in big trouble. Probably more so, now that Sadie was gone from home and Mamma missed her so. "They belong to the public library," Mary Ruth answered.

"Why is it you have to go behind my back—mine and Dat's?"

"I *like* books, Mamma. I enjoy stories that take me to places I can only hope to see . . . and the story people, ever so different than me." *And some not so different, too,* she thought, thinking of poor Eliza, the slave girl who had very few choices in life, except to mind her mistress. She couldn't go on to say that looking forward to reading a book was one of the best things about getting up in the morning. Could she?

"You ain't so much studyin' with this sort of book but readin' lies, Mary Ruth, don't you see?" Mamma meant, of course, the novels, the made-up stories Hannah had spoken out against, too.

"Books like that have plenty of truth in them. Sometimes it's what the characters learn from goin' through a trial; other times it's—"

"My dear girl," Mamma interrupted, "you best be holdin' your tongue."

"Aw, but, Mamma, you could see for yourself." She hurried to her mother's side and removed Harriet Beecher Stowe's book from the pile. "Just look." She opened the pages to the beginning, hoping against hope Mamma might give her an opportunity to explain.

Her mother gave her a stern look. "You must return the books before they start you thinkin' like the English."

"All the books, Mamma?"

"If they ain't for studyin', then I'm 'fraid so."

That was the last word on the subject. Mary Ruth knew better than to continue to argue. She collected the four novels from Mamma's hands. Suddenly she thought of a place she might store them till it was time to return them to the library. Would Dottie Nolt mind if she kept some books at her house? Since she was headed to the Nolts' after the noon meal tomorrow, the timing was altogether perfect.

"Will you be tellin' Dat?" Mary Ruth hoped to be spared his wrath.

Mamma's eyes softened. "Your father has enough on his mind now, what with Sadie off in Ohio. As long as there are no more books like that kind in this house, he won't know this time."

Sighing, Mary Ruth thought yet again of Dottie, who was as understanding a woman as any she'd known—even if Dottie was an Englisher.

Leah took Dawdi John to another appointment with Dr. Schwartz late in the afternoon. If she got the chance today, she would thank the doctor yet again for allowing her to use his office telephone before clinic hours to make her long-distance call to Jonas. He had even been kind enough to step out of the small room, giving her a bit of privacy. Carefully following Sadie's instructions to tell the phone operator David Mellinger's name and home address, Leah had thought placing the call had been nearly as easy as preparing a picnic. She had been rather astonished at how much Sadie knew about the English world, though in this case, her sister's understanding of the telephone had turned out to be downright helpful.

Until Dawdi would return to the waiting room, Leah

wandered over to the bulletin board near the receptionist's alcove. There she scanned the many personal ads—baby-sitting needed, lost dog, and suchlike.

It was the typewritten notice regarding fall cleaning, a request for window washing, that caught her eye. When she looked closer, she saw the person posting it was none other than Dr. Schwartz. Then and there, she decided if he was willing to hire her to wash the clinic windows, she could earn back the money she'd borrowed from Mary Ruth. In short order, maybe. Truth be told, she was also downright curious about the doctor, who seemed altogether kind and gentle—a far cry from his son, if it was his Derry who had fathered Sadie's baby.

When Dawdi John came out of the examining room leaning on the doctor's arm, she quickly went over and asked what she must do to apply for the job. She turned and pointed to the bulletin board.

Dr. Schwartz lowered his glasses and smiled, narrowing his gaze to focus on her alone. "I'd like to think I'm a man who knows an honest face when I see one." He turned to Dawdi. "Can you vouch for your granddaughter?"

Dawdi John beamed from ear to ear. "Leah's one responsible young woman."

"Then, I say she has the job."

"When would you want me?" she asked, feeling good about this already.

"This Saturday, first thing."

She said she must first help her father with the morning milking but that she could arrive shortly thereafter. "Is that agreeable to you?"

He seemed pleased. "I'll look forward to having clean windows."

"Awful nice of you to lend me your telephone before," she remembered to say as she helped Dawdi to the door.

"Anytime," the doctor replied.

On the ride home, Dawdi asked, "Do you think your father will approve of you working for Dr. Schwartz? He's English, after all."

"Well, why not?" she replied quickly. "Mary Ruth is lots younger, and Dat lets *her* work for Englishers. Besides, it's just a one-time job, not every week like Mary Ruth's work at the Nolts'."

That evening when Leah approached her father about the job at the clinic, Dat said he didn't mind if she wanted to earn a bit of pocket change. She was both glad and relieved, for she desired to continue her peaceable working relationship with Dat. But, more and more, she felt it wrong to hold out on both him and Mamma regarding Sadie's plight.

Her baptism day was soon upon her—hers and Jonas's—and it was time to be honest with herself about just what sort of girl she truly was, deep down. Far as she was concerned, she'd had no right to speak out pointedly to Sadie about repenting, not with her own heart so tainted.

She swept out the barn, then went out to the pasture, fixing to bring home the cows for milking. All the while she battled within herself, feeling more wicked with each passing

hour. Here she was learning from the ministers all the Scriptures pertaining to baptism, even memorizing the articles of
faith, and what was she doing but concealing a secret sin. Not
her own, true, but in a way it might as well have been. The
secret pact she'd made with her sister had come between herself and the Lord God. This she knew, sure as the harvest.

Almost immediately on this first full day in Millersburg,
Sadie made the surprising discovery that the area postman
delivered the mail at four o'clock of an afternoon—the Mellinger spread being the last house on his route. The Widow
Mellinger had written out a list of chores for Sadie to do,
"once you're settled in a bit." One of the things expected of
her was to bring in from the mailbox the widow's many letters
coming from Sugarcreek and Walnut Creek, Ohio, and even
some from Shipshewana, Indiana. Edith loved hearing from
her Friendship Circle, all of them Plain, including several Old
Order River Brethren women. Sadie didn't blame Edith—
after all, the woman could scarcely move about the Dawdi
Haus, what with her asthma acting up. Still, Edith Mellinger
went at her correspondence as if her very existence were in
jeopardy if she would but dally only a few hours before
responding to her beloved pen pals.

David and Vera Mellinger's farmhouse was laid out much
like the Ebersol house, with several exceptions, one being a
connecting doorway between the large kitchen in the main
house and the small kitchen in the Dawdi Haus, where

David's mother, Edith, resided. Back home, the connecting doorways were between the two front rooms, making it a longer trek for Dawdi John to get from his rocking chair to Mamma's table.

Sadie's bedroom was situated on the second floor of Edith's Dawdi Haus—a secluded sanctuary, to be sure, since Edith could barely negotiate the main-level rooms, let alone the stairs. Once Sadie ascended the wood staircase in the evening, she felt as if she were heading off to a vacation of sorts, and glad of it.

Graciously, Vera had urged her to come over "next door" any time at all and help herself to whatever she could find in the icebox. Sadie had felt altogether comfortable around both David and Vera from the start. The three Mellinger children were as delightful and well behaved as any youngsters she'd known. Jonas, too, seemed to be going out of his way to be kind, beginning with his warm smile when he greeted her at the pint-sized train depot.

Today she had just opened the icebox to get some ice cubes for the sun tea Vera had set out on the back porch when here came Jonas into the kitchen. "Would you care for some tea?" she asked.

He nodded. "How'd you know that's what I wanted?"

"By the thirsty look on your face." She felt a little silly saying so.

He chuckled at that. "David sent me in for a Thermos full."

"I'll be glad to fill it for you anytime," she offered.

He stood there, still smiling. "First time away from home?" he asked.

The peace of Millersburg had caught her off guard, and so had Jonas Mast. "Well, jah, I s'pose it is."

"Anytime you're homesick and want to take a walk, just let me know. After all, we're soon to be brother and sister, ain't?"

She was a bit startled by his disarming smile and cordial ways. "Denki," she managed to say. "I'll let you know."

———◆———

Weary from a long and busy day cleaning the clinic windows, Leah headed upstairs after evening prayers and was quite surprised to discover a small notebook lying open on her bed.

"What's this?" she whispered, picking it up and realizing it was the makeshift diary Hannah wrote in most every day. The note, attached with a paper clip, caught her eye.

> *Dear Leah,*
>
> *I feel anxious and peculiar asking you to read one of my recent diary entries, but when you do, I hope you'll understand. I've wanted to share this with you for a few days now, but I've been back and forth with the notion . . . ever so confused, really.*
>
> *Maybe we should talk privately after you read this.*
>
> *With love,*
> *Your sister Hannah*

Well, she'd never encountered this before. What could be so important her shyest of sisters should invite a peek at her secret musings?

Dear Diary,

    This is a sad day for our family. How awful strange not to know what to think or do first. So I'm writing what I know, or believe to know, in this notebook.

    To begin with, I innocently overheard my eldest sister say some frightening things to baby Lydiann this morning while Mamma was gone from the house. Sadie was holding Lydiann in her arms, talking ever so softly about another baby. A baby boy Sadie had supposedly birthed—but he had died for some reason, she said. I'm guessing I must've heard wrong. Surely none of this is true. Is my Sadie suffering in the head? I'm ever so worried for her!

    Now I fear I must tell Mamma . . . or Leah, maybe. Otherwise, I cannot live with this knowledge. Please, dear Lord God heavenly Father, may Sadie understand that by my recording these words here, I am doing what I believe to be right for her sake. Not for any other reason would I reveal any of this.

                      Respectfully,
                      Hannah Ebersol

Leah looked around the room she'd shared with Sadie her whole life. The place seemed too empty just now. *What am I to do?* she wondered.

But she knew she must nip in the bud those things Hannah had overheard. She took the diary notebook with her and headed down the hall to Hannah and Mary Ruth's bedroom.

Leah knocked and poked her head in after one of them said, "Come in." Turned out both twins were dressed for bed, and Mary Ruth had begun brushing her strawberry blond locks.

Hannah was sitting on the cane chair near the dresser,

removing her white head covering. "What is it?" she asked, glancing nervously at Mary Ruth.

Leah motioned with her finger, trying not to call too much attention to herself, carefully keeping Hannah's diary behind her back. "Can you come to my room for a minute?" She hoped Mary Ruth wouldn't trail along as she often did. Where one twin went, the other seemed content to follow.

Once Leah had quietly closed her door, she opened Hannah's notebook to the revealing page. "I just read this. You did the right thing, sharin' with me this way."

Hannah was silent, brown eyes blinking.

"Best keep mum about this for now." She paused. "No need worryin' Mamma and Dat."

Hannah nodded, seemingly willing to keep both her diary closed and her lips locked tight.

Such a sorry situation this was. Not only did Naomi Kauffman and Adah Peachey know something of Sadie's sin, but now Hannah knew—and knew the worst part of it. *Goodness' sake*, Leah thought, *it won't be long before everyone knows!*

Chapter Eighteen

Ida sat next to Abram in the front seat of the open spring wagon, brooding over Sadie, now absent more than a week. The sun was exceptionally warm for the second to the last day of August, and there was precious little breeze as they rode to Grasshopper Level for a Saturday afternoon visit with Peter and Fannie Mast. Ida was awful glad to have received word from Millersburg, though not directly from Sadie. Vera Mellinger, David's wife, had taken time to pen a quick note, saying, *All is well here with your eldest. We'll take care to see she attends church with us, as well as Bible study on Wednesday nights.*

Neither Ida nor Abram had figured Jonas was involved in such a forward-looking church. The Amish here shied away from organized study of the Bible. So now Sadie, too, would be attending a more open-minded community. Still, Leah had said Jonas spoke favorably of the bishop there, so Ida tried to set aside her concerns and simply look forward to Sadie's return in time for the Mast-Ebersol wedding. She would pray all was well with her dearest girl.

In the second seat of the wagon, Leah and Aunt Lizzie sat together, with Hannah and Mary Ruth on the bench behind them. The wide cart was still full despite having a bit more breathing room, given Sadie was absent and Dawdi John had decided to stay home and rest. In no time Lydiann fell asleep in Mamma's arms, lulled by the swaying and the peaceful *clip-clopping* of the horse's hooves.

Leah watched the landscape drift slowly by—plentiful trees, songbirds, grassy fields, and acres of cornstalks standing sentry. She wished she might relive the day she'd gotten herself so mixed-up in the forest—embarrassingly lost. Thinking back on it, she felt downright peculiar about Gid making over her like he had. She hoped to goodness he hadn't gotten the wrong notion from her. Still, it was awful kind of him to find her and help her home, weary as she'd been.

Sighing, her thoughts flew to Sadie, as they often did now, and her sister's final words to her at the Strasburg trolley. *I'll be missing your baptism. . . .* Sadie had said it so convincingly, as if it truly mattered she wouldn't be a witness to Leah's life covenant.

She wondered how long before a letter from her sister might arrive. After all, Sadie had offered to write, and Leah was glad about that. She felt she might burst into tears, the whole of it was such a troubling thing, even now.

Aunt Lizzie touched her arm, patting it gently. "Best not fret, Leah," she whispered.

Leah knew she must trust in the Lord God heavenly Father on behalf of Sadie. She would try harder to pray more often for her sister. That and encourage Jonas—in her very next letter—to look after Sadie, though there was little time before he'd be home for his baptism. She could hardly wait! Having Jonas back even for a weekend would lift their spirits—all of them—for he would surely tell how Sadie was getting along at the Mellingers'.

As the minutes wore on she watched the clouds glide across the sky. How eager she was to see and hold Cousin Fannie's twin babies. She and Mary Ruth would be the ones most captivated by the twins' sweet babyhood, she was sure. Hannah, on the other hand, was somewhat unsure of herself around young ones, infants especially.

Mamma must have been thinking along the same lines, for she said, "Girls, be extra careful if you hold either of Fannie's babies. 'Specially Jake. He's not nearly as robust and healthy as his sister Mandie. Nor Lydiann, neither one."

"We promise to be gentle, Mamma," Mary Ruth quickly replied from the back of the spring wagon.

Once they arrived Dat let them off within a few yards of the back door, then drove up to the barn. Peter Mast was waiting there to help unhitch and water the horse. "Hullo, Abram. I see you've got one less mouth to feed," Peter was heard to say.

Leah paid little mind to his comment and walked across the yard and up the back steps, along with Mamma, Aunt Lizzie, and the twins. Cousin Fannie, all rosy cheeked, greeted them splendidly as always. Leah had to grin, wondering why they didn't visit here more often, so pleasant it was. Fannie, her mother-in-law-to-be, was smiling at each of them, offering some ice-cold peppermint water for "whoever's thirsty." Imagining the wedding-day feast they'd be putting on before long, Leah clasped Fannie's outstretched hands.

"Just look at you," Fannie said, eyes aglow. "How's our next young bride?"

Leah felt her cheeks turn instantly warm, and Mamma spoke up right softly. "Best not be sayin' such things just yet."

Fannie gave a nod of the head. Leah, ever so glad none of the Mast boys were within hearing distance, went and sat at the table with her cousins Rebekah and Katie. Young Martha came over quickly and perched herself on the edge of the long bench, eyes alight with curiosity. Surely Jonas's family had some idea of their plans to marry, though it wasn't their custom for couples to speak openly of their engagement this many weeks before the wedding season.

"Didja pick your bridesmaids?" Rebekah piped up, surprising them all.

Thankfully Mamma intervened yet again. "Now, Becky . . ." Her eyes turned solemn and her voice a bit prickly.

Aunt Lizzie added more tenderly, "Let's just wait on that," with a peculiar, even restrained, smile.

Jonas and the upcoming wedding aside, the high point of the visit was all of them tiptoeing upstairs to have a look-see at Jacob and Amanda. "Ach, they're but wee ones," Aunt Lizzie was first to say, reaching with outstretched arms for fair-haired Mandie. She received her from Fannie and set to cooing like a contented mamma chick. Mamma's arms were full up with Lydiann, who looked nearly twice as big as Fannie's twins, though she was younger.

Leah was hesitant to step up when Fannie held up the next bundle, one a mite smaller—tiny Jake. "Do you mind if I hold him first?" she asked Hannah and Mary Ruth.

Fannie clucked warmly at this, and Mary Ruth frowned, as if impatient for her turn.

Jake's awful cute, Leah quickly decided, cradling him and looking down at his miniature button nose, closed eyes, and wee, oval-shaped mouth. His fingers were the smallest she'd ever seen, his nails nearly the size of raindrops.

"He's small but mighty," Fannie spoke up, coming over to touch his wrinkled brow with her pointer finger. "His squeal can rouse me out of the deepest slumber—right up out of bed and onto my feet! Peter thinks he'll catch up with his twin sister in no time." She paused for a moment, then—"We were a bit worried at the outset, truth be told."

"Oh, why's that?" Mamma was next to Aunt Lizzie, with Lydiann blinking her bright little eyes at her youngest girl cousin.

"He had quite a lot of trouble . . . couldn't suckle so well—just awful tiny—didn't seem ready to face the world. Yet the twins weren't said to be premature."

Leah noticed Hannah's eyes grow wider with Cousin Fannie's every remark. "Do you think . . . um, Mandie took away some of the nourishment from Jake . . . that is, before they were born?"

Since Hannah scarcely ever spoke up, all of them turned their heads toward her at once. "Well, now, I gather that's altogether possible," Fannie replied. "I never thought of it thataway."

Mamma nodded in agreement. "Jah, there are times when one twin snatches the food away from the other during the developing. But such was not the case with you and Mary Ruth."

Leah couldn't help but smile. Mamma's eyes sparkled with love just now.

Quietly Leah slipped out of the room and into the hallway, still holding Jake, who was beginning to stir. Aunt Becky Brenneman in Hickory Hollow had once said—and quite adamantly—that talking about an infant in front of him or her "makes for a self-conscious and shy child," and she felt she ought to spare baby Jake.

"Just look at you," she whispered, smiling down at him, his eyes blinking up at her. "I think you're right handsome myself . . . ev'ry bit as healthy as any baby round here. So what if you're small. Babies are s'posed to be, ain't so?"

He gurgled at her, wiggling, too. She wandered down the hallway, cooing all the while, thinking it providential Sadie was in Ohio instead of here with Fannie's babies.

"My turn." Mary Ruth tapped her on the shoulder.

"Aw, I just got him," Leah protested but reluctantly handed over the sweet bundle. "Careful, now."

Mary Ruth nodded. "Didja forget already that I help with Lydiann . . . and Carl Nolt?"

"I know," she replied, still eyeing the full head of brown hair framing Jake's miniature face. Her heart was ever so drawn to the delicate boy, and she wished she could help protect him somehow, though it wasn't her place. Still, if she and Jonas lived at all closer, she had the feeling she would be over here quite often.

"In all gut time I 'spect you'll have your own little ones to love, jah?"

Leah truly hoped so. Many a bride gave birth nine months after the wedding day. But whenever the Good Lord saw fit to bless her future union was right fine. Truth was, she wouldn't mind having a son first, someone to carry on the respected Mast name and help with Jonas's carpentry work or yard work. But then again, she refused to do as Dat had done, wishing too hard for a boy and getting another girl—like when she came along after Sadie. No, she would be grateful for any son *or* daughter the Sovereign Lord chose to give her once she and Jonas were wed.

They had all gone walking, the five of them—Leah, the twins, and Rebekah and Katie Mast. They talked and strolled barefoot across a low ridge near the barn, past the windmill, and up to the high meadow, leaving the farmhouse far behind.

Right off they talked about piling into the pony cart for a laughing good time. But both Katie and Rebekah suggested they best not be too rowdy, what with the Lord's Day just around the bend. Leah could hardly disagree, and they heeded the call of prudence and headed toward the apple orchard for a lighthearted romp through the trees.

Rebekah was grinning as she asked, "When do you's start goin' barefoot over in Gobbler's Knob—in the spring, I mean?"

"Whenever it's warm enough." Mary Ruth was first to answer.

"My feet are so callused it scarcely matters," Katie spoke up.

"Well, let me tell you when Mamma says *we* can run

barefoot," Rebekah said, walking just ahead of Leah and Hannah, with Katie and Mary Ruth on either side of her. "We wait till the bumblebees fly," Rebekah announced as if it were some important revelation. "You know, the big, fat ones?"

"*Our* mamma says the same," Mary Ruth added.

Leah agreed. "Jah, 'cause too soon in the season, and your toes might get frostbit."

To this, the girls let out a peal of unrestrained laughter. They felt a convincing sense of freedom out here, far from the ears and eyes of their elders.

"Looks like we'll be seein' each other several times this year . . . with Jonas and Leah's weddin' coming up," said Rebekah, glancing at Leah.

" 'Course, us girls—and Dat and Mamma, too—are s'posed to be in the dark about it," said Mary Ruth, grinning now. "But as fast as Jonas's letters keep comin', well, we'd all have to be blind not to see the handwritin' on the wall."

"Just think," Katie spoke up, "once they marry, our parents will be in-laws together 'stead of just cousins. But what will that make us girls?"

Mary Ruth clapped her hands. "Second cousins and then some, I'm thinkin'. Glory be!"

Leah smiled with delight. The Mast girls were evidently eager to be as closely connected as they could be. After all, Cousin Peter and Fannie Mast, along with their ten children, were soon to become her second family. Five more sisters. And four *brothers*—a first!

When they'd quieted down a bit, Rebekah asked, "What's Sadie doin' out in Ohio?"

Leah's heart jolted. She bit her lip and remained silent.

She would wait for either Hannah or Mary Ruth to say what Dat had shared with all of them. She guessed Mary Ruth would be the one to answer.

And Mary Ruth it was. "Most everyone, at one time or 'nother, needs some thinkin' time. Sadie will be home soon, you'll see."

Leah was relieved. Seemed Mary Ruth most certainly had accepted their father's explanation—hook, line, and sinker.

"But ain't it strange she should be livin' so near to *your* beau, Leah?" Rebekah said, turning around and looking right at her.

"How do you know this?" Leah asked, standing still with the others.

Rebekah seemed eager to volunteer the information. "Vera Mellinger, Mamma's cousin's wife, wrote and said how worried she was over Sadie."

"Jah, Sadie cries most ev'ry night, Vera writes," Katie added, joining arms with older sister Rebekah. "Just why would that be?"

"Could be she's missin' home, but if so, why'd she go all the way out there in the first place?" Rebekah asked, eyes wide.

Leah shook her head and was starting to speak when Mary Ruth said, "There's nothin' wrong with Sadie that a little rest won't help. And that's all there is to it."

"The same kind of rest your aunt Lizzie Brenneman needed back when *she* was a teenager?" said Rebekah.

Perplexed and uneasy, Leah said, "Seems to me we're talkin' foolishness now. What can you possibly mean?"

"Well, if you don't know, I best not be the one to say."

With that Rebekah spun around and headed on her way.

"Come back!" Mary Ruth called to her, exchanging bewildered glances with Hannah and Leah.

"There's only one reason your parents would send a courting-age daughter away!" Rebekah hollered back. "Think on *that*."

Heartsick anew, Leah suggested she and the twins return to the house. "Let Rebekah say what she will," she said softly. "Come, let's go."

Mary Ruth and Hannah followed, but Katie Mast turned and bounded after Rebekah, deep into the orchard, the opposite direction from the house. "What do you s'pose she meant to imply about Aunt Lizzie?" Mary Ruth asked.

"I wonder . . ." said Hannah.

Leah felt she ought to put a halt to this. "Sadie needs our understandin', not hearsay."

For a short while they trailed the creek as it fell over rock and twig, looping past small oak trees and patches of moss.

Then, when the house and barn were again in sight, Hannah stopped walking. "Last year Dawdi John told me the strangest thing," she said. "Did either of you know Aunt Lizzie lived in our Dawdi Haus at the tail end of her rumschpringe?"

Mary Ruth looked startled. "You sure?"

"Since Dawdi has a clear mind and wouldn't think of lyin', I tend to believe him," Hannah replied. "He said Lizzie joined church in Gobbler's Knob 'stead of the Hickory Hollow district."

"News to me," Leah said. "Did Dawdi say why that was?"

"I guess 'cause for a time, Lizzie needed Mamma's love to

get her through some rough days. Just what . . . I don't know."
All at once Hannah turned pale.

"What is it?" asked Leah, her own mouth suddenly dry.

"You don't s'pose . . . the reason Aunt Lizzie never married was—"

"Uh, don't let's be speculatin'!" Mary Ruth interrupted, her face crimson red.

"I should say." Leah deliberately took the lead and began walking faster than they had before, hoping her sisters might follow her back to the house—and quickly at that.

Chapter Nineteen

Sunday, following Preaching service, Sadie climbed into the Mellinger family two-horse carriage. She sat in the second seat with Edith Mellinger. Edith's grown son, David, his wife, Vera, and their young family—Joseph, Mary Mae, and Andy—sat up front, the two smaller children perched on their parents' laps.

The ride back to the Mellingers' farmhouse dragged on and on. She had already sat through the main sermon, which was miles long, much like the Preaching service back home. Yet today she'd felt the hot pangs of conviction from the first hymn and *Zeugniss*—testimonies—till the benediction. The passages of Scripture read were some not so emphasized by either Bishop Bontrager or Preacher Yoder. Today's main sermon had been about Galatians, chapter six, verse eight—*For he that soweth to his flesh shall of the flesh reap corruption*—which put the fear of the Lord God in her. Did this mean "sowing wild oats," like she had done during rumschpringe and beyond? The part about the flesh reaping corruption had her stumped, really. Did it mean she could be punished further for her immorality, even more than she had been already, losing her baby and all? Ofttimes she worried God might not allow her to have more children if she was ever to marry. Oh, she trembled at the thought!

The minister had also preached on the latter half of the verse: *but he that soweth to the Spirit shall of the Spirit reap life everlasting.* That part had caught her attention but good, and she pondered it still.

She didn't know what it was about the church out here. Honestly, she wished she might put her finger on it, might know exactly why she'd felt so disgraceful sitting there with the other women—even corrupted, just as the Scripture stated. Was this what both Leah and Aunt Lizzie had been talking about for so many months?

Thinking back to Leah's repeated pleas for her repentance, and today's meeting, Sadie fought hard a feeling of utter sadness. But out here in the fresh air and sunshine, her guilt was beginning to lessen again. She had thoroughly enjoyed the common meal and some good fellowship with the young people. Just today she'd met two handsome young men, Ben Eicher from Walnut Creek and John Graber from Grabill in Allen County, Indiana, both here for oat harvesting and shocking. Recalling their spontaneous smiles, she felt she just might manage through yet another Lord's Day this far from home.

Does Mamma miss me? Does Leah? She thought of picking up a pen and finally writing letters to them. *Tonight I will*, she decided.

"How long are you gonna visit?" David's youngest son brought her out of her musing. The little boy, a miniature of his father complete with a wide-brimmed black felt hat, turned round in the front seat and was smiling at her with inquisitive blue eyes.

"Now, Andy, that's not polite to ask." His mother helped turn the towheaded youngster back around in his seat, saying, "Our boy's awful sorry, Sadie."

"No, I *ain't* sorry, Mamma," said Andy outright. "I like Sadie, and I hope she stays put here for a good long time."

So do I, she thought, smiling in spite of herself. She was not eager in the least to return to Lancaster County with Jonas in October. How could she go back only to witness her younger sister's wedding service before her own? Of course, Sadie knew that if she'd chosen to, she could have been courted by a respectable boy from Gobbler's Knob. It was her own fault that when Jonas had first started courting Leah, Sadie herself was secretly seeing an English beau.

'Tis past history, she thought. Now there was only one thing to cling to: her recurring dream of being happily married and coddling her baby boy. Before coming here she had been hopeful the sound of a crying infant might cease once she got settled into her new surroundings, but it had continued, haunting her wherever she went—if not stronger than before. However, she was fully convinced now that what she'd been "hearing" was no more than her imagination.

Sitting next to her, Edith made a slight moan. Sadie turned to look at the snoring woman, her long chin nearly bumping the cape of her dress as she slept.

In order to stay on here, I'll have to live with poor, ailing Edith, she thought. Not much of a life, really, till Sadie got married. If she ever did.

◆

Once she was alone in her room, Sadie began to write her promised letters, beginning with Mamma's.

Sunday evening, August 31
Dearest Mamma,

   Greetings to you and Dat from Ohio. I should've written sooner, but the Widow Mellinger needs near constant looking after. Honestly, I don't know how much time Leah would've had to spend with Jonas if she was doing what I do here. Except courting couples always tend to make time for each other, no matter.

   How is everyone? Are the twins enjoying school? I hope all of my kitchen duties haven't fallen on your shoulders, Mamma.

   I'm guessing Lydiann is rolling over already, ain't so?

With the mention of her baby sister, she felt overcome with sadness. She was beginning to miss little Lydiann, missed working alongside Mamma, too. And Leah? A close and caring sister could never be replaced, that was sure. The evening hours had always been best, when they talked most personally in their bedroom.

She continued her letter.

   The Preaching service here is a lot like at home, but the Scriptures are new to me. The ministers here say teaching from the whole Bible is necessary for us to reside quietly in Christ, so I guess it's time I learned more about the sayings of God's Son. Bishop Bontrager might take issue with this, espe-

cially since he preaches the same favorite Scriptures sermon after sermon.

She felt she best not go on too much about that. If Mamma shared the letter with Dat, which she more than likely would, such news might stir up even more concern about her being gone from home.

> *No doubt you were upset when I disappeared with Leah's help . . . and I ought to be saying how sorry I am if this caused you stress, Mamma. I'm thinking long about many things here while I keep busy with Edith, as well as having fun with the Mellinger children.*
>
> *Tell Leah I'm still considering hard her request I be one of her bridesmaids. Next letter I'll say for sure, one way or the other.*
>
> *I'll write again soon. Tell Dat I love him, too!*
>> *With loving affection,*
>> *Your daughter Sadie*

Finished, she folded the letter and left it on the little writing desk near the window. Then, too tired to think of writing yet another letter, she undressed quickly for bed.

I'll write my sister soon enough, she decided, feeling certain Mamma would share this letter around with the family.

◆

On Monday evening Leah accompanied Dawdi John next door after supper. Unable to dismiss Hannah's haunting words about Aunt Lizzie, she wanted to ask a tactful question or two of Dawdi.

For a time they sat quietly in his front room. She lingered there awkwardly till he spoke at last, worrying aloud over the prospect of colder weather setting in "here 'fore too much longer." Nodding, she listened with the hope of putting him in a favorable mood.

After a solid half hour of weather talk, she rose and went to his alcove of a kitchen just a few steps away and poured a glass of water for herself. "Would you like somethin' to wet your whistle?" she asked.

"I'm fine, Leah. Come sit with me." His voice seemed suddenly strained.

She brought with her the glass of cold well water and hurried back to sit across from him on a cane chair. "What is it, Dawdi?"

He leaned his head back as if glancing at a particular spot on the ceiling. For the longest time he sat that way, his untrimmed gray beard cascading down to his chest. Then, ever so slowly, he lowered his somber eyes to meet hers. "I mayn't be the smartest soul on earth, but I know when my granddaughter's fit to be tied." He paused, still holding her gaze, then continued. "Truth is, you've been wantin' to talk with ol' Dawdi for some time now. Ain't?"

She wondered how he knew. "Guess I have."

"Your perty face gives you away. Them hazel-gold eyes of yours, well . . ." He smiled then, a slow, soft smile that made his gray eyes shine.

She decided to forge ahead. "I *have* been thinking an awful lot about Aunt Lizzie. For the longest time, I've won-

dered why she never married. She's fun lovin' and kind—
would make a right gut wife and mother."

"Well, why not ask her all this?" Dawdi said.

"In so many words, I s'pose I have."

" 'Tis safe to say not every maidel ends up married. Sometimes just ain't enough husbands to go round."

She decided to press the issue further. "But there were
plenty of young men durin' Aunt Lizzie's courtin' years. She
told me so." Truth was, lots of church boys had been interested in Lizzie. In fact, there was one special boy who had
declared his love for her, but he didn't wait for Lizzie to settle
down from rumschpringe.

"I'll admit, there were several interested fellas," said
Dawdi. "In Hickory Hollow, 'specially. I wished to goodness
she'd paid more attention to some of them. . . ."

Leah waited, hoping Dawdi might say more, but his voice
faded away. They sat there together in awkward silence a few
minutes.

Finally Leah felt she must speak up once more before
returning to the main part of the house. She had to stick her
neck out just a bit farther, since she didn't know when she'd
ever have another opportunity. Not with both Hannah and
Mary Ruth vying for Dawdi's attention after the evening
meal, too. Come dessert time, the twins always seemed to get
to their grandfather before Leah could here lately. She didn't
know what it was, but Hannah, especially, and now Mary
Ruth was awful eager to spend time with Dawdi.

She breathed deeply, then asked, "Is it true . . . well, that
Aunt Lizzie came to live here in this addition when she was
a youth?"

Dawdi nodded his head without catching her eye. "Jah, 'tis."

"And was there . . ." She faltered, then managed to continue. "Um . . . was there somethin' wrong that . . . required Mamma's attention?"

Dawdi reached for his old German *Biewel* on the table nearby and opened to a marked page without speaking. She was aware of the whistling sound in his nose as he breathed in and out. And she had a peculiar feeling Dawdi was, right now, preparing to give her a message from the Lord God. If that wasn't true, then why were his eyes so intent on hers as he held the Good Book in his gnarled hands?

He opened his mouth and began to read. " 'When my father and my mother forsake me, then the Lord will take me up. Teach me thy way, O Lord, and lead me in a plain path, because of mine enemies.' " Dawdi sighed, and if Leah wasn't mistaken, there was a tear in his eye. "Your aunt Lizzie was taken in by Abram and Ida 'cause she had need to be."

Leah didn't quite understand what Dawdi meant to say. Why didn't he speak his mind clearly? "I'm ever so puzzled," she admitted. "Did you and Mammi Brenneman . . . well, did you send Lizzie away from Hickory Hollow?"

He closed the Bible as slowly as he'd opened its fragile pages. "I don't s'pose I can explain this to you without stirrin' up even more questions." He paused, his wrinkled hands folded atop the Good Book. "Lizzie and her older brother, your uncle Noah, simply did not see eye to eye back then."

She was staring at him now, grasping for some meaning. Why had he read such a startling psalm to her?

For truth, she couldn't begin to imagine why Aunt Lizzie

would have come from her home in Hickory Hollow all the way to Gobbler's Knob to live absent from her immediate family. Unless . . . could it possibly be what Cousin Rebekah Mast had hinted at in the apple orchard? Could it be Lizzie *was* with child back then?

Nee. She rejected the notion. Not good-hearted and decent Aunt Lizzie.

Feeling terribly uneasy, she said at last, "Is it possible Aunt Lizzie thought of Uncle Noah as her enemy, like in the psalm you just read?"

"Best to simply say the plain path of the Lord God led Lizzie here to Gobbler's Knob . . . and to her sister's arms."

She watched as Dawdi's lips moved, the whites of his eyes glistening. Somewhere between what Dawdi was trying to tell her and what she'd observed all her life in Aunt Lizzie, a line of unspoken truth had been drawn. Surprisingly, what was and what seemed to be appeared even more mystifying than before.

◆

Abram spent the evening with his nose in the Good Book. He refused to go sour faced on Ida, who sat darning an old sock while Lydiann slept in the crook of her arm. He might have allowed his emotions to run unchecked, getting the best of him, because Leah was next door with Dawdi this very moment. From what he remembered saying to his father-in-law just this afternoon, well, there was no way anything good could come of such a visit. Not the way John had laid

211

into him earlier, threatening to "blow the top off this whole family hush-hush!" not so many hours before.

He'd done his best—what he could, at least—urging John to "hold his tongue" till he and Ida could discuss things further. But then, somehow or other, Leah had wormed her way over to Dawdi immediately following Ida's dessert. She'd gotten to him first, offering her arm to steady his gait long before either of the twins had, which was downright disheartening, since he'd taken both Hannah and Mary Ruth aside not so many weeks back and told them to look after their Dawdi right close after supper—" 'tis mighty important," he'd said. Mary Ruth had frowned, no doubt questioning his urgency— she had that way about her—but Hannah, thankfully, had succumbed to his request, ready obedience alight in her soft brown eyes.

All in all, the twins had been doing a right fine job of scurrying over to John the second he wiped his mouth on his handkerchief after eating the last morsel of Ida's apple crumb cake or whatnot.

Till tonight. And now Abram was ever so anxious over what things were being said from the lips of an impatient grandfather to his naïve and softhearted granddaughter.

Hannah hurried upstairs to the bedroom she shared with Mary Ruth. There she began to pour out her anxieties onto the pages of her diary notebook.

Monday, September 1
Dear Diary,
*   I shouldn't be writing this, probably, but Dat's fretful about something. He wore the concern on his dear face tonight*

after Leah helped Dawdi John next door after supper. Still can't quite understand Dat telling Mary Ruth and me to "hurry over to help Dawdi, following the dessert." And he insists we do this every night till he says otherwise. So strange it is!

I miss Sadie something awful, and Mary Ruth's much too busy with the Nolt family and her schoolwork these days for my liking.

Leah spends more time indoors with Mamma now, so there's scarcely any chance for my sister and me to talk privately. I have a hunch Leah had something to do with Sadie going to Ohio. Maybe it's the sad look in Leah's eyes every now and then, especially since there've been no letters from Sadie. I thought by now she would've sent Mamma one, at least.

What an emptiness is in me when we sit down for a meal anymore. Sadie is off in another state, mourning the loss of her baby—or at least imagining she had one. Oh, it wonders me if she's in her right mind or not.

Honestly, I can't say which way I would feel most sorry for Sadie, really. If she's not right in the head . . . that's terrible. But if she was immoral and birthed a dead baby, then that's heartrending. Nothing less.

Respectfully,
Hannah Ebersol

◆

More than two weeks after she'd sent her letter to Mamma, Sadie was returning to the Mellingers' large farm,

having taken one of the buggies to the general store to purchase some items for Edith. Looking up, she noticed the sky
was a resplendent blue, nearly the color of a spanking new
piece of blue cotton fabric, the shade of Leah's soon-to-be
wedding dress.

Pausing at the back stoop, she again stared up at the heavens, wondering if the same hue might also be evident in the
sky in Gobbler's Knob, where Jonas was headed come this
time tomorrow. She felt her heart beating its muffled, secret
throbs, wishing she could be a fly on the wall, privy to the
things Jonas might soon be saying to Leah. But would Leah
let on she'd spent time in the woods with Gid Peachey after
getting lost for hours on end? Sadie couldn't imagine *that*
being discussed. Still, she'd seen Leah and Gid with her own
eyes, coming down out of the deep of the forest together.

Since arriving here, and on the long train ride, she'd
thought several times of what she'd seen that day—so confusing it had been. Hadn't Gid taken a shine to Leah all these
years? They *had* been holding hands the day she'd spied them,
laughing and having themselves a mighty nice time together.
What could it mean?

She'd thought of asking Leah about it later that night, and
then again as they said their good-byes at the trolley, but she
hadn't. Now she wished she had.

Pity's sake, Leah had nearly pushed her out the door to
Millersburg. Why? Was it for the reason she said . . . or to stay
home for Gid?

Impossible, Sadie thought. *Not the Leah I know.*

She was altogether nervous. The kernel of doubt
remained. If true—if Leah *was* two-timing her beau—well,

then Jonas deserved better. Much better.

Yet another thought crossed Sadie's mind. Could it be that even at this late date, Leah was having second thoughts about Jonas? Was she leaning toward doing Dat's bidding, after all?

She could only guess at Leah's true motive for sending her here, but she did wonder a little if something wasn't fishy.

As for Jonas, he had been right kind since her arrival here. An outgoing sort of fellow, he occasionally gave Sadie a welcoming smile across the kitchen table when the family gathered there, especially if the subject of his return to Pennsylvania for baptism rose out of a mix of conversation that included the weather, the next canning frolic, and which of the farm families in their area was growing oodles of celery these days. This during the Mellinger family's eventide hours when David read aloud from the Good Book while katydids chirped in the fields. If she interpreted Jonas's thoughtfulness correctly, she wondered if he felt sorry for her being there, so far removed from her family. Did he assume she was homesick? Maybe that was the reason for his wide-eyed gaze on her from time to time, since he had no knowledge of her past sins. Surely not. And she'd just as soon keep it that way.

Part Two

• • • •

They that sow in tears shall reap in joy.

—Psalm 126:5

Chapter Twenty

On Friday, September 19, Leah stood waiting out at the end of the long lane at dusk. She watched with devoted eyes for Jonas to come riding down the road in his open buggy, his dashing steed brushed spanking clean for the occasion.

Her heart thumped fast and hard, and she felt she might not be able to stand there much longer, so jittery she was. In his last letter from Ohio, he had written he could arrive in Gobbler's Knob at twilight on this night. *Will you be waiting for me, dear Leah . . . near the road?*

Over the shadowy hills a splinter of a moon crept up; its cambered rim cast an ancient white light over the fertile valley below. She gazed at the hollow band of road, feeling all trace of time was lost. Gone—the ache of days, the summer of loneliness, endless weeks of missing her beloved's smile, the touch of his hand on hers, his strong but tender embrace.

And then she spied him, his horse and carriage two shadowy silhouettes moving in the distance, heading in her direction. She felt her heart might burst with growing joy.

"Oh, Jonas," she whispered to the honeysuckle-scented air even before he jumped down from the courting carriage and ran across the road to her. They fell into each other's arms.

"Dear Leah . . . Leah, it's you at last!" He held her so close she felt his breath on her neck. "I missed you so," he said, not letting her go.

Her tears fell onto his shirt as she clung to him. "Jonas . . ."

"I was crazy, out-of-mind missing you." Gently he released her, but only for a moment, his eyes searching hers. "My darling girl . . . perty as a bride on her weddin' day."

The horse let out an impatient neigh, tossing his mane back in the fading light. "Whoa, steady there," Jonas called softly over his shoulder.

Leah found it both comical and comforting—Jonas's unruffled tone attempted to soothe the horse as if he were talking to a human. She fell in love with her beau all over again, appreciating his tender heart toward even an animal.

"Wouldja like to go for some ice cream?" he asked.

"Where you are, that's where I want to be," she replied. And before she could protest, he reached down and lifted her up into his shining carriage.

She couldn't stop smiling as he set her down on the front seat, then fairly flew round the buggy and leaped up into the driver's seat to her right. "Ice cream it is!" He paused, smiling at her. "Guess I oughta pay attention to the road," he said at last, turning slowly to pick up the reins. "We have all night, ain't so?"

"Just so I'm home in time for a few winks before milkin'," she reminded him, though she wished she didn't have to say a word about what tomorrow's duties required of her, including the final meeting with Preacher Yoder prior to baptism. With her whole heart, she would much rather ride off with Jonas, never to come down to earth again, so to speak.

She thought of her husband-to-be's name in front of her own—Jonas's Leah—and it brought such gladness. She whispered it right then and there.

"Didja just say what I think?" he asked, reaching for her hand.

She nodded, unable to repeat it.

"Remember, that's who you'll be for always . . . *my* Leah."

They rode slowly all the way to Strasburg, where he bought ice-cream cones for them. They sat high in the carriage, enjoying the treat in an out-of-the-way spot in the parking lot, away from cars.

When her ice cream was half eaten, Leah brought up the subject of her sister. "How's Sadie doin' in Ohio, would you say?"

"I guess she's all right. She does seem awful dreary, though. Must be she's pining for your family."

His comment startled her. "Jah, that could be. . . ."

"Then, she's not there for her health?"

She felt the awkward hesitancy of his words. Surely he didn't suspect Sadie might be in the family way? Yet there was that unspoken concern in his eyes. She mustn't let on that her sister had indeed experienced such dreadful heartache already, in both her soul and her body. She refused to expand on the scant information.

"Sadie needs a little time away, is all." She considered

what she might say further. Then she knew. "My sister needs a friend, I daresay."

"I've had only a little contact with her, which is the way I prefer it, Sadie bein' single and all."

She felt he was being overly serious. "Aw, Jonas, you're not timid around my sister, are you?"

His face broke into a warm smile. "You mustn't worry on my account. I'm going to marry *you*."

His words hung in the air, a promise for a lifetime. She could rest in such a pledge, and this made her think about the vow they would be taking on Sunday. "It's awful nice of you to be baptized with me."

"We'll mark the day," he said, blue eyes shining.

"Jah, for sure and for certain."

He nodded, holding his now dripping ice-cream cone in his right hand. "Just as we'll commemorate our weddin' day for always."

Silently she finished her own melting ice cream, her heart racing as fast as when she'd first spied him tonight, coming up the road in his handsome courting buggy.

"What wouldja think, Leah, for us to marry on the last Tuesday in November, the twenty-fifth? Would that suit you and your family?"

The combination of ice cream and the lump of happiness in her throat kept her from answering promptly. At last she managed to speak. "Jah, that will be a wonderful-gut day of days. With all of my heart, I'm lookin' forward to bein' your wife."

He must have sensed the anxiety of a young bride-to-be.

"Are you also a little bit nervous?" he asked softly, drawing her near.

"More relieved than anythin', really." And she confided in him how eager she was to discuss the date with Mamma.

They talked of this and that, Jonas sharing something of his work with David Mellinger. "I'm tryin' to complete a year's worth of apprenticeship in six months or thereabouts so I can return to help my father in the orchard at harvest time. That bein' the case, Cousin David expects me to be in the wood shop as early as if I were milkin' cows of a morning, workin' alongside him. David's mighty helpful, but let me tell you, he makes me earn my keep."

She felt it was all right to bring up something else, the way they were sharing so openly and all. "How is it you ended up learnin' the carpentry trade clear out in Ohio?"

"Nothing less than providence is how I look at it," Jonas said. "The Lord God heavenly Father works all things together for our gut. Believe me, it was downright perfect timing."

"Has your mother's cousin always known of your keen interest in carpentry? Is that why he contacted you in the first place?"

Jonas shook his head. "I can't say it was, really. I scarcely knew of David and Vera Mellinger."

Then, how was it Jonas had been invited to do an apprenticeship with a distant relative? Unless, could it be David had heard of Jonas's lifelong dream to be a carpenter through the Amish grapevine? If so, how had it gotten all the way to Ohio, and right around the precise moment the two of them were betrothed last spring? She had always wondered about that, though she'd never told a soul.

"What is it, love?" he asked.

"Oh, I'm all right." She put a smile on her face. But the hard facts were that Jonas was to be the only young man round these parts who chose to earn his living doing something other than farm related. Practically unheard of for the firstborn son of a farmer not to follow in his father's own footsteps. Having hinted at her curiosity in a letter, she was eager to ask all this of Jonas, but she held her peace. For now, she would cherish their time together, wanting nothing to spoil this night.

Chapter Twenty-One

One more day till baptism, Leah thought as she awakened early Saturday morning. Her time with Jonas the evening before lingered fresh and sweet in her mind, yet she worried her beau must surely suspect something was amiss with Sadie.

With Naomi counting the hours until she talked to Preacher Yoder today, and with Gid's sister Adah wondering what in the world Sadie was doing so far away, Leah dreaded Jonas might get wind of something. After all, unsuspecting Hannah had learned the *full* truth from Sadie's own lips. Wasn't it just a matter of time before Sadie's secret leaked out?

For sure and for certain, the things Naomi would tell Preacher at the final instructional class paled compared to what Leah knew of Sadie's wild side. *Naomi doesn't know the half of it,* she thought, embarrassed anew. Her heart beat heavily in her chest.

She felt the Lord God's urging ever so strong and could no longer resist on the side of honoring her sister's wishes. She must cast aside her promise, difficult as that would be, to answer a holy call.

Making her way to the barn in the predawn hour, she found Dat busy watering the driving horses and the field mules. "'Mornin', Leah," her father said, glancing over his shoulder at her.

"'Mornin', Dat." She forced her bare feet to move quickly, lest she lose heart and falter. "I need to talk with you," she blurted.

He looked at her with solemn eyes. "What's on your mind?"

When she didn't answer immediately, Dat rubbed his beard. "Your mamma and I feel you may have done the right thing by Sadie, after all . . . if that's weighin' on your mind."

"Then, you aren't so upset?" she asked.

"'Tis not easy, all this happenin' so suddenly. Heaven knows . . ." He paused for a moment, looking back at the house. "And your mamma's goin' to need some extra attention from you—all of us, really."

"I 'spect so. . . ." How easy it would be to simply go and wash down the cows' udders and dismiss what she'd set out to do. "I . . . uh . . . must speak with you about something else," she said, stepping forward. "It's about my baptism . . . makin' ready for it in my heart."

Dat removed his black wide-brimmed hat, holding it in both hands. "'Tis all right, Leah. If something's causin' a stir in ya, 'tis best to air it."

She nodded, aware of a lump in her throat.

"Are you prepared to follow the Lord in holy baptism?" he came right out and asked. "Or is there some resistance on your part . . . about the ordinance?"

"I simply want to ask your forgiveness, Dat."

"Well, now, whatever for?"

She paused, the tug-of-war awful strong, then plunged forward. "I need to tell you I've known of somethin' . . . of a terrible sin Sadie committed and had me promise not to tell."

Dat stood mighty still just then. "How terrible do you mean?"

She glimpsed the pain that registered in her beloved father's eyes and had to look away. "Sadie had a baby," she whispered, reliving the frightening truth of it. "I was there the night she birthed a baby boy. And if Aunt Lizzie hadn't helped, well, I hate to think what might've happened. Sadie was in such an awful bad way."

Dat's face grew ever more solemn. "Lizzie was on hand, you say?"

"She had a part in savin' Sadie's life." She went on to describe how she'd ridden bareback on one of the horses "to fetch Dr. Schwartz, though I knew ridin' thataway was a sin of my own makin'—and I'm right sorry 'bout it. There was just no other choice to make . . . unless 'twas to let my sister die."

Dat stared down at his hat, moving it slowly around in his hands. "Do you mean to say Lizzie knew Sadie was in the family way?"

Leah was afraid of this. Dat seemed miffed, even angry. "Sadie didn't tell Aunt Lizzie till the night the baby came. Ach, don't be upset at Lizzie, Dat. She did only what she had to."

"And what of the baby? What became of *him*?" Dat's

words hung in the air for a moment before she could answer.

"The poor little thing gave up the ghost . . . and died." Fighting back tears, she pressed on. "Oh, Dat, with all of my heart, I had to tell you these things. I've waited much too long, I fear."

His eyes, wide and moist, were fixed on her. But he said no more.

"When I make my confession of faith and join church, I want to present myself a clean and willin' vessel. . . ."

He surprised her by reaching for her right hand and holding it in both of his.

"May I have your mercy for keepin' this dreadful secret?" she asked.

A single, slow nod came from him, and she knew he was offering his understanding, even forgiveness, at her burning request.

———◆———

Hours later Leah met with both Preacher Yoder and Deacon Stoltzfus, along with Jonas and the other baptismal candidates. Upon first entering the Yoders' farmhouse, she caught a glimpse of Naomi talking quietly with Preacher in the front room. As expected, Sadie's former best friend had followed through with her warning. More than likely, Naomi was reporting Sadie's misconduct and deceit this minute.

Naomi turned to look at her, and the blood instantly drained from her face. Sadie's former best friend had come clean, all right.

Leah waited her turn to speak with Preacher Yoder, not willing to call attention to herself. It was true, there had been plenty of time for Sadie to repent on her own. But today, before Leah filed into the Preaching service with the other candidates and offered her life as a "living sacrifice" to the Lord God heavenly Father, she, too, must open her mouth and confess. She and Sadie—Aunt Lizzie, too—had made a hasty, even unwise covenant last year; it was past time to set things right between herself and God. Because if the day ever came that Sadie bowed her knee at last, she would realize what Leah was about to do was right and good in the sight of the Lord. When all was said and done, this act of obedience on Leah's part might just turn things around more quickly for Sadie.

When it was her turn to speak to Preacher Yoder, he offered her a handshake that could make a man out of a boy, she decided, careful not to wince. She began to acknowledge her sins of omission. "It is my understanding certain transgressions have been committed by my baptized sister. . . . Sadie Ebersol. For some time now, I've known of them," she began. "Yet I have failed to bring them to light. . . ." She went on to tell all she knew of Sadie's sinning, grievous as it was.

Here the minister glanced at the deacon and nodded his head slowly. "I commend you, Leah," he said. "May you find your forgiveness in Jesus Christ, our Lord and Savior."

Now, upon Sadie's return from Ohio, there would be a serious confrontation with the brethren. She would be given a chance to confess or be shunned. Sadie would no longer have the consolation of simply biding her time. Her sin had found her out.

When the final instructional meeting got under way, the ministers discussed with great sobriety the difficulty of "walking the straight and narrow way." Leah soaked up every word, steadfast in her decision. She and the other applicants were given ample opportunity to turn back from the baptismal covenant, but she sat tall in her chair and said *jah* with confidence when asked.

Jonas answered with a similar assent. When the young men were asked if they would pledge to accept the duties of a minister if the lot should ever fall to them, Leah noticed he was emphatic in his affirmative response.

The heaviness she'd carried for nigh unto a year was lifted, and she felt as light as a driving horse without its harness. Only one nagging worry remained: How would her confession affect Sadie?

Ida felt so awkward, there in the cramped phone booth. The fact that Abram was squeezed in with her made it even more confining. Abram was still smarting over the truth of Sadie's iniquity, having shared with Ida Leah's confession in the barn this morning. Both were suffering, truth be known.

Now here they were in the one-horse town of Georgetown. They felt it of great necessity to speak to Sadie without delay, and to use an English telephone, of all things. Ida found it altogether curious Abram already had David's woodworking shop number in his possession. Leaning around her, he wasted no time in dialing.

When David answered, Abram told who he was and that he wanted to speak to Sadie "right away, if at all possible." Ida thought he might've at least chatted some about the weather, not been so quick to get off the phone with the man who was making it possible for their Sadie to have a roof over her head.

"Hullo, daughter? Jah . . .'tis your mamma and me callin'," Abram said.

There was a short pause; then Abram asked, "How're you getting along there?"

Abram waited for Sadie's answer.

"We're fine, just fine," he said back to her.

Then Ida heard him get right to the point. "It's sadly come to our attention that you were guilty of improper courtship practices. Is this true, Sadie?"

Ida held her breath for the longest time. She simply couldn't bear to listen to only one side of the conversation. And about the time she felt she could no longer contain her frustration, Abram turned and held out the phone to her. "Sadie's cryin' . . . wants to talk to you."

She put the black receiver to her ear. "My dear girl . . ." So eager she was to hear her daughter's voice again. *Please come home to us,* she thought.

"Oh, Mamma . . ." was all she heard from Sadie, then a bit of sniffling.

"We best talk over some things. Can you speak freely?"

More sniffles. Then, "Jah, I can."

"It's come to light since you've been gone that you were . . . well, that you birthed a child," she managed to say.

"Did . . . Leah tell you . . . this?" Sadie sputtered.

231

"I best not say just yet."

"Well, I won't go before the ministers. I hope you didn't call to ask me to—did you, Mamma?"

"It's the only way, the only thing to do." She inhaled, looking to Abram for moral support. "You wear a stiff upper lip, Sadie, but I've heard you weepin' in the late-night hours. Dat and I . . . we both hope you'll return home and make things right."

"I don't see how . . . not now."

Ida ignored the comment. "This pain you carry . . . let it lead you to repentance, Sadie."

"I'm a lot like Aunt Lizzie, ain't so, Mamma?"

It was Ida's turn to sputter. "What—whatever do you mean?"

"Lizzie sinned in the selfsame way." Sadie was silent for a moment, then—"It's ever so foolish for me to repent."

" 'Tis foolish *not* to. If you refuse, then I'm sorry to say, but Dat and I—oh, it'll be ever so difficult—we'll have no choice but to go along with *die Meindung*—the shunning—if it should come to that."

The shun . . . Ida went cold at the thought. Surely such harsh discipline could be prevented.

"I don't care." Sadie's words echoed in her ear. "Let the People do as they must."

Ida began to weep and Abram comforted her as best he could, the two of them nearly nose to nose in the cramped space.

"This is all my sister's doin'," Sadie said. "I'll never speak to her again!"

"Oh, Sadie . . . no." The dreadful words tore at Ida's heart, and she could talk no longer.

Abram kindly took the telephone and spoke slowly into the receiver. "We best be sayin' *Da Herr sei mit du*—the Lord be with you, Sadie. Good-bye."

Then he hung up.

Sadie was distraught as she returned the phone to its cradle. It was a good thing David Mellinger had made himself scarce while she spoke on the phone. Hearing Dat's voice on the telephone line seemed mighty peculiar. But nothing could compare to the realization Leah had betrayed her!

Mamma, no doubt, would hope to shield Hannah and Mary Ruth from the pitiless reality. This, when Sadie thought of it, gave her the slightest bit of comfort, except she wondered how long the twins could be kept in the dark.

Such a blight she was on her family name, in more ways than one. Even so, her father had offered a blessing before he'd said good-bye. This, along with Mamma's pressing remarks—from a compassionate and concerned heart— helped to quell Sadie's anger.

But it was the knowledge Leah had broken her promise that was most troubling. Resentment lingered long after supper, deep into the night.

Chapter Twenty-Two

At first rosy dawn, Leah was awakened by robins tweeting out a "Lord's Day . . . Lord's Day" pronouncement. Dozing off and on, she dreamed that upon arrival at Preaching, she discovered Jonas gone. Cousin Peter Mast was there, telling the ministers his son had changed his mind and returned to Ohio. Brokenhearted even amidst her grogginess, Leah lay in bed, tears trickling over the bridge of her nose as she struggled to escape this partial wakefulness. She felt herself brush away the tears, fully awake now. Such peculiar and troubling imaginings on this most reverent day!

Truly, she could not conceive of Jonas leaving Gobbler's Knob without following the Lord in joining church. What the sacred ordinance meant to her, it also meant to him. Baptism was the essential next step in being allowed to marry with the blessing of the People. This was nothing more than a fuzzy-headed predawn stupor.

She sat upright in the bed, shaking her head and pushing sleepiness and the alarming dream aside. Reaching over, she placed her hand on her wayward sister's pillow. *Will you understand what I had to do?* she wondered, missing Sadie.

Leah chased away her troublesome thoughts and embraced this most blessed day.

Almost immediately upon dressing for church, after milking and breakfast were finished, Leah heard a knock at her door. Quickly she went to see who was there.

"Do ya have a minute for your ol' auntie?" Lizzie said, standing there smiling wistfully.

What with this being an extra-special Sunday, Leah wasn't too surprised to see her. "Come in, come in. And since when are you old?" She reached for Lizzie's hands and pulled her gently into the bedroom.

Strangely enough, Lizzie closed the door firmly behind her. Then she turned back to face Leah. "I'm old, jah . . . when my nieces have grown up enough to join church and give themselves to the Lord God. Ain't so?"

"No . . . no, no. You're as young as you've always looked to me."

Apparently there was more on Lizzie's mind than talk of growing older. "I'm here to offer a heartfelt blessin' to you, Leah."

She sighed. "If only Sadie were here to witness the day."

Aunt Lizzie nodded. "I daresay we should never have promised to keep that wretched secret of hers."

"What's done is done," Leah said. "Now we must forgive

ourselves, just as the Lord God has forgiven us through Jesus Christ."

"Abram told me you confessed quietly of Sadie's baby boy," Lizzie said.

Leah had wondered when Dat might reveal this to Aunt Lizzie. He surely had not wasted any time.

Sighing deeply, Leah continued. "I must tell you I feel ever so light now—a burden's lifted from me, truly. Yet in the selfsame way, I bear such heaviness in my heart for Sadie."

"Surely our Sadie knows how dearly loved she is," Aunt Lizzie said, embracing her.

"And I pray my confession will bring her heart home to the People, once and for all," Leah replied.

Suddenly tears welled up in Lizzie's eyes. "Let me look at *you*." She paused, reaching for Leah's hands. "Oh, my dear girl, I've waited so long for this day of days, when you would choose to follow in obedience the path of righteousness. The way of the People. May the almighty One bless you abundantly."

Leah was greatly touched by her aunt's thoughtfulness and, most of all, by her unexpected blessing—something a father ordinarily bestowed upon his son or daughter.

"Oh, Aunt Lizzie, it's good of you to come up here just now." She was at a loss for more words.

"'Tis a day to 'come out from among them, and be ye separate,'" Lizzie quoted the well-known Scripture. She continued. "'Be a light to the world,' honey-girl. Without spot or wrinkle."

"With the help of the Lord above, I will," Leah replied.

Then, as quickly as she'd come, Aunt Lizzie turned, opened the door, and hurried down the hall to the stairs.

Downright edgy, Mamma brushed Dat's black felt hat as Leah and the twins gathered in the kitchen. Mary Ruth insisted on making a fuss over Leah's freshly ironed white organdy *Halsduch*—a triangular piece of cloth, also called a cape—and the long white apron over her long black dress. Mamma kept looking at Leah, an odd glint in her eyes. And all the more when Lizzie went and stood right next to Leah.

It wasn't long, though, and they heard Dat calling to them to "come now, and let's be goin' to the house of worship."

They heeded the call and hurried out the back door.

Leah stooped to pet her dog quickly, wondering how awkward things might be for Smithy Gid *this* day. Undoubtedly, he'd be watching—and praying, too—when Leah filed into the service with the other girls who were to be baptized.

She spied Dat standing near the horse, talking low and soft to the animal, the way he often did, while the family stepped into the spring wagon for the short ride.

"Be a light to the world. . . ." Aunt Lizzie had said upstairs.

"Mustn't keep the ministers waitin'," Dat was heard to say as Leah climbed into the backseat with Aunt Lizzie.

She prayed silently as they rode along a bit faster than was a typical Sunday go-to-meeting pace. Dat must be eager to get her into the Fold, she thought, lest something should surface to keep that from happening. No doubt he was terribly upset over Sadie's wrongdoings—probably hoping Leah would remain pure before the Lord God.

Looking out at the pre-autumn landscape—tobacco fields reduced to green stubble and cornstalks rising to new heights—she thought of the personal matters she and Jonas had discussed well into the night on Friday. For one, he was planning to approach her father—this very afternoon—about the possibility of purchasing a corner of his land to build a house, possibly in the spring of next year. As newlyweds they wouldn't need a place to call their own just yet. Jonas wanted to follow the Old Way of doing things. They would simply visit amongst their many relatives, staying with different ones for the first six months after marriage. During this time they would be given free lodging, as well as an assortment of wedding gifts at each house, as was the People's custom. Just yesterday Mamma had hinted she hoped they might spend their wedding night in the spare bedroom downstairs.

Naturally the biggest hurdle of all would be whether or not Jonas and Dat saw eye to eye on the matter of land. The more she thought on it, the more she felt embarrassed Dat had not initiated such a plan, offering to *give* his son-in-law and daughter a bit of land as a dowry . . . a blessing on their marriage. But she had an irksome hunch Dat was still holding out for something to go wrong between Jonas and herself . . . even at this late date.

Sometime this afternoon they would know one way or the other what Dat's reaction to Jonas's request might be. She hoped her years of working closely alongside Dat might somehow make a difference.

In contrast to last year's baptism Sunday, which was overcast and gray—when Sadie had been one of six girls baptized—*this* Lord's Day the sky was a spotless blue with no indication of a single cloud. A good sign.

And now here were this year's applicants, eight girls and six boys—Jonas being the only one who had not grown up in the Gobbler's Knob church district. Leah was grateful to Bishop Bontrager for making it possible for Jonas to be baptized along with her. She hoped to have the opportunity to tell the bishop so at some point, when the time was right and with Dat by her side.

The massive barn doors gaped wide, propped open for the Preaching service to allow for additional ventilation. The People poured into the meeting place, some with additional family members and friends from other church districts for the special ordinance. Latecomers were assigned to sit on the back benches, near stacked bales of hay, which often poked the spine—a sure incentive not to be tardy.

With head bowed, Leah sat on the middle bench with the other girls, up front near the ministers. Across from them on a wooden, backless bench, the boys sat, their spines straight as ladders, while the next hymn was sung in unison by the People.

Seven ministers entered the area set up amidst the long granary and alfalfa bales, including Bishop Bontrager, Preacher Yoder, Preacher Lapp, Deacon Stoltzfus, and three other visiting ministers and deacons. They removed their large black hats and shook hands with different folk nearby, on their way to the ministers' bench.

After two sermons were given, each an hour long, Bishop

Bontrager stood and offered personal remarks directed to the candidates. This was Deacon Stoltzfus's cue to leave the meeting and bring back a pail of water, along with a tin cup.

The bishop continued. "You are to be reminded that your lifelong vow is being made to the Most High God . . . not only to the ministers here and this church membership."

Fully aware of the meaning of the covenant—what it required of her all the days of her life—Leah was eager to go to her knees when the bishop said, "If it is still your intention to be baptized and become a member of the body of Christ, then kneel before Almighty God and His church to obtain your salvation."

As she knelt, Leah prayed silently for the strength to take this holy step.

The bishop asked the first question. "With the help and grace of our Lord God heavenly Father, are you each willing to renounce the world, your own flesh, and the devil and to be obedient only to God and His church?"

The repeated jah was heard as each of them answered.

"Now, can you promise to walk with Christ and His church and remain faithful through life and until your death?"

Again the answer came in a stream of jahs.

"Do you confess that Jesus Christ is the Son of God?"

When it came Leah's turn, she said, "I confess that Jesus Christ is the Son of God."

The membership and children in the congregation stood for prayer after the last vow was audibly sealed. Leah and the others had been instructed to remain in a kneeling position, in an attitude of humility. The deacon's wife untied the ribbons of Leah's prayer cap; then the bishop laid hands on her bare head as Deacon Stoltzfus poured water into Bishop Bontrager's cupped hands. She felt the water dripping onto her hair and running down her face and neck, and at that moment she wept.

"May the Lord God in heaven complete the good work He has begun in each of you and strengthen and comfort you to a blessed end," prayed the bishop. He reached out a hand to Leah. "In the name of the Lord God and the church, we extend to you the hand of fellowship. Rise up, Leah Ebersol."

She rose, struck by the solemn responsibility she now had to the People under God Almighty. The deacon's wife greeted her, then offered the Holy Kiss. Leah and the other newly baptized church members took their seats, and each girl retied her prayer veiling once again.

Leah sat motionless, mindful of the lifetime commitment she had just made. Understood within the vow was the promise she would help to uphold the *Ordnung*—rules and order—and forsake not the exceptionally strict church of her baptism.

Chapter Twenty-Three

Mary Ruth felt more at ease today than she had the last time she'd stumbled upon Elias Stoltzfus after Preaching. Today the People had gathered at Uncle Jesse Ebersol's farmhouse. Though older than her father, Uncle Jesse was on hand after the meeting to pump well water to quench the thirst of a good many folk while a half-dozen women headed for the house to help with the common meal. Mary Ruth and Hannah helped Leah and some of their girl cousins set out the food—bread and butter, two kinds of jam, sweet and dill pickles, red beets, fruit pies, and black coffee. She knew they'd be setting and resetting the table three or four times, and the youngest children would eat last.

Still, encountering Elias had occurred quite unexpectedly—out in the barnyard, once again on her way to the outhouse. Not so embarrassed this time, she had been the first to say, "Hullo!" And he had returned the smile and greeting in kind.

She was more than pleased when he said he'd seen her walking on the Georgetown Road several different times in the past weeks. "Wouldja ever let me take you to where you're goin'?" he asked.

She was markedly aware of other people milling about the backyard. "I . . . well, do you think that's a wise thing?"

"Why, I'm thinkin' it's a mighty gut idea. It'll save your feet, for one thing."

She had to cover her mouth quickly to halt the laughter that managed to break loose anyway. They stood there, both of them laughing.

"I s'pose I can take your smile as a jah?" he asked, still grinning, his black hat off and resting flat in his hands.

Goodness' sake, this is abrupt, she thought. What would Dat say if he knew she was agreeing to let Elias take her to the Nolts' house in a pony cart?

"When will ya be out and 'bout again?" he asked, not one bit shy.

"In a couple-a days."

He returned his hat to his head and gave it a pat. "Well, then, I'll just plan to be happenin' by of an afternoon."

She felt her face grow warm. "I'd say if you were to be around the stretch of road 'tween my house and 'bout a mile west of there—round four o'clock or so—you might see me walkin'."

He nodded. "Done!" he said and was on his way.

"What have I gone and agreed to?" she whispered to herself.

"Hullo, Dawdi!" Leah called to her grandfather where he sat rocking on the small, square porch at home.

Dawdi John's eyes lit up as Leah and Jonas walked toward him across the backyard an hour or so after the common meal at Uncle Jesse's place.

"Well, now, who's that you got with ya?" he said, grinning.

"Jonas Mast . . . my beau. And one of the few young relatives you've yet to meet."

Jonas leaned down and extended his hand to Dawdi. "I'm mighty pleased," he said.

"John Brenneman's my name. I hail from Hickory Hollow, the reason I've never laid eyes on you, I daresay." Dawdi slowed down his rocking. "Welcome to the family."

"This is Mamma's father," Leah told Jonas. "Soon to be your grandfather-in-law."

Slipping his arm around her, Jonas stood tall, eyes beaming, as the three of them exchanged comments about the weather and, soon after that, the baptism. " 'Twas a right nice group of young folk this year," said Dawdi. "I daresay all of 'em will be hitched up by December."

Leah smiled at his bluntness. "Now, that's not the *only* reason to join church, is it?" Even though it might appear Amish young folk had marriage on their collective mind when thinking through their lifelong covenant, they best be heeding the promises made for more than just the purpose of marriage. She felt ever so sure about that.

"Well, it won't be long and the two of you will be man and wife, jah?"

Jonas smiled down on her. "Not long at all."

"Where do you young ones plan on livin', come next spring?" asked Dawdi.

Leah expected her grandfather to ask this. "Jonas and Dat plan to talk through that in just a bit."

"Well, I have a notion Abram won't make it any too easy for you, Jonas . . . just a warnin' from your ol' Dawdi-to-be." With that he winked at them both. "Used to be a Lancaster County bride could expect her father to offer expensive gifts, but anymore—"

"Dawdi! Remember, Dat's got to be prudent in the matter," Leah interrupted but quickly covered her mouth, realizing what she'd done.

"Go on, speak your mind, honey-girl." Dawdi lifted his black hat and scratched his head underneath. "What were you sayin'?"

"Sadie should be the recipient of such a gift, really—bein' the eldest daughter. And the twins are comin' along close behind . . . and someday, Lydiann. If Dat gave each of us girls a parcel of land, wouldn't be long and there'd be none left for him to farm."

Dawdi was nodding his head, pulling on his gray beard. "You've got a point there, but I doubt Abram will use that as his excuse today." Here he looked up with wise and gentle eyes. "Best steel your heart, young man. Don't expect anything from Abram Ebersol, and you won't be disappointed."

Leah's hopes fell a bit. Truly, she didn't want her Jonas feeling the same way. After their visit with Dawdi, Leah walked with Jonas out to the bank barn. They headed all the way around the back, where the second-level door opened up to the haymow. They stood outside, some distance from the gaping entrance, lest Dat overhear them.

"Dawdi John makes Dat sound like a hardhearted man. Dat can be difficult, to be sure, but he's also compassionate," she said.

Jonas nodded, reaching for her hand. "It's not necessary for me to ask anything of Abram. I'm a frugal sort; we can manage fine without land."

She felt ever so glum. "Maybe it's best to wait an' see if Dat offers on his own." That was unlikely. Dat would want to hold on to as much land as he possibly could for all the reasons she'd given earlier. Maybe it *was* wise for Jonas to forget about talking to Dat—at least this afternoon.

"We can always rent the house you wrote about," Jonas suggested. "Save up our money and buy land later to build on."

"Jah," she said, still wanting her father to treat her as special as she'd always felt she was to him.

Looking up, she noticed Aunt Lizzie running down the mule road, waving and calling to them. "Oh, look who's comin'," she told Jonas. "You remember my aunt Lizzie, don't you? Come, let's chat with Mamma's sister."

Before Lizzie, Jonas, and Leah could greet one another there in the barnyard, here came Dat hurrying out of the stable toward them, and Mamma running out the back door, skirt on the wing.

Leah found it both humorous and odd as they stood in a small but not so cozy circle in the barnyard. High in the sky behind the barn, the windmill creaked and whispered as Leah reintroduced Jonas to her aunt. "You remember Jonas from our visits to Grasshopper Level, jah?"

Aunt Lizzie grinned. "Why, certainly I do."

Mamma nodded, forcing a smile. Dat looked green around the gills, and Leah wondered what on earth that was all about. She felt the mood was severely strained, with most of the tension coming from Dat, though Aunt Lizzie's face looked awful pink, too.

After a while Dat suggested he and Jonas "walk out to the field for a spell," and with that, Mamma, Leah, and Lizzie strolled toward the house, the three of them linking arms.

"I have a feelin' Abram might talk to Jonas concernin' a dowry," Mamma whispered as they went.

"Can you be sure?" Lizzie asked.

"Well, I s'pose not, but I wouldn't be surprised."

"I'd say 'tis past time for Abram to show some charity," Lizzie piped up.

Leah glanced at her aunt and gave her a frown.

"Honestly, I'm wonderin' . . . what's Abram been waitin' for? After all, Jonas is the man of Leah's hopes and dreams," Aunt Lizzie continued, talking now more to Mamma than Leah.

Mamma pursed her lips like she wasn't sure what to say, and Leah was ever so glad her mother was quiet. If Mamma got started, no telling where any of this might lead.

Glancing over her shoulder, she saw Dat and Jonas heading for the tallest stalks of corn, Dat moving slowly as he went, and Jonas swinging his arms carefree-like. They walked together a ways; then—much too abruptly—they stopped and faced each other, silhouetted like two tall blackbirds against rows and rows of corn.

It might not have been the best timing for this man-to-man talk with Jonas. For some months, Abram had been calculating the risks, wondering just when he ought to take the lad aside. Should he speak straight from the hip this far removed from the wedding season, as Peter Mast had demanded back in August? Or wait till closer to November, maybe? What was best?

The risks were ever so many. His relationship with Leah was on the line, not to mention his and Ida's. And what a lip his wife could have at times, though he knew she had every right to be outspoken about *this* matter.

All that aside, he wanted to know what Jonas Mast was made of—if the boy had a speck of grit in him. He wanted to observe this blue-eyed boy Leah had fallen for when she was but a girl, witness for himself the kind of reaction the startling truth, so long held, might trigger in Jonas. And if Leah's beau hightailed it for the hills, all the better.

"No doubt the two of you have picked your weddin' date," he began as they walked.

Jonas nodded. "Leah and I discussed it Friday night."

"I 'spect Leah will be talkin' to her mamma 'bout all of that."

"Seems so."

They meandered to the edge of the cornfield and turned and stood there, still wearing black hats and Sunday-go-to-meeting black trousers and frock coats, the long sleeves of their white shirts rolled up.

A waft of wind came up, and cornstalks hissed as the two slipped through the golden fringe. They followed a narrow path single file through a maze of straight rows.

When they were completely cloaked by tall shoots of near-ripened corn, Abram stopped walking. Jonas, barely a yard away, looked almost too young to be taking Leah as his bride. "The time has come to speak bluntly," Abram began.

Another current of air rustled the stalks so strongly they thrashed against the wide hat brims the men wore. Quickly Abram secured his with one hand while Jonas tilted his head against the gust, his hands still deep in his trouser pockets.

"The dear girl you have chosen to be your bride is not who you may think," he continued.

Jonas fixed a silent gaze on him.

Where had the wonderful-good years flown? It was mind-boggling that he should be standing here, on the verge of revealing this momentous news to Leah's young beau.

He straightened a bit and pressed on. "When Lizzie Brenneman was in her rumschpringe, she was found to be with child." With his next breath, he laid out the truth. "For nearly seventeen years now, my wife and I have raised Leah as our own."

Eyes blinking steadily, Jonas scarcely moved. "Why do you tell me this?"

" 'Tis only fair that you know. And . . . if this truth in any way discourages you from marryin' the girl who believes herself to be Ida's and my daughter . . . well, then, I give you this chance, here and now, to reconsider."

"I love Leah" came Jonas's emphatic words. "This information doesn't alter how I feel."

Abram expected as much.

Just then thousands of blowing cornstalks threatened to flatten him. He leaned his head back and looked up at the sky, blue as the ocean, with flimsy white cotton for clouds. *Oh, Father in heaven, help this your defenseless servant. . . .*

Attempting to compose himself, he looked directly at Jonas. "Ida and I will talk with Leah tonight concerning this."

"Do you mean to say my Leah is unaware of her own mother?"

My Leah . . .

Put off by Jonas's quick tongue, Abram said, "She looks to Ida as her mamma . . . so I ask you not to speak of this to her." He paused, reflecting on the precarious circumstance. "Do you plan to spend more time with Leah today?"

"Maybe so . . . to say my good-byes."

"It was Lizzie's hope Leah be spared this knowledge till she reached the age of accountability. Which has now come, her bein' a baptized member of the church." He didn't go so far as to reveal the recent stress between himself and Lizzie and, more recently, Ida regarding the how and when of telling Leah. That was of no concern to Jonas.

Removing his hat, Jonas ran his long fingers through his light brown shock of hair. "Are Leah's sisters also in the dark 'bout this?"

"In due time they will know." He paused, then—"I repeat myself: If this causes you grave concern—Leah's life havin' issued forth from a corrupt union—speak now or forever hold your peace."

Jonas inhaled and appeared to grow an inch or more taller. "I won't be speakin' my mind on this issue just now. There'll be plenty of time for Leah to share with me her feelin's. . . ."

Abram was perplexed. "By letter, do ya mean to say?" Such a weighty matter for written correspondence.

Jonas nodded. "Until that time comes, I'll be makin' this a matter for prayer." He returned his hat to his head and said, "Is there more to discuss?"

"You have not asked for my blessing on the marriage."

"I have my Father's blessing," Jonas said. "And if Leah is strong enough to follow through with our wedding, I will ask for your blessing, as well." With that he turned and headed straight out of the cornfield, toward the house.

Abram suffered a sudden and fleeting light-headedness. He had lost this round with Peter Mast's son, that was clear. Wishing for a piece of straw to put in his mouth, he yanked on a cornstalk instead, bending it and pulling off a handful of tassel. Staring down at it, he frowned and changed his mind. He tossed it onto the ground, then stamped his hard shoe on it, muttering as he did.

Jonas had felt downright sure of himself while being sheltered by lofty cornstalks. But now, as he walked over the grazing land toward the house to Leah, he was somewhat befuddled. He could see her where she was sitting on the front porch, beside the woman whom she'd known all her life as her aunt Lizzie but who, in all truth, was her biological mother. And also next to her was Ida Ebersol, who had taken Leah in as her very own baby daughter but who was, in brief, her aunt.

How *would* Leah take such shocking news? He hoped his sweetheart would not be distressed—and to think he would not be anywhere near when Abram broke the news. He would be too far away to offer any reassurance, too far to hold her when she cried for all the years her family had deceived her.

Certainly, he did not know all the particulars or just why it was Abram and Ida had abided by Lizzie's wishes and withheld the truth from Leah. It might not be such a good idea for him to second-guess the wisdom of it.

Leah spied him from her cozy spot on the porch and stood to wave. *My dear girl*, he thought, waving back. Oh, the urge to run to her was nearly uncontrollable, yet he kept his pace, lest Ida and Lizzie notice how compelling his attraction was to Leah. Yet, here she came running across the rolling green turf to him, her bare feet flashing white beneath her long skirt.

Darling Leah . . .

"Did Dat offer us a bit of land?" were the first words out of her mouth.

He had completely forgotten she expected her father to have discussed the dowry. This the supposed reason for their walk in the first place.

Before he could admit no such topic had been brought up, she was nestled in his arms. He embraced her gladly, noting Ida and Lizzie must have slipped inside, for they were now nowhere to be seen.

"What did Dat say?"

He hadn't actually promised not to tell Leah the truth of her parentage, yet he would honor the elder man's request. "Let's go for a ride," he said, taking her hand.

"Where to?"

"Somewhere quiet—away from here—where we can walk and talk awhile." He wanted to hold her close and never let her go, to shield her from the coming revelation.

"I'll go an' get my shawl." She pulled away from him and scurried to the house.

While hitching up the horse, he struggled with the reality of Abram's words. Leah was the outcome of Lizzie Brenneman's youthful lust. What would his family think? Would Dat advise him against marrying his second cousin . . . if *he* knew? And Mamma, would she weep with the news? Or did she have the slightest inkling? After all, Mamma and Ida Ebersol had been fairly close through the years, sending letters back and forth occasionally, and Abram and Peter were known to put their heads together at farm auctions and the like.

A stern yet somewhat compassionate man, Abram had given his life for a secret, possibly turning a dreadful situation into a seemingly happy one for all concerned. Till now.

What *would* become of Leah once she was told? He'd have to await her letter—surely by this coming Wednesday he would have some indication. Such a dear she was about writing and sharing her thoughts with him. Soon enough Jonas could expect to know her heart on this.

Chapter Twenty-four

Leah and Jonas spent what was left of Sunday afternoon sitting side by side in a grassy, unfenced area not far from the perimeter of smithy Peachey's farm. Long and unpaved, the one-lane road had led them to a vast meadow with a small pond in the north corner of the property. Seemingly, this area was not used for grazing land, though Leah wondered why.

"Who owns this acreage?" asked Jonas.

"I don't know, really. For as long as I remember, no cows or horses have ever been on it." Her mind wasn't fully on Jonas's question just now. She was thinking about him leaving tomorrow . . . and what, if anything, Dat had said to Jonas earlier. But she'd decided while running to the house to get her shawl that she would be patient and not press for answers. Knowing Dat, it was possible he'd had other things on his mind than the dowry.

"Most any piece of property can be had for a price." Jonas leaned forward, resting his arms on his knees.

So . . . Dat must not have offered Jonas land as a wedding gift, she thought sadly. Just looking at Jonas, she knew. The brightness was gone from his eyes. Something was troubling him, all right.

"Do you think the smithy might know who owns the land we're sittin' on?" he asked.

"Maybe. You could ask, if you want."

He turned to her and smiled hesitantly. "Well, no, that could be awkward, ain't?"

She knew what he was getting at, of course. Gid's father, if he owned this land—well, then, they were trespassing—and Jonas was thinking it would be right tricky to approach the blacksmith, given the circumstances. "Did you want me to find out?" she asked.

He picked a blade of grass and held it between his fingers, staring hard at it. "I'll think on it."

Not only troubled, Jonas seemed a bit aloof, too . . . and this just since his talk with Dat. She'd watched for him to come back from the rows of corn with Dat, wondering why they'd had to go in so deep she couldn't see them at all. To talk man to man? But she stuck to the promise she'd made herself—she wouldn't put her nose where it didn't belong.

Jonas let the long piece of grass fall from his hand and looked at her. "Will you write to me . . . like before?" he asked suddenly.

"Jah, and will you, too?"

He nodded and was quiet for the longest time. Turning back to gaze toward the southern horizon line, he sat there amidst the grassland and a thousand insects, some of which kept crawling up her legs. She remembered the time when Jonas, but a boy, had slipped her a pair of his work trousers, bringing them out in a makeshift backpack to his father's milk house. She had asked if he had a pair he'd outgrown, some she could borrow for the summer because she hated being bit by mosquitoes and other insects, working out in the fields with Dat. Besides, back then, she'd felt more like a boy than the girl she was. Nobody, not even Sadie, ever knew of the trousers. One of the silliest things she'd ever done. But even then she'd recognized the irresistible bond between herself and her second cousin.

After a time Jonas turned to look at her again, searching for her hand. Finding it, he smiled with both his mouth and his eyes. She felt the sweet warmth of his hand; then he lifted it to his lips and kissed the back of her wrist, oh, so gently. She had to smile; he was ever so dear and certainly not distant now. Not in any way. "I truly wish you were comin' back to Ohio with me." He pressed her hand against his face.

"Mamma couldn't begin to manage with both Sadie and me gone. It's best for Sadie. . . ." She paused, biting her lip. "I'm sorry, Jonas, honest I am. I wish things had worked out differently."

"You never said why it was more important for Sadie to go than you." His eyes were trusting, yet questioning.

"Someday . . . things will become more clear" was all she dared say.

That seemed to satisfy him, and he sat there enfolding her hand in both of his. "I'll count the hours till I see you again." He turned and gathered her into his arms. "Oh, Leah . . ."

Leaning her head on his shoulder, she felt both happy and sad. "November twenty-fifth will be our day for always," she whispered.

Then, she didn't know quite how it happened, but his head was close to hers, ever so near. "My precious girl," he whispered. "Dearest Leah." He nuzzled her nose slowly, yet playfully with his own, and before she could resist, his tender lips found hers. She was startled at first but did not pull away. The kiss was sweeter than she'd ever imagined, and, oh, she longed for more. No wonder Mamma had said to save lip-kissing for after the wedding!

When briefly they pulled away from each other, the longing in his eyes could not be denied. Truly, he adored her.

His arms encircled her yet again, and she was enraptured by his affection, even fervency, as she snuggled near. His second kiss led to yet another, till she felt breathlessly woozy.

"Oh, Jonas . . ."

"Are you all right?" He touched her cheek.

"Maybe not."

They smiled then, faces aglow. She laughed a little shyly and leaned away from her darling beau. "I love my husband-to-be," she told him.

His eyes were intent on her, and he shook his head slowly. "I am the happiest man on earth." He caught her hand in his and looked down at their entwined fingers.

She thought she might cry. "Nothin' dreadful will come of this, I hope."

"Ach, Leah . . . never. No . . . no. How can it be? We've sealed our engagement with three kisses, our mutual promise to wed." He was frowning now, his eyes searching hers. "Don't you agree?"

"So . . .'tis not a bad omen, then?"

He shrugged his shoulders. "I honor and respect you, dear.

You're the light of my eyes. I can't say I believe in omens, really."

"Well, gut," she said, and because she was convinced what he said was true, she leaned over and kissed *him* square on the lips.

"Let's walk," he said, standing now. He lent a hand and pulled her up, and they went strolling happily together, talking over the ins and outs of their wedding day soon to come. A warm breeze caressed their faces, and Jonas leaned down and picked a wild yellow daisy. "What a happy day it will be," he said, giving the flower to her.

"Jah, ever so happy." She lifted the delicate petals to her cheek.

They walked a bit farther, and Jonas pointed out a curious, rectangular-shaped mound. "What is that, not three yards away? Do you see it?"

She squinted, looking hard in the direction of his hand, quickening her pace to match his.

"How peculiar." He stooped to examine what looked to her to be a small grave. "Someone must've buried either a little child or a pet dog here," Jonas said.

She saw where the ridge of grass had been cut away, and the slight rise. "But who would bury someone here and not in a cemetery? 'Tis awful strange."

Jonas agreed. "And seems to me, a private burial place would require at least a simple marker."

"You'd think so, jah."

"But why a grave dug here in the middle of a deserted pasture?" he mused aloud.

"This is wasted grazing land," she spoke up. "I can't

imagine it should become a cemetery, can you?"

Jonas shook his head. "Hardly. But fancy folk do the strangest things sometimes, ain't so?"

She wondered why Jonas now assumed the owner was English. Right surprising it was, really.

◆

Jonas drove Leah home and walked with her to the back door. They said their good-byes rather swiftly—no lingering, so the family had no opportunity to observe, the way of the Old Order. Serious courting was done in secret, under the covering of night.

Not wanting to shed a tear in front of him, she waved and hurried inside, bypassing any conversation with Mamma and the twins, who were rushing to get supper on the table. She headed straight to her bedroom and lay down, thinking back on her afternoon with Jonas and their kisses, hoping the Lord God would not punish them for disobeying Mamma's strict wishes.

Recalling the warmth of Jonas's embrace—his face ever so near—a small part of her began to understand how it was Sadie had succumbed to forbidden hours with the Schwartz boy, one thing leading to another till she'd found herself in an awful bad way.

Leah was most thankful Jonas was an upstanding young man and that they were now baptized church members. They had made their promises to God and *her* church this very day. Realizing the reality anew, she felt even worse for having lip-kissed on the day of holy baptism.

She went to the window and looked out toward the woody hillock, wishing she might visit with Aunt Lizzie. But in a few minutes Mamma would be calling for supper. For now she must put on a smile or else her family might wonder what she'd been up to. Kissing Jonas, beau or no, would not be fitting supper talk. Besides, Leah wanted to be a shining example to Hannah and Mary Ruth, who would experience similar feelings in the not-so-distant future.

'Tis a gut thing Jonas and I will be married soon, she thought, blushing as she hurried down to the kitchen. *I must tell Mamma the date we've chosen for the wedding.*

Jonas hurried his steed toward Grasshopper Level. He hadn't spent much time at all with his family this visit, though his twin baby brother and sister held great fascination for him. His married sister, Anna, and her husband, Nathaniel King, had been vying for his attention, as well as Mamma. Next month when he returned, he hoped to make up for lost time. Along with Dat, his brother-in-law, Nathaniel, and younger brothers Eli and Isaac, they would all help bring in the apple harvest, as planned. There would be plentiful time for some good fellowship then. He hoped he might be able to complete the apprenticeship he and David had agreed upon— a few weeks shy of seven months. Though he was working diligently to make that happen, if he could not, he would simply extend his stay in Ohio and trust his father could make do without him during harvest. If so, his final return home would fall very close to his wedding day.

Tonight, however, he looked forward to an enjoyable time

around the long kitchen table. Mamma, more than likely, would put on a big spread for him, another sure reward for riding all that way on the train and back. At supper he must let Dat know there was a slim chance he might not make it back home by apple-picking time.

The horse whinnied and he settled back in the carriage. He thought of Leah's vague comment about Sadie, made without so much as a blink of an eye: *Someday . . . things will become more clear. . . .*

He was somewhat apprehensive, having heard a few rumors over the years about Lizzie Brenneman—all confirmed this day. Could it be Sadie suffered a related problem? Certain sins ran in families, his father often said.

It wasn't fair to point fingers, if only in his mind, not the way his own passions had flared this afternoon. He should have stopped with a single kiss, yet Leah's eager response had taken him by surprise. She loved him greatly, that much was clear.

So his sister's unexpected letter a month back, warning him of Leah's interest in Gideon Peachey, had to be false. Still, he planned to speak to Rebekah tonight, hear her out about whatever she thought she'd witnessed at the August singing in Abram Ebersol's barn. Not that he had ever given her foolish letter a second thought, anyway.

He let the reins rest loosely across his knees. Recalling the afternoon's pleasures, the time he'd spent with his darling girl, he determined it *was* best, even wise, that Leah remain here in Gobbler's Knob for the next four weeks or so. A separation of hundreds of miles was a good idea for now. He could not imagine anything more embarrassing than having to answer no to the deacon's appointed question, "Have you remained pure?" prior to the wedding service. At all costs, he must protect and keep as sacred his love for Leah.

Abram sat at the head of the table and bowed his head. He took his time saying the Lord's Prayer in his mind, following the silent blessing for the meal Ida had cooked for them. He knew full well his time had run out. Lizzie had been demanding the truth be revealed ever since Leah turned courting age. And because Jonas Mast was now aware of it, Abram could no longer put off what he had to do. Tonight the story of Lizzie's sorry rumschpringe was to unfold.

Sometime after supper he and Ida would arrange to speak privately to the girl they considered to be their second child. To Abram, she was all a daughter should be—everything he and Ida could hope for and more. And considering the shameful path their firstborn, Sadie, had chosen, having to talk to Leah weighed even more heavily on him.

Short of asking her to go with them to the barn or for a walk over to Blackbird Pond, behind the smithy's barn . . . well, he didn't know how things would play out. Still, he could wait no longer; otherwise, Lizzie might take matters into her own hands, jump ahead, and talk to Leah about the circumstances of her birth.

His father-in-law would be of no help with any of this, Abram knew. It had been John's desire ever since he'd come to live in the Dawdi Haus last spring for Abram to "face up to the hard facts, and the sooner the better." John's attitude hadn't set well with Abram, and as a result they'd exchanged some heated words, the last of which seemed to cause a flare-up in John's bad hip. No longer could he lift a hand to harvest or to fill silo. With Leah soon to be hitched, Abram hadn't the slightest idea how he was going to keep the farm running at all, let alone soundly.

Mary Ruth broke the silence. "Please pass the mashed potatoes, Mamma."

Ida did so quickly, then handed the large platter of baked pork chops to Abram. "Your favorite," she said with a quick smile.

Abram looked to see where Ida had put Lydiann, who usually spent the supper hour in Ida's arms. "Is the baby upstairs sleepin'?"

"Jah, she has a low-grade fever. . . ."

"End of summer flu?" Mary Ruth asked.

"Oh, I hope not," Hannah spoke up.

"No, no, no." Ida was adamant. "Lydiann's just trying to cut her first tooth."

Leah had slumped down in her seat, awfully quiet—more so than usual. Abram observed her discreetly between bites of meat. *Did Jonas defy me today and speak to Leah about Lizzie?*

He shuddered at the thought.

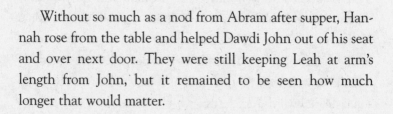

Without so much as a nod from Abram after supper, Hannah rose from the table and helped Dawdi John out of his seat and over next door. They were still keeping Leah at arm's length from John, but it remained to be seen how much longer that would matter.

Abram breathed deeply. John's relationship with his granddaughter Leah would not change one iota once she was told of her true beginnings. As for himself, Abram's parental status would be reduced to merely *Onkel*. With that woeful thought, he curled his toes inside his shoes.

He got up from the table and found *The Budget*, a newspaper published in Sugar Creek, Ohio, and distributed by mail to the Old Order communities. Meanwhile, Leah and Mary Ruth cleared the table and cleaned up the dishes.

After a bit Leah said she was feeling "awful tired tonight" and turned to leave the kitchen.

"I hope you're not cutting teeth like the baby," Mary Ruth teased.

This brought a peal of laughter from Mamma, as well as Hannah, who'd just now returned from the Dawdi Haus.

"Ach, Mary Ruth, best leave your sister be," Abram spoke up in Leah's defense.

Leah smiled weakly, even gratefully, and headed upstairs.

Hearing from Leah's lips that she was under the weather gave Abram pause. Tonight just might not be the best time to reveal such life-altering information, after all.

He drew a sigh and settled back in his hickory rocker. *One more day won't hurt none*, he decided.

But what if Leah had already been told by Jonas? The thought continued to nag him through the evening and later as he lay down on his bed and had to contend with Ida's steady snoring. His back pained him enough to make him restless. He stared out the window at the moonlit sky, afraid that once Leah was told of her roots, he and Ida would never regain what they'd lost.

———— ◆ ————

Sadie helped Edith off to bed early, as was the older woman's custom. "Lanterns out" usually came by eight o'clock of an evening, which gave Sadie plenty of time to read or think. But this night she planned to write a letter.

> *Sunday, September 21*
> *Dear Mamma,*
>   *Hello from Millersburg.*
>   *I suppose Leah and Jonas are glad to have joined church today. You and Dat must surely be grateful. Was there a big crowd?*

She wondered when or if she might hear that a letter from Preacher Yoder had been sent to the Millersburg preacher. Or worse, from Bishop Bontrager to the Ohio bishop. Church discipline, after all, followed closely on the heels of the unrepentant soul. Naomi Kauffman, if she'd kept her word, had already set things in motion for Sadie to be disciplined, at least in the Gobbler's Knob church. With Leah having spilled the beans to Dat and Mamma, as surely she had, no doubt Preacher Yoder had gotten an earful from her, too.

> *You might think me uncaring, Mamma, if I say Leah shouldn't count on me to be a bridesmaid. You can tell her for me. There's so much going through my mind now. Better to ask Hannah and Mary Ruth. Or . . . Adah Peachey, since she and Leah have been bosom friends. Yet I daresn't be so bold as to suggest whom Leah ought to pick, for goodness' sake. Still, I'm awful angry at her these days.*

Mamma, I know it was ever so awkward for you and Dat to use the telephone yesterday. I know, too, that your words—both of yours—were meant to encourage me to confess. Truly, they have gone round and round in my head. And, if I'm to be honest, in my heart.

I best be signing off for now. Write when you're able. I hope Jonas Mast might tell me of his and Leah's baptism.

With love,
Your daughter Sadie

Chapter Twenty-five

Abram rose and dressed in his work clothes before the rooster's first crow. He rolled up his sleeves and headed promptly to the barn, where he wiped down the bloated udders of his two milk cows before sliding the wooden stool up to Rosie.

Leah was late in getting out to help, which was unusual for her on a Monday morning—if she was coming at all, considering her departing words in the kitchen last evening. Ida would surely alert him if Leah was, in fact, ill.

The last time one of his daughters had been said to be "under the weather," no one guessed she was expecting a child. Sadie had been both immoral and successful at concealing it for a time. Even now, thinking about Sadie's deception made him want to go out and find the *Lump* who'd done her wrong. He hadn't asked who had been the father of the baby. Best not to know.

The unexpected clatter of a carriage coming up the long lane caused him to crane his neck to look; Abram was flabbergasted to see Preacher Yoder in the faint morning light.

"*Wie geht's*," the brawny man called to him from the side yard.

"Hullo! I'm in the barn milkin'."

"I know where you are, Abram" came the reply, reminiscent of the Lord God calling Samuel of old.

He looked up and saw Preacher walking at a brisk pace, following the outline of the barnyard where the gravel met the back lawn. "Looks to be another mild day on the way," Abram said, keeping on with his hand-milking chore beneath Rosie.

"Better weather I haven't seen for September twenty-second."

"We mark this day?" he asked, puzzled. "What's on your mind, Preacher?"

Not only stocky, but taller than most Plain men in the area, Preacher had a fearsome way of filling up the space he occupied. Young folk, mainly those in danger of church discipline, often whispered that the strength of Jehovah God was sketched on Preacher's countenance. He had been only thirty-two years old when the lot of ordination fell on him; it was soon after that he became the divinely appointed shepherd for the Gobbler's Knob flock. Now he was fifty-five and as forthright as ever. "Leah spoke with me on Saturday mornin', just so you know, Abram. Are you privy to what she had to say?"

He nodded. "That I am."

"Then you know your eldest—soon as she returns home— will have to face Deacon Stoltzfus, Bishop Bontrager, and myself." Preacher stepped back as if eager to exit. "When do you expect the girl back?"

The girl . . . not "your daughter." Preacher Yoder was making a severe point, and Abram should have expected as much. Preacher, along with Bishop Bontrager, was known to dig in his heels. Little or no mercy was the rule, and baptized church members were fully aware of the consequences of missing the mark.

"Sadie is visiting in Ohio. As far as I know, she'll return in a few weeks. When she does I'll instruct her to follow the Ordnung in submission to the church."

"That is your word on this, Abram?"

"Jah, 'tis."

Standing at the upstairs window, Leah had seen Preacher Yoder's buggy through the lane and into the barnyard. She decided it best not to head out to the barn, what with somber talk of Sadie going on. Must be the reason why Preacher had come here so early of a morning. She'd half expected him to come calling yesterday afternoon, even while Dat and Jonas had gone to talk privately in the cornfield. But Preacher Yoder had his own way of doing things, and no one ever questioned the time of day he chose to drop in.

She carried around in her at least a speck of hope. After all, Sadie hadn't yet turned down her request to be a bridesmaid in the wedding, an honor Sadie knew was wholly tied to a confession. Now, with the church brethren involved, it might be that the way was paved for her sister's redemption.

After Preacher Yoder left the barn to return to his carriage and hurry out to the road, Abram finished the milking and stumbled across the barnyard, heading for the house. The tantalizing aroma of bacon sizzling and Ida's scrambled eggs with cheese welcomed him, discouraged as he was.

"Abram?" His rosy wife met him at the back door.

Before she could say more, he was nodding his head. He sensed her concern. "Jah, Sadie best be gettin' herself home. And mighty soon."

"Then, she's in danger of the shun?"

"If she doesn't hurry and confess, she is."

"Ach, what'll we do?" asked Ida, hovering near as he hung his hat on the wooden peg in the utility room.

"When it comes to our daughters, we never give up on 'em."

Ida gave him an encouraging smile, then leaned on the crook of his elbow as they headed for the kitchen. "I'll keep this in my prayers."

He wanted to ask about Leah in the worst way but held his peace. The fact she wasn't anywhere around led him to think she might be upstairs tending to Lydiann.

About the time he might have asked, here came Leah carrying his wee daughter. "Let me have that baby of mine," he said, sitting down at the table.

Leah, smiling now, gently offered Lydiann to him. "She's dry and ever so happy."

"Then her tummy's full, too?" He glanced over at Ida, who was scooping up the eggs and dishing them onto an oval platter.

"Oh my, did she ever eat." Ida came over, carrying the platter. She set it down and gave him a peck on the forehead, then smooched Lydiann's tiny cheek, making over their little one. "Can you believe how fast she's growin'?"

Abram touched Lydiann's soft face with his thumb. "Who's she take after, do you think?"

"Hard to say, just yet," Ida replied. "But I daresay Lydiann's most like our Leah."

Our Leah . . . How much longer will she be considered ours alone? he wondered. Everything within him resisted telling Leah now. If ever.

Leah's eyes shone with delight at Ida's comment. She hurried to set the table, catching his eye. "Sorry I didn't get out to help you this mornin', Dat. What with Hannah and Mary Ruth dressin' round for school and all, Mamma needed my help with the baby."

Just then the twins rushed to take their places at the table. "Aw, lookee there," Mary Ruth said, grinning at Lydiann in Abram's arms. "She's her father's baby girl, ain't so?"

This brought plenty of smiles, and Abram figured he knew why. Truth was, he'd spent hardly any time at all with Lydiann. Not because he didn't want to. He was just far busier than he'd hoped to be at this phase of his life. Looking to slow down some, he'd been hoping for the longest time Smithy Gid might take over the heavy farming duties once married to Leah. But Jonas Mast had seen to it those plans had gone awry.

"No . . . no, I say Lydiann's *Mamma's* girl," said Ida, cooing now and taking the baby from Abram. "I daresay she'll be mighty content to sit on my lap while you feed your face, dear."

Quickly Leah and Ida took their seats. When Abram

bowed his head for the blessing over the meal, he added an additional prayer. *O Lord God, may your watch care rest on our Sadie. . . .*

He breathed in audibly, signaling the end of the prayer.

Leah reached for the platter of eggs near her and noticed Mary Ruth helping herself to three long strips of bacon across the table. "Won'tcha save some for the rest of us?" she joked.

Mary Ruth gave her an apologetic look. "Sorry. Guess I thought I needed plenty of energy today."

Hannah nodded her head.

"And why's that?" Dat asked.

"We're havin' the first test in mathematics," Mary Ruth explained, all smiles. "I s'pose to see what each pupil recalls from last year."

"In arithmetic, you say?" Dat said.

"It's hard work," Hannah said softly. "Takes a lot out of certain pupils." She smiled at Mary Ruth and they tittered.

"If a *certain* daughter of mine didn't fret so over grades, I doubt she'd need any extra bacon a'tall." Dat chuckled a bit. "Ain't so, Mary Ruth?"

Mamma looked up just then, jostling Lydiann, who was reaching for the nearby breakfast plate. "Better learn all you can this year, girls. Next year I'll be puttin' you both to work here at home."

Mary Ruth's smile faded instantly. Leah suspected it was an indication of how her sister's heart had just sank, to be sure.

Feeling like it might be a wise thing to change the subject, Leah stuck her neck out and asked, "Dat, would smithy

Peachey happen to know who owns the grassland northeast of his property line?"

"*I* know who does," Dat replied. "That land belongs to the good doctor."

"Dr. Schwartz?"

"Henry Schwartz has done nothin' with it all these years. Why do you ask?"

Leah was caught like a driving horse in the path of a reckless automobile. "Jonas and I were there yesterday afternoon, is all."

"So then you know it's perfect grazing land and a cryin' shame not to put animals on it." Dat shoveled another spoonful of eggs into his mouth. While chewing, he managed to say, "You were trespassin' if you's were over there."

She recalled Jonas had suspected as much. How peculiar that an English doctor, of all people, wanted to let that land just sit there with no intended purpose.

Then it struck her hard as a bushel of potatoes falling on her head. Dr. Schwartz owned the land where someone had dug a tiny grave. Awful strange!

She reached for her glass and drank down half of the creamy milk, straight from Rosie to Mamma's table. Could it be? But no, surely not. Had *Derry's* father buried Sadie's blue baby in his own field?

"What is it, Leah?" Mamma was asking, staring at her.

"I guess I'm not feelin' so gut right now." She slid off the bench and rushed out of the kitchen.

She heard Dat say as she headed upstairs, "Goodness' sake, Leah was sick last night, too."

Well, she couldn't help how she was feeling. She had to

take herself off to her room for a while. She needed to breathe slowly . . . think this over carefully. Besides, what *could* she say was wrong with her later, when she went out to hose down the milk house, feed the chickens, gather the eggs, and mow and fertilize the yards? How could she begin to say that Dr. Henry Schwartz must have buried his own grandson—and Dat's, too—on that fertile plot of land? How could she confess that Sadie had conceived the dead baby with the doctor's wicked son?

Nearly worse than all of that, Dr. Schwartz hadn't had the decency to tell Sadie about the burial. He could have done so in confidence, one way or another. Mercy knows, this might have helped ease Sadie's desperation and suffering, even given her a place to privately kneel and ponder her great loss.

Henry Schwartz was a licensed physician and a trusted family friend. She'd seen the framed certificates on the wall at his medical clinic, felt the steadfastness in his handshake. So why should such a smart doctor give a stillborn, premature baby a burial? If he indeed had done so. Made hardly any sense.

She felt helpless and sad at once. Helpless to know what to think . . . and awful sad for Sadie, who knew nothing of this, and just as well.

Chapter Twenty-Six

Lizzie was helping Ida put up the late cabbage the Tuesday after Leah's baptism, making sauerkraut in her sister's kitchen. "'Twas my understanding you and Abram were plannin' to speak openly to Leah two days ago." With both Hannah and Mary Ruth away at school and Leah safely outside with Abram, she felt at ease bringing this up.

"We changed our minds, is all," Ida explained. "Leah wasn't feeling so well."

"Oh? Leah's ill?"

Ida nodded, absentmindedly it seemed. "Abram decided we should wait a bit."

Wait longer?

Lizzie didn't like the sound of this. Both Ida and Abram had used the selfsame remark as an excuse too many times over the past months. Honest to goodness, she didn't think it fair to wait one more day. After all, Leah was old enough to be courted and marry, so why not acknowledge her maturity in *this* important matter?

"I say it's past time" was what she felt like saying, and did so flat out.

"Well, now, Lizzie, is it your decision to make, do you think?" Ida's blue eyes could grow dark with displeasure on occasion, and this was clearly one of those times.

"If you're draggin' your feet—scared of what Leah's response might be—well, I'm willin' to tell her myself."

"I'm sure you are." Ida straightened and then continued to stir the wilting cabbage in the kettle of boiling water. "But I think you best be waitin'."

"Waitin's all I've been doing Leah's whole life long." Lizzie wished to push back the years. Back to when her daughter was but a toddler—so cute Leah was—and Lizzie wished she might whisper it was *she* who was Mamma. But with the help of Bishop Bontrager, the three of them had made an agreement to last until Leah reached courting age. Lizzie had stuck by her word, keeping the hardest promise of her life.

"Just when do *you* think Leah should know 'bout me?" Lizzie asked hesitantly.

"Soon as Abram says" came the expected answer.

Wanting to say more, she bit her tongue. She was distressed these days, even worried, knowing the wedding season was just round the bend—desperate, really, to share her maternal affection with Leah. Not that she hadn't always demonstrated her love to her birth daughter—to all of Abram's daughters, really.

Abram's daughters . . .

Oh, there she'd gone and forgotten the truth yet again. One of the Ebersol girls was really *her* daughter. Would heart and head never agree?

Honestly Sadie had been glad to see Jonas Mast return to Millersburg. She didn't let on to anyone, and certainly not to Edith, who nearly every day now was telling about one "nice Amish boy" or another, several of whom had come in from surrounding counties for the potato and corn harvests. "All kinds of young fellas are here. My goodness, Sadie Ebersol, you picked a right gut time to visit!" The frail woman had a clacking tongue, except when she was deep in slumber for the night or napping during the day, which was much of the time, depending on what was happening in the house.

"What sort of lookin' boys are they—the ones from surrounding counties?" Sadie found herself asking.

"Oh, blond or dark haired, it don't matter none. All of 'em be mighty attractive, same as you," the widow said. "You'll see for yourself if you go to one of the singings. That's where the lookin' gets the strongest, ya know." Edith sighed, her slight chest heaving. "I daresay the most wonderful-gut thing on God's green earth is a match well made."

"I s'pose so" was all Sadie said in response.

A rumble was heard next door in the main house, and Sadie went to see if one of the children had fallen. But Vera signaled all was well—"just a bit of confusion 'tween Joseph and Mary Mae" was the excuse. Which meant there must have been a scuffle, a battle of wills common to any household with children.

Vera Mellinger had her hands full with three lively youngsters and another on the way. Young Andy suffered with severe asthma, the reason a telephone was permitted in the woodworking shop. As if she weren't busy enough, Vera often hosted Bible studies for the church women, too. Sadie had repeatedly been invited to attend but felt she should look after Edith next door, a right good excuse for not sitting a full hour while reading Romans or Corinthians, epistles written by the apostle Paul the People here liked to study.

So many things were different here in Millersburg. She was still becoming accustomed to the pitch-black color of the buggies, instead of the gray color of Lancaster County, not to mention the curious shape of the carriages. Men's hat brims were only three inches wide, and the single, baptized young men grew beards right away, instead of waiting till they were married, like in Gobbler's Knob. Here, too, the men's hair was medium-length and notched—squared off at the ear—compared to the bowl-cropped, shorter style back home.

The local women wore their bodice capes more frequently, and their prayer caps had numerous ironed pleats in the back. She was the only girl with a pleasant-looking, even pretty, heart-shaped head covering, she realized. This fact alone attracted plenty of attention from young men—also, that she was visiting the Mellingers, a well-respected family.

The flourishing countryside reminded her of home, for sure and for certain, except there were more rolling hills. Once chores were done, Sadie often walked the back dirt roads, dodging the deep grooves made by the metal wagon wheels and looking out over the miles and miles of ripening corn.

She felt like a foreigner with a name like Ebersol. More common were the surnames Schlabach, Hershberger, and

Stutzman, and she sometimes wondered why Mamma had never mentioned David Mellinger's family was connected to Fannie Mast's side or that their ancestors had put down early roots here.

If asked, Sadie might have said she liked being round a whole houseful of shirttail cousins who doted on her at times, embarrassingly so. It was as if they felt somewhat sorry for her but at the same time liked her for who she was. Still, if they'd had any idea what she'd done and refused to repent of, they might have packed her up and sent her home promptly. She was awful sure of that, seeing as how they were forever discussing Scripture—sometimes even in heated debates, which she found to be curious.

One such conversation had taken place last night, when Jonas returned from Pennsylvania. He and Cousin David were having themselves a fine time disputing the cut of a man's hair. "The rounded style looks mighty fancy to me," David had said, staring at Jonas's bowl-shaped cut.

"Not to me, nor to the brethren back home."

"But there's a problem with it, I'd have to say," said David, looking serious. "For one thing, if you were ever stuck out in the middle of nowhere and had no way to shape the curved ends, you'd be in a pickle, jah?"

Jonas's eyes had brightened. "I guess I can see your point, but I'd have to say the notched style would be that much harder to keep up . . . if you were away from civilization, so to speak."

This had brought rousing laughter. Even Vera and droopy-eyed Edith were smiling.

"What about the length?" Jonas asked. "Ain't it a solid issue in the Bible?"

David got up and went to get the Good Book. Then, sitting back down at the table, he began to read. "'If a man have long hair, it is a shame unto him.'"

"I agree, 'tis a sin and a shame," Jonas said, a twinkle in his eye. "The longer the hair is, the more shame, I'd say."

David had agreed with a smile, his own hair at least two inches longer all around than Jonas's cropped style.

Sadie wondered if the Lord God paid any attention to a Plain man's hair. Wasn't it a person's heart that made the difference? That's what Dat and Mamma had always said. Maybe four inches or more too long was an issue if a man wanted to follow hard after the Word of God. But two inches?

She tried to imagine Dat sitting here talking over such things, but she knew her father had no use for nitpicking Scripture.

Jonas, though, had seemed to enjoy the debate. *Such fun I'd have with him as my brother-in-law,* she thought, knowing she'd never have the chance to enjoy the relationship because the Bann and eventual shunning would put a wedge between her and Jonas, as well as her entire family.

◆

The afternoon found Sadie on her way downtown to the old general store, where Vera and other Amishwomen sold their handmade wares. This day there was a whole batch of potholders, aprons, sunbonnets, and embroidered dish towels to deliver.

The air had the slightest chill to it, and she was glad she'd worn Vera's navy blue sweater, though she missed her shawl from home. Being it was now toward the end of September, she should have planned for the change in weather. But she'd packed quickly to come here, so fast she hardly had much of anything to choose from. Soon, though, she would be sewing more dresses, and she'd have to figure out a way to bring in some spending money for fabric and sewing notions. She couldn't expect Vera and David to pay her way in life, though she was providing a live-in care service for their mother.

Rain was forecast, so she hurried the horse just a bit, eager to get where she was going.

It was on her way back to the Mellingers' that an almost eerie wobble made the buggy shake and groan . . . then *bang!* Somehow the hitch either broke or came loose, and she sat helplessly while the horse, complete with its harness dragging, kept on going, trotting away in spite of her calling, "Come back! Ach, you mustn't leave me here like this."

Still, the mare hightailed it down the road, paying her no mind. So there she was, cockeyed in the wagon, fortunately on a dusty side road where scarcely any automobiles dared to venture.

At first she considered getting out of the now slanted buggy, its front pitched forward so that it was impossible to sit in the seat. She thought of getting out to walk the long way back. Too far. Still, she couldn't just sit there and wait for night to fall.

Gazing out at the fields of corn on all sides so similar to

those back home, Leah came to mind. What nerve, her younger sister sending her off on a train to the Midwest, then telling Dat and Mamma on her once she was gone! How could Leah up and betray her like that?

Irritated to no end, Sadie managed to climb down out of the horseless carriage. She went and balanced herself on the split-rail fence by the side of the road. She knew it wouldn't be right to abandon David's family carriage—wasn't the kind of thing a visiting relative, though awful distant, would do. Sooner or later she hoped someone would miss her and begin to wonder where she was, especially come suppertime, which, best as she could guess, was in another two hours or so.

❖

Sadie might have sat and fumed for the rest of the day about her situation if Jonas Mast hadn't happened along in David's market wagon an hour later.

"Well, now, where's your horse, Sadie?" He jumped down and hurried over to her.

She told him what had happened, and he was surprisingly calm. "Wasn't your fault," he said. "I'll get you back to the Mellingers', then go lookin' for the horse. David can help fix the hitch."

Glad for his kindness, she got settled into the wagon. She was ever so relieved and anxious to talk to him, but she wanted to be careful about appearing too forward. "Your baptism—and Leah's—was the weather nice for it?"

" 'Twas a sunny day . . . and the best day of my life, so far," he said, holding the reins. "Aside from weddin' Leah, I can't think of anythin' I'd rather do than kneel before the bishop and promise my life to the Lord God and the church."

His answer got her goat; she wasn't prepared for this. Yet she should expect him to say such things, shouldn't she? After all, he was just as devout as Leah seemed to be. Maybe more so.

"How was Leah? Did she shed a tear?"

He clucked his tongue, urging the horse to hasten along. "Leah was ever so happy. Too bad you weren't there for the ordinance yourself."

"Jah." Suddenly she was at a loss for words. The People would have expected her to be present at her sister's baptism, no question. But soon enough they'd all know why she'd left—and why she was never going back.

They rode along in silence, except for the chirping of the birds, too loud for her liking. She longed for the quietude of Edith's back porch, where no one could bother her and the barn cats could roam up and purr their soft contentment while she held them in her lap.

It was then that Jonas spoke again. "Next week I plan to drive Sarah Hershberger, next farm over, to the Sunday singing. A girl with not a single brother to drop her off. I'm doing it only as a favor for her father, a carpenter friend of David's. She's about your age, I'd guess. How would you like to ride along?"

She had to laugh a little. Jonas was as kind as he was well-mannered, acting as a big brother to David's close friend . . . and to her, as well. She liked the idea of going somewhere in the coming week, so she said, "Jah, I'll go," and left it at that.

Beverly Lewis

◆

On Wednesday Jonas received Leah's first letter since their baptism. He wasted no time in beginning to read it, hoping she might indeed share her thoughts on what she'd learned Sunday night from Abram and Ida. But surprisingly, there was no mention of anything out of the ordinary. Had Abram decided against telling her? For what reason would he not?

One thing was quite interesting: Leah had written that the local doctor was the owner of the property where they'd spent the sunniest part of Sunday afternoon.

> Dat says Dr. Henry Schwartz, down Georgetown Road a mile or so, owns the land. We best not go back because it's trespassing, just as you said.
>
> Lydiann is babbling a lot now, and today I almost thought she said, "Mamma." Sadie won't know her when she returns home next month.
>
> I asked Mamma if she thought November twenty-fifth was all right for our wedding, and she agrees it will be just fine.
>
> I'm missing you already, Jonas. Something awful, truly!

Reading this, he almost wished he'd stayed on in Lancaster County. How could he have left his sweetheart-girl to deal with the harsh reality of her birth without his loving support? She might think him coldhearted, though by his kisses she knew better.

Without a doubt, he felt all but guilty for knowing what Leah did not. His bride-to-be was Lizzie Brenneman's own daughter! Once Abram and Ida revealed the truth to her, she

286

would be sorting through a gamut of feelings. Alone.

Mary Ruth had been anxious for the chance to see Elias again. Scarcely had she stepped out the front door of the Nolts' house when here he came in his pony cart. Nearly flying down the road, his black felt hat was high in the air as he waved and beamed a smile at her. *He likes me,* she thought, her heart racing as she walked barefoot along the road.

"Hullo, there, Mary Ruth!"

"How are you, Elias?" she said, feeling oh, so comfortable with him.

He leaped down and went around to help her into the small cart, which wasn't at all necessary, since it was considerably lower to the ground than a buggy.

"Didja think I'd remember?" he asked cheerfully.

She wanted to say, "I knew you would," but instead replied, "I'm glad you did."

The russet pony pulled them much faster than she thought possible. Too fast, maybe, but it wasn't her place to say so. She must learn not to talk so much, to let others speak their minds, especially a young man as interesting as this jovial boy next to her.

"When will you turn sixteen?" he asked, as if he didn't know.

She smiled, keeping the laughter inside for now. Once she got home, she'd tell Hannah all this, and they'd giggle together. "Well, not till February tenth, year after next."

He wasn't a bit shy about his answer. "I'll be waitin' for that, Mary Ruth."

"Hannah will be sixteen the same day," she offered, wondering if he might think to include his older brother, Ezra, in his plans—whatever they might be—so far ahead in time.

"I hope you like ice cream." He made a high-pitched sound that his pony recognized as a signal to speed up even more.

"Jah, I do. Mamma makes it homemade. Do you?"

"Sometimes, if we have blueberry pie to go along with it."

She didn't know why that sounded funny to her. "A little pie with your ice cream, then?"

"That's right, Mary Ruth." His pony was working up a lather, and she felt a bit uneasy, the two of them speeding along in the cart. Yet she kept her peace, not wanting to spoil the delight of this special afternoon.

Chapter Twenty-Seven

After leading the animals out to pasture, Leah helped Dat shovel manure, then mowed the front, side, and back lawns—fertilizing them for the final time this year.

That done, she followed Aunt Lizzie's markings, heading for the honey locust tree, a letter from Jonas in hand.

> Friday morning, October 3
> Dearest Leah,
>
> I am always glad to receive your letters, and I cherish each one. Often I read them over again before drifting off to sleep after a long day of work; that way I can be sure you will show up in my dreams.
>
> Even so, there are times when I wish I received only one letter each week from you. Why, you may ask? In all truth, it is difficult for me to bear your sweet letters because they fill me with longing for you, dear Leah. Especially now, when the memory of our kisses still lingers. . . .
>
> My heart beats only for you. There is no other way to put it.
>
> Now, I hesitate to tell you this, but I've just been offered

*the prospect of establishing a partnership with David Mellinger
here in Millersburg. This may be God's providence at work,
and I wanted you to hear this good news directly from me.*

*I don't mean to alarm you, but what would you think of
us living in Ohio after we're married? We would have to get
Bishop Bontrager's permission and blessing on such a thing,
but we'll cross that bridge later.*

I look forward to your next letter!

> *All my love,*
> *Jonas*

Leah's hand shook as she finished reading. Jonas was surely
excited, and his words—*this good news*—clearly indicated her
beau was more than willing to pull up stakes and leave Pennsylvania permanently.

Yet how could *she* leave her family behind? Jonas knew
firsthand how close she was to her sisters . . . and to dear Dat
and Mamma. Aunt Lizzie, too. And how empty would her life
be without her lifelong best friend, Adah Peachey? Besides, at
the time of baptism, she'd made her promise to both her
father and the bishop that she would never permanently leave
the Gobbler's Knob church district—as had Jonas.

A graceful lark swooped down from high overhead before
it soared up again, disappearing from view over the treetops
and toward the densest area of the forest. She pondered what
to write to him, how to share her heart yet not hold back on
her happiness for him—for this remarkable chance to own a
carpentry business. Most any girl would be thrilled at such a
prospect, were it not for leaving everything she knew and
loved behind. Except for Jonas, of course.

Ach, what can I say to you, my beloved? A woman's obedience to her husband came first after her submission to almighty God and the church. This had been ingrained in Leah since childhood, having been taught by Mamma's example and in nearly every sermon.

It was kind of Jonas to ask her in such a manner as to make her feel she had a choice. But truly, Leah knew she had none at all. Only one way could she possibly reply; this she knew instinctively. She must write back quickly and say she was ever so glad for him, that if he was able to obtain the bishop's go-ahead and blessing, and he believed the Lord God was leading them to live and raise their future children in Ohio, then so be it.

◆

Jonas had begun to think perhaps Abram was counting on a measure of moral support—waiting till Jonas made Leah his wife—before revealing Lizzie to be Leah's mother. It seemed strange to him that Leah had not written a word about it. Her silence on the matter was unlike her. Undoubtedly, Abram would have informed Leah that he'd also told Jonas the facts regarding Lizzie—on their baptism Sunday, no less. And Leah would just assume he was waiting for some word from her, wouldn't she? Unless there was some other reason she seemed so evasive.

He'd thought of writing Abram to inquire, but that might put his future father-in-law on the spot. No need to open the door to a clash. There was enough potential for that, with

Smithy Gid still lurking in the wings and Abram Ebersol all for it.

Was it possible Abram had confided in Jonas hoping the news of Leah's parentage might cause him to abandon his wedding plans, leaving Leah in the dust? Was it for the purpose of running him off? If so, this would definitely make room for Smithy Gid. But Jonas rejected the notion as absurd.

Based on the things his sister Rebekah had told him the last evening he was home, he might have had reason to think hard and long about getting right back to Lancaster County to spend his final weeks as a single man closer to Leah. But the memory of his darling girl's fervent kisses persuaded him otherwise.

Still, he put enough stock in Rebekah's observations to be somewhat concerned. He did hope to question Sadie soon, when he helped her with some chores tomorrow evening. They would go downtown together in the market wagon to make a delivery of quilted goods for Vera. This time he hoped the wagon might stay hitched to the horse. It wouldn't do for him to get stuck somewhere at dusk with Leah's beautiful blond sister. People talked. Everyone here rumored he was betrothed to marry a girl from back home . . . and that the girl was not Sadie, but her younger sister.

Leah gathered eggs and fed the chickens the next day before helping Mamma with the washing that hadn't been completed on Monday washday. Yesterday the skies had darkened, making down rain, and she'd rushed to take in the near-dry clothing. Because of the change in weather, Mamma had decided to break with the schedule and wash the rest of the clothing today.

"Cousin Fannie wrote me a nice letter," Mamma said as they worked together at the hand-wringer. "She wants to invite you and me to a quiltin' bee in your honor."

"Really?"

"I guess this is Rebekah's idea—hers and Katie's."

Leah couldn't help but recall the last time she'd spent time with Fannie's daughters. Downright uncomfortable, it had been . . . such pointed questions about Sadie and all. She'd had a difficult time dismissing the cutting remarks, especially from Rebekah.

"Why do you think they want us to quilt with them?" she asked.

"They're welcomin' you into the family as a sister." Mamma gave her a smile. "We'll make whatever quilt pattern you like."

So Rebekah and Katie wanted to make amends—was that it? How awkward, otherwise, to marry their brother with such unsettled feelings. "I'll go, sure. Sounds to me like fun."

"The first week in November it is," said Mamma, holding on tight to a pair of Dat's work pants as the wringer did its work.

"Won't be long after the quiltin' frolic and Jonas and I will be wed." She remembered, too, that Naomi's wedding service was coming up soon. Naomi had said no more about it, but Leah had heard from Mamma that Luke was putting pressure on Naomi to see a doctor. Leah didn't quite understand what Mamma had meant by that. But when she asked, Mamma indicated in hushed tones the bishop himself had taken steps to determine just how pure the young woman who was to become his grandson's bride really was. Evidently, he had taken to heart Naomi's rumschpringe with Sadie.

Leah blushed to think the bishop had that much say. Dat had often indicated by dropping hints along the way that this "minister with full power" ruled somewhat mercilessly amongst the People. But this? She didn't care to dwell on it. She assumed it remained to be seen whether or not Naomi Kauffman would end up becoming Naomi Bontrager.

"When do you think our bishop will contact the Ohio ministers?" she asked softly, thinking now of Sadie.

Mamma could not respond. She simply shook her head, eyes filling with tears.

By this reaction from dear Mamma, Leah understood the letter of warning had most likely already been written and sent. The wheels of excommunication and shunning had been set in motion. The People did not slap the Bann on a church member easily or swiftly unless the nature of the offense allowed for no other alternative. In Sadie's case, once she returned home, the six weeks probationary shunning would go into effect so she could have a taste of it and want to repent of her sins. Whether Sadie returned home or remained in Ohio, if she did not repent, she would end up shunned. Just as Leah and Jonas would be if they left Gobbler's Knob and Bishop Bontrager did not rule on the side of leniency.

Leah's greatest dread was that Sadie might simply decide never to come home.

◆

Promptly at four o'clock the mail arrived, and Sadie hurried out to bring in the bundle of letters. She made her stop on David and Vera's side of the big brick house, depositing a third of the mail in the designated spot on the corner of the kitchen counter. She noticed yet another letter from Leah to Jonas and shoved it down toward the bottom of the pile. Then she hurried to the Dawdi Haus to bring great joy to Edith with five letters bearing the widow's name. Edith had begun to share many of her pen-pal letters with Sadie. One of the women she wrote to had a grandson, a courting-age boy Edith wondered if Sadie might like to get to know. Even though courting amongst the People was kept secret, it seemed to Sadie that Edith was bound and determined to play matchmaker.

Sadie also held a letter from Leah to her, along with one from Mamma. She was fairly sure Mamma's letter would carry the same urgent message she'd stated by telephone. Precisely, Mamma was making a determined, obvious plea for Sadie to *come home immediately and repent. Spare yourself the shame of the ministers there having to contact you. Oh, Sadie, my dear girl, you must do this! Dat has also requested this of you.*

She cast aside Mamma's letter in favor of the one from Leah. The first letter her sister had bothered to write to her . . . another sure sign Leah had helped to get her out here, only to betray her once she was gone. What both Mamma and Leah didn't know was that there were plenty of interested fellows here, something she could never now hope for in

295

Gobbler's Knob. Both Ben Eicher and John Graber had scrapped amongst themselves to get Sadie's attention at the last singing. She'd ended up riding home with Ben, having secretly promised John her presence at the following singing. Either of them would do just fine for her to marry. She didn't mind that Ben lived over in Walnut Creek or that John made his home much farther away in Allen County. Indiana, Ohio—wherever she ended up meant she didn't have to be a *Pennsylvania* maidel. It would be all right with her not to be within earshot of either Leah or Mamma—especially Leah, though Sadie did miss Aunt Lizzie terribly. One of these days she must write Lizzie a long letter.

Seeing the smile on Edith's face, Sadie helped open each of the pen-pal letters for the old woman, then excused herself to the light and airy bedroom that was for now her home away from home.

The second-floor bedroom was smaller than the one she'd shared with Leah back home. Still, it was all her own, with a double bed to stretch out in and a wide oak dresser with plenty of space for her few clothes. She had already started sewing some new dresses and aprons for the coming autumn using the dress patterns from the Millersburg church district, with Vera's input on style and cut. Easily, she had stitched up the long seams of two blue dresses in short order. Since Vera was soon to give birth, Sadie felt she ought to do this sewing herself, as well as some for Edith.

Now she pulled the only chair in the room over next to the tall window and tore open the letter from her sister.

Dearest Sadie,

How are you? All of us here are all right, except we miss you something awful. I've waited to hear from you, but when you didn't write, I worried you were miffed. And rightly so.

I did not tell Mamma about your baby on a whim. Honestly, it was the hardest thing I've ever done, breaking my promise to you. You must believe me. In one way I despised it, but in doing so I felt the burden of guilt lift from me. Our sisterly covenant was ever so wrong. I see it clearly now. Oh, Sadie, I can hardly ask your forgiveness.

For all the time I did keep mum, I thought hard about those things you shared with me, especially that day in the garden. I weep sad tears, knowing how you struggle to forgive yourself, dear sister. And I pray you will let God, our loving Father, restore you to the church. He alone can grant grace and mercy.

I know (and you do, too) that soon you will be called upon to make things right with the brethren here, and I'm worried this will cause a terrible rift between us. Surely you must live in fear of the shun; I myself tremble to think of it. It seems all of Preacher Yoder's sermons nowadays call us to live as a holy generation. How could I possibly do so while carrying a heavy weight of deceitfulness?

One thing I hope to accomplish in this letter is to let you know, once again, that I love you and will never stop. What I did I would expect you to do if ever I strayed from the narrow way. Oh, please come home and make amends, dearest Sadie.

Will you write soon?

> *With much love,*
> *Your sister Leah*

Sadie slumped back in her chair, sighing. Obviously her sister had taken great care to write such a heartfelt letter. Torn between fond memories of their early days together and blaming Leah for spilling the beans on her, Sadie let the letter slip from her fingers and drift to the floor.

Chapter Twenty-Eight

The stately trees lining the road had already begun to turn to golden, red, and orange hues. Because of this and the fact he felt rather glum, Jonas did not rush the mare to his final destination. As a boy he had often gone out this time of year, past his father's orchard to where giant maples and oaks dropped their leaves in such abundance he liked to gather up a select few, choosing the most colorful to press between the pages of the largest book in the house, *Martyrs Mirror*.

His mother had once discovered a red sugar maple leaf marking the page where the account of "four lambs of Christ"—a brother and three sisters—had been sentenced to death as heretics, though they were indeed followers of Christ. He was stunned when he read the middle sister came to her death singing, then prayed aloud, "Lord, look upon us, who suffer for thy word. Our trust is in thee alone." All four commended their spirits into the hands of the Lord God, offering up their blood sacrifice, their very lives, for their unfaltering faith.

From that day forth, he had often wondered if he, too,

might be given the heralded "martyr's grace" if ever he were to come to such a fate. For that reason, he had purposed to give his life fully to spreading the goodness of the Lord above, wherever his feet may trod.

This evening, though, there was no need for that kind of grace. But empathy, perhaps. Sitting next to him was a young woman who seemed as sad as she was lonely. The sooner he got her back home the better.

Sadie said not a word as they rode along, evidently waiting for him to do the talking. He held the reins too high, tense as can be. "What do you know of Smithy Gid?" he blurted out his question.

She replied softly. "He's the only son of my father's closest friend, the blacksmith. Our neighbor, as you know."

Jonas contemplated how to phrase his next question. Or should he?

They rode along, too quiet for several minutes. At last he brought up the August Sunday singing held in Abram's barn. "Did you happen to see Leah and Gid together there?"

"I didn't go to the singin' that night." He noticed out of the corner of his eye that she turned to look at him. "I did see Leah and Gid walking through the cornfield over to his house after attendin' the singing."

He could only guess why Leah had even gone to the singing, let alone left with Gid. Nevertheless, this information wasn't earthshaking enough that he should be concerned. Although it did seem odd for a betrothed young woman to spend time with a single man.

"Do you have any reason to believe Leah might be interested in Gid?" Everything within him rebelled against asking such a thing—Rebekah's report made not one lick of sense. He knew Leah was as devoted to him as he was to her. And yet the tone of her last letter made him wonder if something wasn't amiss.

"I saw them . . . one other time, too," Sadie added somewhat hesitantly.

"When was this?"

"Not too many days before I left for here."

Tension spread down from his jaw to his neck and now his shoulders. "Are you sure you saw *Leah* with Gid?"

She sighed, fidgeting now. "It happened the day Leah got herself lost in the woods. When she didn't come home for the noon meal, Mamma sent Gid out lookin' for her, with the German shepherd—a gift to Leah from Gid last spring."

He tried to recall if Leah had ever mentioned the dog. Inhaling, he held his breath before continuing. "Does your father hold out hope for the two of them gettin' together?"

"Oh my . . . ever so much."

That fact still did not establish a reason to suspect Leah of being unfaithful. "Can you be more specific about what you saw the day Leah got lost?" he asked.

"Well, they were walkin' out of the deepest part of the woods. Gid was playin' his harmonica for Leah, and they were laughin' together. And . . . I'm not sure I ought to say much more."

"Go on, please. . . ." he said, her hesitancy causing his heart to pound. "What is it?"

"I . . . I saw them holdin' hands." She paused. "I had an awful hard time believin' it then, but it was so."

He clenched his jaw. No! This *had* to be purely innocent

on Leah's part. Then he remembered how Leah had refused his two invitations to come here . . . to be near him this summer. Why had Leah sent her sister instead?

He had never thought to address the question, not in connection to Leah wanting to stay home for Smithy Gid. She'd indicated her mother needed help with the new little one, though at the time, he *had* wondered why Sadie or the twins couldn't have pitched in, freeing Leah up to make the visit.

Keeping his gaze on the road, he never once looked at Sadie to his left. Could she be trusted? He wasn't certain. Why *was* she here and not Leah?

I'll write to Leah immediately about this, he thought. *I must know her side of things.*

Observing the road ahead as far as he could see, he followed the line of every ridge and valley, each soaring tree, till his eyes found the sky. He was struck by the coming nightfall—something of a lemon color—not the predictable rosy hue of setting sun.

'Tis the end of summer, he thought, hoping it was not also signaling the end of Leah's affection for him. Yet with each dying moment, summer ebbed toward autumn . . . and there was nothing he could do to slow its progress.

When Leah received Jonas's letter, she didn't have time to read it in sweet solitude. Dat expected her to help with as many of his barn chores as possible, more than usual this week since smithy Peachey and several other farmers nearby needed his help digging potatoes. Due to severe back pain, he'd finally given in and paid a visit to Dr. Schwartz "to get me some pain pills." Being able to offer his help with the harvest had always been of utmost importance to her father. He enjoyed the make-work-fun mentality of the People, wanting to be counted on by the neighboring farmers.

She hurried upstairs to her room right after dinner, knowing she must not dawdle. There she read the letter from Jonas.

Right away she determined something was wrong: Jonas wanted to know if she'd "spent time with Gid Peachey at a singing in August" . . . and could she explain his gift of a German shepherd?

> I hope to hear from you as soon as possible, Leah. Since we are betrothed and plan to marry in a few short weeks, I trust you will clear this up for me.
>
> Surely it is nothing more than a misunderstanding. I pray so!
>
> I'll watch eagerly for your letter.
>
> > With love,
> > Jonas

Oh, her heart ached for him. None of this had any bearing whatsoever on their love. She must answer him immediately, even take time tonight to write before going to bed. For dear Jonas's sake, she would write long into the wee hours if necessary.

To think that someone—who?—wanted to cause a falling-out between them this close to their wedding day! She could not imagine how such a thing had come about.

She slipped the letter into the top dresser drawer and

hurried downstairs to help with kitchen cleanup so Mamma could nurse Lydiann.

All of a sudden, a distressing thought occurred to her. Was it possible Sadie had something to do with this?

Getting Edith settled this night was a chore and then some. Edith wanted to sit by lantern's light in the front room and read one pen-pal letter after another aloud—this humorous happening and that event—till Sadie was plain tuckered out. On top of that, she was having trouble giving the woman her full attention, recalling how miserable Jonas looked since their trip to town. He was nearly silent at mealtime, not engaging so much with either David or Vera in the good-natured sort of conversation they'd obviously enjoyed all summer long. Even Mary Mae and Andy, the two younger Mellinger children, weren't successful in getting him to play evening games, she noticed.

Daylight hours were growing shorter, and the family—Edith and Sadie included—spent more and more time together following supper. Edith wasn't in a hurry to be helped back to the Dawdi Haus; she liked to sit in one of the old rockers in Vera's kitchen and listen to the after-meal talk or ask David to read yet another chapter from the Good Book.

Sometimes Sadie slipped into her daydream world, thinking about Ben Eicher or John Graber while helping Vera with dishes, looking forward to the next singing. Neither boy could hold a candle to fair-faced and handsome Jonas Mast, who she was beginning to think was the most desirable young man anywhere. Still, as much as she admired Jonas, she couldn't just out and out steal him away from Leah, could she? The rational side of her pondered this continually, but the compelling desire to lash out and have her revenge made Jonas most enticing. Ever more so as each day passed.

Two days later Sadie found herself sitting on the front porch, waiting to bring in the mail.

She walked down the sloping lawn to the mailbox and thanked the postman for the delivery, then thumbed through the pile of letters on her way up to the house. Right away she noticed an envelope addressed to Jonas from Leah. Seeing her sister's handwriting and name in the upper left-hand corner made her heart pound hot and hard.

Leah broke her vow. She promised to keep my secret forever! she thought. *She doesn't deserve to be happy. . . .*

Quickly, without thinking ahead to what sadness this might cause Jonas, she slipped the letter into her dress pocket. Then, hurrying into the house, she headed to Vera's kitchen and deposited the stack of letters on the counter as usual.

Glad no one was anywhere around, she pulled Leah's letter out of her pocket. Holding it in both hands, she stared at it, aware of the heat in her face, the rage in her heart.

Leah belongs with Smithy Gid, she told herself. *Dat knows it, so maybe 'tis best. . . .*

Vera's trash receptacle was kept under the sink, and Sadie

reached down to open the cabinet door. Jittery with a guilty conscience, yet flush with anger, she held Leah's letter over the waste can, took a deep breath, and let it drop into the rubbish.

Chapter Twenty-Nine

The day came and went with no mail back from Leah, although Jonas was glad for a letter from his mother. She had written of being extra busy with Jake and Mandie. *They bring us great joy, times two.* There was also a cheerful letter from his brother-in-law, Nathaniel, and one from his next-youngest brother, Eli, with talk of the apple harvest.

Jonas was aware, on some level, of the singular squeak of a car's brake as the postman stopped in front of the house each day. Ankle-deep in sawdust out back in the carpentry shop with David, he imitated the master carpenter's every movement, taking great care to craft each desk or chair into a shining example of excellence. All the while he was mindful of the hammering of his own heart.

What's keeping Leah? he wondered.

Thinking back to her response to his earlier letter raising the subject of them living here after the wedding, he wished now he hadn't put the question to her in writing. He should have waited to talk with her in person about the prospect once he returned home. Her return letter, he recalled, had been one of loving words, even of encouragement. She wanted him to be happy in his life's work, as long as Bishop Bontrager would sanction such a thing. She wanted what *he* wanted, *with the blessing of our sovereign Lord and the church.*

Despite her seemingly positive approach to moving, he had sensed an underlying hesitancy, even disappointment. He decided to reread that particular letter tonight. First, though, he must take good care in making the dovetail joints on the dresser drawers for one of David's regular clients. After that he planned to sweep out the workshop and redd up before going to the house for supper.

With no word back from Jonas, Leah began to think something must be wrong. Surely he had understood the things she'd written to him, that she and Gid were merely friends, neighborly and all, as one would expect when families in close proximity work together. *Nothing more*, she had written, still shocked Jonas had been led to believe otherwise. She'd explained why she had been present at the singing, how she'd gone with Adah at her request. Also, she'd told Jonas in no uncertain terms that King belonged to the *whole* family, not just to her . . . and she'd even asked Dat's approval, wondering how prudent it was to accept such a gift.

Even so, in spite of all she'd written him, she felt something was terribly amiss. A single day turned into an agonizing two . . . then three. Jonas was clearly ignoring her letter. But why? Had he read between the lines of her earlier letter? Had he sensed her reluctance to live in Ohio? Surely he did not question the bishop's stern stance on keeping to home or that they had both promised to live amongst the People of Gobbler's Knob, vowing so at baptism.

Worse, had Jonas chosen to believe the near accusations about Smithy Gid and herself?

Truth be known, she had begun to wonder if their premature affection—kissing as they had—might have been a bad omen, indeed, just as she had brought up to Jonas that very day. Yet he'd brushed it off.

She went about her work in a fog. Never having been one to question herself, she began to question everything. She recalled the tiniest details of her life with Jonas, the joyful snatches that had begun with their earliest days and family visits to Grasshopper Level: picnics on the lawn, romps in the meadow, daisy picking, volleyball games—all of it—including their most recent Sunday afternoon together, soaking up sunbeams in Dr. Schwartz's empty meadow.

She decided to send yet another letter to her beloved, to make one more attempt to convince him she was, and had always been, trustworthy—his faithful Leah. She would not cover the old ground previously written—that Smithy Gid had merely found her in the forest and walked her home, that both she *and* Adah had gone with Gid over to the Peacheys' house after the singing that night.

The letter she intended to write this time was meant to state once more how she felt in the deep of her heart, recalling their youthful promises—made so long ago, it seemed—as well as the loving words exchanged during courtship's dearest days.

Do you remember helping me catch that hop toad the

Sunday we were out by the creek all alone? My mamma raised her eyebrows when we returned, awful muddy from having such fun together. I guess she thought at my tender age of eleven I had no business falling in love with you. But Mamma didn't know what we knew, did she? We truly cared for each other, even then. And still we do . . . I do. How can I not write you again to tell you these things within my heart?

Yet you remain ever so silent. Are you displeased, Jonas? Have I offended you? I would return the dog in a short minute if you say the word.

> *My love always, for you alone.*
> *Your faithful Leah*

Desperate to resolve whatever had caused this breach, she scanned her letter before sealing it shut, hoping . . . *praying* Jonas might read her words . . . and see through to the love in her heart.

———◆———

It was well before sunrise when Jonas set out running. Frustrated to no end, he sprinted for a full mile without stopping on a level dirt road near Killbuck Creek. A pain in his side caused him to slow up, so he resorted to walking.

Not a speck of traffic was here so early in the morning. He was glad for the peace before he and David were to head out for Berlin to eat breakfast at Boyd and Worthman's Restaurant and General Store.

With still no word from Leah, he wondered if their plans for marriage were on shaky ground. Was it possible she did care for Gid Peachey and had never had the courage to tell him? But if so, what about their afternoon together, kissing and sharing their hearts so openly in the flower-strewn pasture . . . and their talk of the wedding?

He walked more briskly, getting his wind back. The thought crossed his mind Leah might possibly have some of the same inclinations Lizzie Brenneman had as a fickle and lustful youth. Was it possible—could it be—Leah was in any way similar to her birth mother? There had never been any indication of that. Leah had convinced him of her love, that she was true blue.

He picked up his pace and began to run again, soon turning to head back to the Mellingers' place just as dawn broke over distant hills. Desperately he tried to outrun the exasperating thoughts, such wretched ones they were.

Leah awakened feeling all wrung out, so scarcely had she slept. She had argued with herself all night, going back and forth about whether or not to send the last letter she'd written to Jonas, dear to her as it was.

She got up and dressed, brushed her hair, and pinned it back in a tight bun, finally setting her prayer cap on her head. Forcing herself down the stairs and out to the barn, she decided to wait till after breakfast to think more about the letter. Dat had always said never to make an important decision on an empty stomach. Mundane as it was, she felt she needed sustenance—some of Mamma's scrambled and cheesy eggs, maybe—to hold her together. With still not a single letter arriving from Jonas, she felt short of breath, concerned she might not be able to perform her many outdoor chores this day.

Plain and fancy men alike were feeding their faces at the well-known Berlin restaurant. Some sat at the long counter, others settled in toward the back, sitting around tables. The atmosphere was charged with farm talk and the coming cold snap, a change of pace to be sure. But David seemed to have more than home cooking on his mind. "Something's bothering you, Jonas," he said.

"Is it that obvious?"

David smiled quickly. " 'Tis all over your face."

Jonas couldn't say what was on his mind, couldn't reveal the torture he'd lived with each day the mail came and went with no word of explanation from Leah. "I'm thinkin' I might need to cut short my apprenticeship, if that's agreeable to you."

David nodded. "Well, now, you've come a mighty long way in nearly six months, to be sure. We'll miss you round here, but jah, that's all right in my book."

Jonas paused, staring down at his plate. "I need to get home right quick." He wasn't so keen on saying what was on his mind just now. He could think only about seeing Leah again, talking with her face-to-face ... hearing the truth directly.

"We've had gut fellowship since you've come here," David said, his eyes registering sympathy. He poured two heaping teaspoons of sugar in his black coffee, stirred it, and slurped the hot drink. "I hope things are all right 'tween you and your sweetheart back home," he said.

Jonas drew a deep breath. "Jah, I hope so, too." He stopped for a moment, then continued. "And while we're speaking bluntly, I've been wonderin'—do you have any idea how my apprenticeship came about? Any inkling at all?"

David nodded. "I shouldn't say . . . prob'ly. But between you, me, and the fence post, 'twas your father-in-law-to-be who set it up with me."

"*Abram* did?" Jonas was taken aback.

David had another drink of his coffee. "He called on the telephone to tell of your keen interest in carpentry and wondered if I might not take you on—help you get your feet wet."

His head was spinning. "When was this?"

"Round the end of March."

Just as I began to seriously court Leah, he thought. *So Abram wanted me gone all along.*

Leah happened to meet up with Gid, of all people, as she was closing the door on the chicken coop, having just gathered the eggs.

He removed his black hat as he came near, offering a boyish grin. "Bein' more careful in the woods these days, Leah?" He slowed a bit and glanced toward the forest.

She had to smile. "Jah, I am that," and she thanked him again for rescuing her that awful day.

"Well, I best be gettin' back to work," he said, heading off in the direction of the mule road.

She stood there, basket of eggs in hand, observing his long stride. He reached up and put his hat back on his head, going up toward Aunt Lizzie's. Probably to clean out her chimney flue before the cold days set in, Leah assumed. Lizzie had been saying as much, though Leah hadn't expected her to ask Gid to do it. Lizzie would insist on offering him something for his work, of course. More than likely, it would be a nice, plump fruit pie or suchlike, instead of money.

Carrying the eggs carefully to the house, she wished Jonas could have seen her just now with Gid, seen there was nothing except pure friendship between them. She placed the basket on the kitchen counter and hurried upstairs to her bedroom. From her dresser drawer, she pulled out her latest letter to Jonas. Still unsure of what to do, she read it again.

Finished, she refolded the letter. She knew she must not further plead with him to believe what he surely already knew in his heart. If he didn't trust her by now, when would he ever?

She pushed the letter back into the drawer. Hurt and discouraged, she headed downstairs.

Will we ever be truly happy again? she wondered. *Will I?*

David was already in the workshop hand sanding a table leg when Jonas arrived promptly at six-thirty the morning after their talk in Berlin. The day felt slightly cooler than yesterday's dawning hour, and he smelled woodsmoke lingering in the air, a sure sign of autumn.

Jonas greeted the master carpenter and set to work, using a doweling jig on the eight-inch oak boards, soon to be a trestle-table top. He was anxious to throw himself into the work to drown, if possible, the disappointment that cut away at him. He must help David catch up on a half dozen or so projects for eager customers, enduring the wait till his father got word back to him with some dependable answers regarding Leah.

Feelings of near despair had begun to set in during the past week. The letter he had written to his darling girl had offered him no solution, having been met only with maddening silence. Though he could hardly hold back his urgency, he knew it was not prudent to assume the worst or to be impulsive and rush home unannounced. Instead, he'd written a letter to his father asking him to pave the way for the unplanned visit with Leah. He'd spelled out his dire concerns, pleading with Dat to get a feel for the situation with Abram Ebersol—*because I can't go on this way, not knowing for sure about my Leah.*

He had sent the letter off in yesterday's mail. *Dat won't ignore my request,* he thought. *He'll go right away to Gobbler's Knob. I know he will.*

Now he must attempt to be patient till he received word back regarding Leah and his impending trip. The hours stretched long before him.

Chapter Thirty

It was chilly in the barn, even with the wide doors all closed up this morning. After a short time Abram went back into the house for his work coat while Leah milked Rosie.

Returning to the barn, he heard a horse and carriage rattle into the lane. Walking over to the side yard, he was surprised to see Peter Mast waving a greeting to him. "Hullo, Abram!"

"*Willkumm!*" he called back.

Peter got out and tied the horse to the post. They exchanged a few words about the change in weather, then they walked toward the barnyard, where Peter asked if they could speak privately.

"Oh?"

" 'Tis concerning your daughter and my son." Peter sounded downright serious all of a sudden. "Ain't the first time we've been mighty plainspoken, as you recall."

"Leah's within earshot," Abram replied, jigging his head in her direction. "Why don't we mosey up to the pasture?"

Instead of taking things slow, they walked at a hurried

pace, Abram noticed, all the way out past the barn to where the windmill stood guard over his prized property. He looked toward the woods and thought he saw Lizzie out sweeping her front porch, a thin line of smoke curling up from the log house chimney.

Peter seemed overly eager to get to the point. "It's come to my attention, namely from Jonas, that Leah and the smithy's son may be carryin' on romantically."

Abram bristled and Peter stopped talking, glancing at the ground, as if to let the information settle in. *How could Jonas suspect such a thing?* Abram wondered. *Why is Peter here on the boy's behalf?*

This made no sense, but he waited for Peter to continue, hard as it was not to spew forth the questions rapidly gathering in his mind.

"Now, Abram, I know you and I know Ida, but I can't vouch for Leah . . . and I think you can guess what I'm gettin' at here."

Can't vouch for Leah . . .

Abram suppressed the fire in his bones. What kind of nerve! Peter and Fannie Mast had known from the beginning of Lizzie's unwed pregnancy, even though the bishop had put the shush on things early on for little Leah's sake. Still, it wasn't Peter's place to throw around insults like this.

"You best be speakin' straight with me, Peter," he urged.

"All right, then—is Smithy Gid warmin' up to Leah?"

Abram set his chin. He was tempted to give Peter what for, and then it came to him . . . the *real* reason Peter was here. Well, now, wasn't this curious? Jonas must be having second thoughts about marrying Lizzie's illegitimate daughter after all. Most likely, Peter was here to help Jonas wiggle out of his betrothal, using as an excuse what Abram had shared with Jonas man to man. If that was the case, then he *had* found out what Peter's son was made of, and none too soon. "Who's askin' this—you or Jonas?" Abram said.

"I'm here at my son's request. But I have a stake in this, too."

Abram straightened, recalling the day Gid had gone in search of Leah in the woods, bringing her home wearing an unmistakable grin. "Seems to me Gid would be a right fine man for my Leah," he replied. "Ain't no secret how I feel 'bout that. If he wants to spend time with Leah, I have no problem with it."

"So . . . it's true, then?"

"Gid's awful fond of her. As for courtin', well, 'tis hard to be exact about what goes on under the coverin' of night."

"Gideon Peachey has your blessin', is that what you're sayin'?" Peter's face had turned as red as a ripened beet.

"He's had the go-ahead since he turned sixteen." There, he'd said it all, though clouded over with a shade of gray.

"Then, I guess that's that." Peter turned tail and headed back through the paddock without so much as a good-bye grunt or a tip of his black hat.

Heading toward the barn, Abram felt torn. He was fully persuaded Gid was Leah's best chance for happiness. Even so, he could not bear to see her heart broken. He was caught between his dear girl's hopes and wishes and what a father knew best. Downright angry he was at Jonas Mast for instigating a breakup. No doubt in his mind—Peter's boy had made a deliberate turn away from Leah, starting that day in the cornfield.

The telephone in the woodshop was jangling as Jonas hurried to answer it. David was nowhere around, so he picked up the phone. "Mellingers' Carpentry."

"Jonas? Is that you?"

He perked up his ears. "Dat?"

"Jah, thought I'd make a quick call to you, son."

"Gut to hear back from you." He wondered if his father had some important news. Why else would he resort to using a telephone?

"I don't want you to waste any more time troublin' yourself over the likes of Leah Ebersol."

The words slapped him in the face. "You spoke to Abram?"

"This morning . . . and, believe me, you're better off this way than findin' out your girl was disloyal after you married her."

Jonas was aware of the pounding of his heart. His precious Leah untrue? His throat went dry. How could this possibly be?

He recalled again Leah's decision not to spend the summer here with him. How frustrating it was not having solid answers for why she had refused. Yet he'd trusted her, respecting her right to remain in Gobbler's Knob as she wished. Then, when he'd invited her a second time, what had she done but call him on the telephone, of all things, to ask if he could make arrangements for Sadie to come in her stead! Just why *had* Leah sent Sadie to him? He could only imagine.

Feelings of total frustration flooded him, and he knew not what to say or think. Knowing Leah through all the years of their friendship, he would never have thought she might purposely set out to betray him. Such a thing was unthinkable, truly.

"Son, are you there?"

He drew in a breath and expelled it suddenly. "I can't begin to understand this, Dat."

" 'Tis essential for you to come home. You made a covenant with the Gobbler's Knob church. . . ."

I can't think of living anywhere near Leah if I can't be with her myself, he thought. But to his father he said, "David's offered me a partnership and perhaps I oughta be thinking on that."

"Jonas . . . son, you'll be shunned if you don't return."

Bishop Bontrager was one of the most austere ministers in all of Lancaster County, the spiritual head of the Gobbler's Knob and Georgetown church districts. Responsible for recommending excommunication and shunning, the man of God had the power to seal Jonas's fate.

"I'll write to him and plead my case if I have to," he said. "But if he refuses, I'll make a life here for myself without Abram's Leah. . . . Somehow, I will. With God's help."

His father continued to argue for Jonas to return home, saying he couldn't think of going on without him.

When the time came to say good-bye, Jonas offered, "God be with you, Dat. Tell Mamma I love her . . . and my brothers and sisters, too."

"Son, please think hard about this. You mustn't throw

away your life. . . ." There was great heaviness in Dat's voice. Then he said, "I'm through with the Ebersols, kin or not, for what they've done to us!"

Jonas stared at the telephone after hanging up. It seemed unbelievable. Leah must have given in to Abram's wishes . . . and now preferred Gid.

———◆———

It was going to be a warm afternoon, much nicer than the morning had started out to be; this was clear to Sadie by well past the noon meal. She helped not only Edith with some light cleaning but also Vera, offering to dust the front room and bake a pie for supper while Vera read to Mary Mae and Andy before putting them down for a nap.

With the cherry pie nestled safely in the oven, she hurried back to the Dawdi Haus through the connecting door. She saw Edith dozing in her rocking chair, white-gray head tilted back, mouth gaping open. Tiptoeing past her, Sadie headed for the stairs.

In her room, she sat near the window, looking out. She felt at once guilty and even sad for having thrown away Leah's letter to Jonas. But the very next morning, after a sleepless night, she had gone to look through the kitchen trash, only to discover someone had gathered up the refuse in the house and taken it out to the large trash bin. When she inquired of Vera about the trash pickup, she was told the county collectors had already come and hauled it away.

For more than a week, she struggled immensely. She'd had

no business taking Jonas's letter, nor should she have thrown it in the trash. Angry or not, though, she could reason Leah had it coming—her telling on Sadie and all. She honestly felt she could overlook, even forgive Naomi Kauffman for going to Preacher Yoder to rid herself of sin prior to baptism. Naomi's knowledge of Sadie's rumschpringe was scant in detail compared to what Leah was privy to. Besides, sisters were supposed to keep vows of the heart. And Leah had not.

What misery I've caused Jonas, she thought, having daily witnessed his despair firsthand. And the act of tampering with mail was a crime, she knew. The all-seeing eyes of the Lord God heavenly Father roamed to and fro over the earth. Her list of sins was ever lengthening.

She had wrongly interfered in the fate of two people's lives, delving into the most personal regions of the heart. Yet she felt helpless to confess her wrongdoing to Jonas, though she knew she must. She was worried sick what he would think of her.

By being in the kitchen when Jonas came in for a refill on his Thermos of iced tea, she might force herself to come clean. She was prepared to confess the whole thing, and she'd calculated the timing of their encounter, hoping he was punctual with his afternoon break. Since Vera had gone upstairs with the children, this was Sadie's best opportunity.

Now here he came, hurrying across the lawn and up the steps into the house. "Hullo," he said flatly, the smile gone from his face.

His greeting distressed her; she was at fault. Even so, no matter how solemn he looked, she must follow through. "I, uh, wonder if I might talk to you right quick." She leaned hard against the kitchen sink.

"In fact, I'm awful glad I bumped into you," he said, taking her off guard. His eyes were red-rimmed yet unwavering, and he glanced about, as if checking to see if they were alone. "You were right, Sadie. It's true what you told me . . .'bout Leah and Gid. They *are* a couple."

She didn't know what to think and felt her face go flush. "Are you sayin' you heard from someone back home?"

Jonas nodded and told of his father's telephone call. Then he startled her by saying, "I owe you much gratitude."

She could hardly believe what she was hearing. So she *had* been right about what she'd seen in the woods that day? She could see by the stricken look in his eyes that here was a young man in need of comfort.

"I'm ever so sorry, Jonas," she said in a tender voice.

He smiled then, a shattered kind of smile that did nothing to disguise his hurt. "No, no. This is not for you to worry over."

She glanced at the oven. "I baked a cherry pie hopin' to cheer you up at supper."

He attempted to force another smile, she could see. "I'll look forward to your pie," he said. Then he returned to his work.

She watched him hurry toward the back door. *I spared Jonas by discarding Leah's distressing letter,* she thought in amazement. *And surely it was that, because there are no more coming.*

Hours later Sadie was outside sweeping the little box of a back porch to the Dawdi Haus when she saw the ministers walking toward her across the yard.

They've wasted no time, she thought, noting the stern look in both the preacher's and the deacon's eyes. Suddenly she felt as if she were headed to the gallows.

Chapter Thirty-One

Leah came in the kitchen door and saw Mamma sitting at the table, her face stained with tears. "Ach, what is it?" She rushed to her mother's side.

"I worried something like this might happen." Mamma looked down at the letter in her lap. "It's the worst news ever."

"What is?"

Mamma shook her head. "Sadie's not comin' home. Already she's had a visit from the brethren there. But everythin' hinges on her willingness to repent."

"*Still* she refuses?"

"Awful sad, 'tis." Mamma pulled out one of Hannah's embroidered hankies hidden beneath her sleeve and wiped her eyes. Her voice faltered. "If the Bann is put on her—even a short-term shunning—Bishop Bontrager might put a stop to her letters."

"Then we'll lose touch with her. . . ." Leah felt strangled. She laid her head on her mother's soft, round shoulder, keenly aware of her own grief but even more so of Mamma's trembling.

When Dat came indoors for a drink of water and spotted them there, his mouth dropped open. "What's wrong, Ida . . . somebody up and die?"

Mamma said nothing, holding up the letter for him to see.

Removing his hat slowly, Dat planted himself in the middle of the kitchen, his eyes moving back and forth across the page. His lips formed every silent word.

When he finished reading, he frowned. "If Sadie's diggin' her heels in about comin' home, then I 'spect there might be a reason for it." His words sounded convincing, but his voice was right wobbly.

Leah held her breath and Mamma said, "Just what could that be, Abram?"

He folded the letter, staring down at it. "Who's to say, really. But I'm a-thinkin' . . . could be Sadie has herself a new beau."

"Who'd have her if she's to be shunned?" asked Mamma.

Dat fell silent for a time. When he looked up, his eyes were awful watery. Leah felt her skin go prickly. "Maybe Jonas, for one," he said.

"Ach, Abram!" Mamma clasped a hand to her heart.

Leah was devastated at Dat's remark, though the idea *had* crossed her mind. Could it be Sadie was the reason for Jonas's ongoing silence, the reason why his letters had ceased? *Surely not*, she hoped, her mouth going dry.

"What'll become of our Sadie?" Mamma asked, sniffling.

Dat glanced at Leah somewhat ruefully. Unexpectedly, he went and sat next to Mamma at the table. Slipping his arm around her, he stared at the checked oilcloth. "We do as the Lord God calls us—to live as a holy example. . . . Sadie knows the way, Ida."

Leah felt as distressed as Dat and Mamma looked. She leaned hard against the table, wishing the stillness might be broken—if not for happy talk, at least for her burning question.

Finally she asked, "What'll happen if Preacher Yoder has already written and told the preachers there . . . 'bout Sadie's iniquity?"

Dat raised his head and looked at her. "Seems to me, they'll want to keep all that tomfoolery under their ministerial hats," he said. "In fact, I 'spect they'd prefer to keep it hush-hush, them eager to bring new blood to the community and all."

"What about the Proving?" asked Mamma. "Won't Sadie be watched closely for a time?"

Dat nodded his head. "If she passes scrutiny for six months, she'll be welcomed into the Ohio fellowship, as long as they hold to believers' baptism, separation from the evil world, and reject going to war. Far as I understand, anyway."

Leah had heard tell of the Proving. She'd also heard of certain church districts where the People intermarried so frequently the children born to such unions suffered physical problems—sometimes mental.

So, in the process of time, if she repented there, Sadie would be allowed to join the Millersburg church district. But she'd be shunned in Gobbler's Knob.

Mamma spoke up. "Ach, the worst is our girl will be cut

off from us—unless she has a change of heart and comes home."

"Not likely now, I'm afraid," Dat said, getting up.

"What'll happen to Jonas?" asked Leah quietly.

Pulling at his beard, Dat eyed Mamma. "I daresay he must've gotten special permission from the Grasshopper Level bishop to take his apprenticeship out of state."

"Jah, he did," Leah said. "Jonas told me so last spring before he left." She sighed, wondering if she ought to say more. Then she could hold the words back no longer. "Will he be shunned, too, if he doesn't return?"

"That'll be for his bishop to work out with both Bishop Bontrager and the Ohio brethren." His eyes showed deep concern toward her.

A groan escaped Leah's lips.

Dat went on. "Unless Jonas gets himself home by the end of next month, he'll be subject to the vote of the People. But . . . I'd say there's still hope he'll be spared the shun."

Not if Sadie's caught his eye, she thought, cringing inwardly. *I was naïve, sending my beautiful sister to Millersburg in my stead!*

Leah could no longer deny her sorrow. How on earth could she sit here while Dat speculated, when her future with the only boy she'd ever loved was at stake? She wondered if she should now make some attempt to contact Jonas besides her letter. Should she hurry to a telephone and call him?

No, that was much too bold on her part. She wouldn't put Jonas on the spot. Indeed, he must have a reason for not writing, though she couldn't imagine what. Patience . . . and a meek and gentle spirit were of the utmost importance. No respectable Amishwoman would behave otherwise. Hard as it would be, she must allow him to get in touch with her on his own terms.

Without saying more to either Dat or Mamma, she hastened out the back door, hurrying down the lane to the road. She ran so hard she lost track of where she was going, and by the time she slowed to catch her breath, she'd come upon the boundary line where Peacheys' land and Dr. Schwartz's empty field met up—where she and Jonas had exchanged their first kisses not so long ago. What could have gone wrong in such a short time?

Weary now, she sat on a nearby rock, indifferent to trespassing. Moments crept by and it felt that the world—*her* world—had come to a halt. She looked out over the fertile grassland to the approximate area of the small grave, though she could not see it from here. The lonely place, without even a marker, lay in the tall grass, representing the death of everything she had come to hold dear.

There lies my future without Jonas, she thought, realizing just how terribly depressed she felt.

Then, quite unexpectedly, another sad thought crossed her mind. For all she knew, Sadie's little baby lay lifeless and cold in that grave. Such a devastating turn of events this all was, beginning with the sins of Sadie's rumschpringe. Everything—*everything*—had spun out of control, shattering their lives, from Sadie's first curious look at a worldly English boy.

Heavyhearted, she rose and labored back up the long road toward the Ebersol Cottage, as she'd always called her father's abode. The limestone house with its grand front door and wide porch seemed to smile a welcome to friend or foe alike. If the things Dat said were true—and no doubt they were—

the family home would remain a place of refuge for her well into a bleak and lonely future. Not the house of her wedding service, nor her wedding night. Not the happy dwelling place where she and Jonas came for visits with their new babies. . . .

She would remain Abram's Leah for a long time to come. Maybe forever.

———◆———

After outside chores were done, Leah kept busy sewing a blue bridesmaid's dress for Naomi's upcoming wedding—when she wasn't helping Mamma. In spite of her busyness, she could not get her mind off Jonas as each day passed and no more letters arrived.

She and Adah spent their leisure time sewing together. But, though Leah tried to conceal her sadness, she couldn't fool her best friend.

"Oh, Leah, as much as I would like to have you as my sister-in-law, I can see clearly how much you love Jonas."

They had been working side by side at Adah's mother's trestle table, stitching by hand the side seams. With no one in the kitchen except the two of them, it was a rare and quiet moment, indeed.

Leah looked into Adah's pretty green eyes and sweet face. "You'll always be like a sister to me, no matter. . . ."

Adah stuck her needle into the pincushion and stopped her sewing. "If you ask me, I'd say you should go find a pay telephone and call your Jonas."

Leah gasped. "Ain't proper."

"But you can't live without knowin' for sure, can you? I'd be glad to go with you. Honestly, you *must* call him!"

She stared at her friend. "Surely you don't mean it."

"You said you two could talk 'bout anything, jah?"

For sure and for certain, that was true. At least that *had* been the case before his letters stopped.

"So, will you call him?"

Leah sighed. Adah was right: She had to know something one way or the other.

Leah didn't feel the need to take Adah up on her offer to go to the pay telephone booth with her. Not wanting to let either Dat or Mamma know what she was up to, she agreed to borrow some loose change from Adah to place the call, awkward as it was. She had used up all her window-washing pay from Dr. Schwartz to reimburse Mary Ruth. And rightly so.

Having already gone through the process of getting David Mellinger's woodworking shop number before, she felt much more self-confident making a long-distance call this time.

When a grown man's voice came on the line, she realized it was the master carpenter himself. "Uh, jah, I wonder if I might be speakin' to . . . Jonas Mast?" she sputtered.

"Well, I'm sorry to say he's not here just now."

"Oh, I don't mean to bother you," she said.

"No trouble a'tall."

"When would you be expectin' him?"

"Well, can't say that for sure. No tellin' when they'll be back from the singing."

They?

"Do you mean to say. . . ?" She stopped, scarcely able to finish. "Are you speakin' of Sadie Ebersol, maybe?"

"Why, that's right. Sadie and Jonas left here not five minutes ago."

She leaned back against the glass of the phone booth, feeling faint. *So it is true! Just as Dat supposed. Jonas is now seeing Sadie!*

"Is there a message I might give Jonas?" The question jolted her, and she was so hurt and befuddled she found herself shaking her head instead of giving a verbal response.

"Hullo? Are you there?"

"Uh . . . there's no message. I'm sorry." She felt stiff, scarcely able to place the receiver back in its cradle.

I'm sorry. . . .

Why had she said that? Sorry was for a faithless boy like Jonas Mast to be saying to her, for goodness' sake! But sadly, she might never hear those words uttered from her former beau's lips.

Oh, she rued the day she'd ever let him kiss her, especially the fervent way he had. *They* had.

She slapped the reins a bit too hard once she climbed back into the buggy, sending the mare swiftly forward. Only one person she cared to see just now, what with this dreadful pain churning inside. Only one, because Aunt Lizzie must have felt the selfsame stabbing pain when the boy she'd loved had walked out on her, too.

She must get to Lizzie right away. She must sit across from

Lizzie at her little kitchen table and sip some warm, honey-sweetened tea, letting the tears roll down, stopping only to ask what a girl could do when her heart hurt this awful bad.

"Lizzie's over in Strasburg buyin' fabric for your weddin' quilt," Mamma told Leah when she asked.

"When will she be back?" she asked, feeling worse than glum.

"In time for supper," Mamma said, handing Lydiann off to her. "Could you entertain your baby sister a bit?"

Poor, dear Mamma. She'd been wrung out lately, largely due to Sadie. But what would Mamma think if she knew Sadie had beguiled yet another young man? This time Leah's own beau.

Jonas was all mine for ever so long, Leah thought tearfully, holding Lydiann close.

She kissed her baby sister's head, got two spoons for Lydiann to play with, and put her down on the floor. Then, lifting her long skirt to the side, she got down and sat next to the active baby.

Watching Mamma stir a great pot of beef stew, she breathed in the aroma of onions and celery cooking. The smell reminded her of one of the few times they'd ever invited the Mast family over for a Saturday supper. Jonas had sat directly across from her, as he often did—no, come to think of it, as he *always* did. Right from the start, she'd been naïve enough to believe he was as smitten with her as she was him!

Would every smell from now on point her to memories of Jonas? Would it always be so?

"I hope Lizzie can use the fabric for somethin' besides my weddin' quilt," she heard herself saying. In that moment she felt as if she were buried in a straw stack, trying to find an air hole, yet suffocating all the while.

"Aw, Leah, you mustn't . . ." Mamma turned to look at her.

Slowly, Mamma's expression withered as she stood there, potholder in one hand, wooden spoon in the other. "Oh, honey-girl." She set them both down quickly and hurried to kneel on the floor. It was the first time Leah had ever heard Aunt Lizzie's special nickname for her come pouring out of her mother's mouth.

"Oh, Mamma," she cried. "There's not goin' to be a weddin' after all." She told what she'd done at the pay telephone booth and, worse, what David Mellinger had said. "Sadie's gone and taken Jonas from me."

Mamma leaned over and wrapped her comforting arms around her, saying over and over, "My dear, dear girl . . ."

When at last Mamma released her, Leah felt as limp as a dry tobacco leaf. Without saying a word, she picked up Lydiann and carried her upstairs to Mamma's bedroom and closed the door. She lay down with her on their parents' bed while Mamma finished cooking downstairs. Placing her hand gently on her sister's tiny chest, she searched to feel the soft yet steady beat of the baby's heart.

"You must never suffer so," she whispered.

Chapter Thirty-Two

It had come to Ida's attention, by way of Miriam Peachey, that the gossip vine was spreading itself along, heralding the news that Jonas Mast and their own Sadie were a rather odd partnership. And it had all happened so suddenly. Naturally, none of the talk had started with either herself or Leah, but *someone* had gotten the grapevine swinging with the news.

The saddest thing was not only were Sadie and Jonas both in danger of long-term estrangement from the local church community, but they'd never again enjoy the warmth of their families, unless individually they could get Bishop Bontrager to lift the Bann in due time. So both young people were in the same boat, though Sadie's shunning was imminent, Ida knew, and would more than likely be enforced only in Pennsylvania. Jonas, on the other hand, still had time on his side.

Even so, Peter and Fannie Mast, though kin, were clearly not on speaking terms with either Abram or Ida. Fannie no longer answered Ida's letters, and Abram didn't seem to mind one iota. It was as if the two families had shunned each other, and Ida despised it something awful.

◆

Sadie was nearly finished setting the table when Vera let out a sharp cry. "Go and call David," Vera said, pointing toward the back door with one hand and holding her stomach with the other. "Tell my husband to ride quick an' get the midwife!"

Doing as she was told, Sadie scurried out the door and down to the woodworking shop to inform David his fourth child was on the way.

While David took the carriage and hurried down the road, Vera was upstairs preparing to give birth. The task of feeding supper to Joseph, Mary Mae, and Andy now fell to Sadie. And, she just realized, Jonas would also be present at the table.

Somewhat nervous at the prospect of carrying on a conversation with the young man her sister had jilted, she set about dishing up the food, calling for the children to wash their hands and "come to the table."

Fortunately a good portion of the meal was already on the stove or in the oven. She smiled, glad she could truly take credit for the homemade noodles and gravy, and dried-corn casserole . . . if Jonas happened to ask.

Joseph and Mary Mae came quickly. Mary Mae held up her chubby hands for Sadie's inspection before she took her place at the table. "Did I wash 'em clean enough?" she asked, blue eyes shining.

Sadie assured Mary Mae she had done an excellent job of it. Then she said quickly that their mamma would soon introduce them, each one, to a new baby brother or sister. "Won't be long now."

"Best be a boy," Joseph said suddenly. He wore a slight frown, as though worried about the sounds coming from upstairs.

"Your mamma will be just fine," she said in his ear, guiding him around the table to his place.

It was little Andy who dawdled at the sink, sliding the round stool over and stepping up to wash his hands. Jonas glanced at Sadie, then at the food, steaming hot on the table. His eyes seemed to say, *You're handling things very well.*

She caught the message and rose to help the four-year-old dry his hands and get seated. "Now I believe we're ready for the table blessing," she said, looking to Jonas to bow his head and take David's place in all of this.

While her head was bowed, she thought how strange, yet awful nice, this unexpected situation was—she and Jonas the only grown-ups at the table, surrounded by three young ones. She felt she was being given a glimpse of what life might be like as a young wife and mother. Married to Jonas Mast, maybe? Well, that would please her, for sure and for certain . . . if the handsome boy across the table could get her sister out of his head long enough to notice *her.*

Jonas made the quick sound in his throat, just as both Dat and David Mellinger always did, to signal the end of the silent prayer. They all sat up straight, and Sadie passed the food to Jonas first; then she began to serve the children.

While they ate, she waited for Jonas to bring up an interesting topic for conversation, but she wasn't so ready for his remark when he finally did. In fact, she had to stop to think of what to say, she was that cautious.

He spoke to her while the children occupied themselves with feeding their faces. "I saw you had unexpected visitors recently." His voice was rather quiet, softer than usual.

She did not wish to call more attention to herself over this. Thankfully, Edith had snoozed all through the ministers' conversation that day. Still, Sadie was sure both Vera and David had been alerted to the men arriving in the preacher's buggy. It was hard not to stand up and take notice of the sober-looking men wearing their black trousers and frock coats with straight collars. "Evidently, word's gotten out that I intend to stay on here," she said.

Joseph let out a belch and Andy tried to mimic him.

Sadie continued, saying she'd discussed her idea with Edith and the widow was absolutely delighted with the prospect of an ongoing companionship.

"What about your family . . . and your home church?" Jonas held his glass of water, not drinking. "How do the Gobbler's Knob brethren look on it?"

"Bishop Bontrager has issued a warning, is all." She shared with him what she had been told, that, eventually, she could join the church here, "though more progressive than at home." She didn't tell him that Bishop Bontrager had mercifully spared her by not revealing to the Ohio ministers the details of her past transgressions.

"I'd hate to see you shunned for simply stayin' put here."

She said no more, hoping his curiosity had been satisfied. Truth be told, she wanted to keep Jonas's attention on *her*, not on problems relating to church rules and regulations. "I'll be all right," she replied. "You'll see."

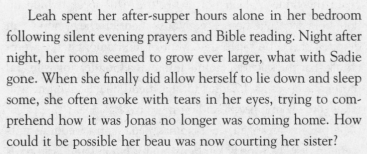

Leah spent her after-supper hours alone in her bedroom following silent evening prayers and Bible reading. Night after night, her room seemed to grow ever larger, what with Sadie gone. When she finally did allow herself to lie down and sleep some, she often awoke with tears in her eyes, trying to comprehend how it was Jonas no longer was coming home. How could it be possible her beau was now courting her sister?

Sitting by her bedroom window late into the night, having long since snuffed out the oil lantern, she stared up at the dark sky. She didn't care that some folk were saying things like "Abram's Leah is pining away, a bride-to-be without a beau" or "just look at Abram's Leah—ach, she grows old before our eyes."

She glanced briefly in the hand mirror on the dresser and observed how awful gray her face was. Gone the rosy cheeks, the bright eyes. She was only seventeen and appeared to be dying. Then and there, her thoughts strayed to Catharina, the martyred Ebersol great-grandmother who had lost everything to follow the Lord God.

Leah couldn't go so far as to think that she, too, had given up all to do God's bidding. But she *had* followed her heart at the prompting of the Holy One, breaking her pledge to Sadie . . . to give her life to the Amish church.

On the day of Naomi Kauffman's wedding, Leah felt as if

she were floating through all the necessary motions, saying all the expected things. She assumed Naomi's doctor must have given the bride a clean bill of health, so to speak, which no doubt pleased Luke Bontrager. Not to mention the bishop. Leah despised the tittle-tattle that went around amongst the womenfolk. For the sake of Naomi's future as a God-fearing wife and mother, she was glad Sadie's former friend hadn't fallen near as far as some young people did during rumschpringe.

Upstairs, arranged on Naomi's bed, many wedding gifts were on display. Mostly kitchenware for Naomi and farm tools for Luke. Careful to show interest in the bride's gifts, Leah went upstairs to look with Naomi before the wedding service began. "What a joyous day," she said.

Naomi smiled, eyes brimming with happy tears. "All's well, now."

Leah was much relieved Naomi did not once mention Sadie's name.

Later, during the preaching, Leah sat next to Naomi, along with Adah—the three young women all in a row, wearing their new blue dresses and white aprons—while Bishop Bontrager gave the main sermon. He focused on the Old Testament marriages, beginning with the story of Adam and Eve, up through Isaac and Rebekah, and concluding with a story from the Apocrypha about Tobias heeding his father's counsel and choosing a bride from his own tribe.

Leah sat still as could be, trying not to dwell on the fact that two short weeks from now, she and Jonas had planned to be standing before the bishop, making their lifelong vows to each other. Her eyes dimmed at the thought. Hard as it was, she was following through with her promise to Naomi, being a dutiful wedding attendant. She hoped no one suspected her pain, though she assumed all of them had heard by now, one way or another.

She took in several breaths and attempted to paste on a permanent smile as Naomi and Luke agreed they were "ordained of God for each other" and would remain so till such time as death should separate them.

Leah and Adah had decided beforehand they would not stay for the barn games, geared toward the single youth and courting couples. Adah had suggested they return home together with Leah's family so she could spend the rest of the afternoon and evening with Leah, helping her through "such a hard day."

Gid sat with the menfolk, unable to keep his eyes off Leah. He wished he might do something to ease her sorrow, which was plainly evident. Leah was a plucky one, but knowing her as he did, he felt sure she was suppressing her grief. At least for the moment . . . for Naomi's happiness.

What a girl! To think she'd lost her beau to her own fickle sister. The thought stirred him up, even though it meant the girl he'd always admired and cared for would not be marrying this month after all. Leah would still live neighbors to him under the covering of Abram's roof. Yet he felt sick to his stomach, enduring some of the pain that such a dear girl must be experiencing this moment as she stood tall and pretty next to the bride and groom.

Dat agreed there was plenty of room for Adah to ride home with them, and Leah was ever so glad. They didn't say much as they rode together in the back of the spring wagon, with Lizzie and the twins in the next seat up, and Mamma, Lydiann, and Dat up front.

Once home Adah followed her upstairs so Leah could change into an everyday dress and apron. " 'Twas nice to see Naomi lookin' so happy, jah?" Adah said.

Leah had to agree. "To think what might've turned out to be." She didn't much care to discuss the aftermath of a reckless rumschpringe.

She hung up her new dress and apron, and the girls hurried downstairs and out the back door, both draped in their warm shawls. They headed through the rows and rows of brown stumps that had once been a cornfield, to Adah's house. There, Adah slipped out of her nice, new dress and hung it up for the next Preaching service. "I'm sorry you had to suffer through today, Leah," Adah said.

"I'm glad you were right beside me," Leah replied quickly. "Such a comfort it was. You just don't know."

Adah suggested they not attend many of the weddings this year. "I can think of plenty of things to do besides goin' from one weddin' to another all November long."

Leah appreciated her friend's thoughtfulness. "Mamma said she heard there were some spillin' over into December."

"No one should expect you to go to all of them . . . or any, for that matter." Adah reached for her hand.

"Still, I'd hate to see *you* miss out, Adah. There'll be plenty of nice boys there, eager to play the barn games and whatnot. You really should go with your sister . . . and Gid."

Adah, it was plain to see, was reluctant to say she would or wouldn't go. Leah knew that if Adah waited too long, she

344

might miss out on having herself a beau. It wouldn't be fair for Adah Peachey to be Gid's age and still single, waiting for the "right one" to come along.

Jonas worked extra hard in the wood shop, recalling Leah was to be a bridesmaid in Naomi Kauffman's wedding this day. He set to sawing with such fervor that David looked up and gave notice, raising an eyebrow, before he returned to staining a table.

Stopping to wipe his face on his sleeve, he shuddered to think Abram had succeeded in getting his first choice in a beau for Leah. So Gid had stolen his bride. Still baffled as to why he hadn't known, or at least surmised as much, he found himself shaking his head in utter dismay. Leah had chosen to let him down by simply not responding to his important letter—by not coming right out and saying that, jah, she wanted to obey her father's wishes.

There was only one thing to do now: try his best to forget her, that and the pain she'd caused him . . . and his family. Best leave the past right where it belonged—behind. Yet that was anything but easy with Leah's beautiful and wide-eyed sister practically living under the same roof. She was a constant reminder of what he'd lost.

Leah and Adah had been walking out near Blackbird Pond and beyond for over an hour. Even though Adah insisted they rest near the willow tree, Leah refused to stop. She had such pent-up energy, yet was nearing collapse at the same time. She wanted to calm down but wouldn't let herself. "How will I ever forget Jonas?" The question poured out of her like vinegar mixed with honey.

She welcomed Adah's gentle touch on her shoulder, and they fell back into their silent, somber walk. The two friends had shared both sadness and joy through their years together, but today Leah's despondency was far more intense than any time she could remember.

"Love must be disappointing at times," Adah said. "I 'spect you'll never forget him."

They walked in silence till Adah spoke up again. "Mamma sometimes says, 'Love is faith with its work clothes on.'"

Leah had heard that said, too. "It's all I can do to rise in the morning, missin' him . . . missin' the life we'd planned. I have no hope in me, Adah." She wouldn't go so far as to reveal that as children she and Jonas had made a love cov- enant of sorts. It was pointless to talk about, let alone con- sider now . . . especially with Gid's sister.

"I s'pose after some time passes, you'll delve deep into your heart and find forgiveness there for what Jonas and Sadie have done to you."

"Forgiveness warms the heart and soothes the sting," Leah said softly. "Aunt Lizzie has said that my whole life, growin' up. Easier said than done."

"The Good Lord will help you, Leah. I'll do my part, as well."

Giving Adah a quick smile, she slipped her arm around her best friend, and they walked one more time around the large pond.

———◆———

Tuckered out, Leah said good-bye to Adah at last and headed across the field to the barn. She went around the back way, toward the earthen barn bridge leading to the second level. The haymow beckoned her.

She stepped inside, taking in the familiar and sweet scent. Looking around, she made herself a spot to nestle in and sank down into the warm hay. Fatigued as she was, she called to mind her conversation with David Mellinger yet again.

Jonas and Sadie . . .

Together.

Jonas's name connected to her sister's. Why? How? *Oh, Lord God heavenly Father, please help this weary soul of mine!* she prayed.

She drifted off to tearful sleep and dreamed she was pitching hay, the raked pile seemingly never ending as she gripped the pitchfork. Her arm muscles and clenched fist throbbed with the intensity of the chore, and she roused herself slightly, only to relax once again and return to sleep.

In search of a shovel, Smithy Gid climbed the ladder to the hayloft and was thunderstruck to see Leah there, fast asleep. Several gray mouse catchers had positioned themselves around her like miniature guards, but by the look of their relaxed and furry bodies, getting forty winks was uppermost in their feline minds.

Lest he disturb Leah's peaceful slumber, he decided against tramping through the hay just now and would have immediately descended the ladder if he hadn't noticed Leah's tear-streaked face. Unable to move away, he stared unashamedly at the curve of her eyelashes, the blush of peach on her cheeks, the relaxed expression on her lips.

Most precious she is. . . .

His heart wrenched and his breath caught in his throat. He would move heaven and earth if he could to let her know, in the appropriate time, that he was eager to offer his hand of friendship. If it should take years, he would wait. For goodness' sake, Leah must not live life as a passed-over maidel due to the outright heartlessness of Jonas Mast.

Two cats awakened and blinked their green eyes at him, staring him down. Pressing his finger to his lips, he hoped to ward off any piercing meows; then he realized how futile the gesture was. Cats cried, even screeched, as they desired. A body could simply look at a barn cat and a ruckus could follow if the cat's mood was just right.

He stood motionless, hoping the cats in question might run off or return to their dozing. *Just keep still,* he thought.

Again shifting his gaze to Leah, he found himself wanting to lean forward, stretch just enough to touch her face . . . even gently press the loose strand of her brown hair between his fingers. But he held fast to the ladder.

Gid struggled, knowing he had always been a distant second in Leah's mind. *Can I persuade her otherwise?* He recalled the coolness of her hand in his that day in the woods. Several times during their difficult trek down the entangled hillock, he had reached for her innocently—steadying her, keeping her from stumbling or worse.

But now it appeared she *had* fallen, having succumbed to the cruelly twisted jumble of her life. And though he was willing, he had been unable to keep her from doing so.

Chapter Thirty-Three

A solid half hour came and went as Leah napped quietly. She stirred in and out of a dream, aware of voices below her.

"No . . . no, Leah can't handle this now. I've just lost one daughter; I won't lose another!"

It was Dat's voice . . . in her dream? But no, she was right here in the hay.

Lost in a sleepy stupor, she tuned her ears to whatever she thought she'd heard.

"Time's run out, Abram. There are people who know the truth. . . ."

Aunt Lizzie? Was she nearby, too? She wondered what on earth Dat and Aunt Lizzie were doing in the barn together.

"There's no need to be rushin' ahead with this, 'specially with the wedding called off," Mamma said. "And 'tis a difficult time for the family just now, what with Sadie soon to be shunned."

"I agree," Aunt Lizzie said. "But wouldn't *you* rather tell her than have her find out through the grapevine?"

Leah rose and shook the hay off her dress and apron, the cats scattering as she did so. Bewildered, she walked to the edge of the loft and peered down. "Dat? Mamma?" she called softly, surprised to see all of them in a huddle by the feed trough.

Dat turned and spotted her, his face paling instantly.

Their eyes held. An awkward silence fell between them, and Leah saw that both Mamma and Lizzie were befuddled, too. Lizzie's hand flew to her mouth; Mamma's eyes glistened, her face quivering.

At last Dat broke the stillness. "Leah, how long have you been up there?"

"I don't know . . . must've fallen asleep." She moved toward the ladder and made her way down.

"Come here to me, child." Mamma opened her arms to embrace her.

She felt the breathless heaving of her mother's bosom and wondered why her heart beat so fast.

Dat turned to Aunt Lizzie, his mouth open as if he wanted to speak, but the words wouldn't come.

Mamma held fast to Leah. "I think 'tis best for Abram and me to be alone with Leah for now, Lizzie. You understand, ain't?"

Eyes downcast, Aunt Lizzie sighed audibly, and Leah observed the intense struggle between what Dat and Mamma were wanting—whatever it was—and what Lizzie must have been hoping for. Lizzie seemed to shrink in size just then. For an agonizing moment her aunt stood next to Mamma, saying not a word, looking forlorn and alone.

When Aunt Lizzie raised her head, she fixed her sad eyes on Leah.

"Sister?" pleaded Mamma softly.

Slowly turning away, Aunt Lizzie wandered slump shouldered over to the wide barn door, leaning hard against it as it inched open.

Leah felt the rush of cool air as her dear auntie headed outside.

Once they were alone, Dat sat down on a square bundle of alfalfa. He looked at her, beard twitching to beat the band. "It's time you heard the truth, Leah." He placed his big hand on the spot beside him. "Come, sit beside ol' Dat."

Just the way he patted the baled forage made Leah tremble.

Lizzie was beside herself. Why had they sent her out of the barn? In all truth, she had every right to be present when her honey-girl heard the story for the first time.

She stumbled up the mule road toward home, continuing to worry. Had they made a mistake deciding to tell Leah? Poor thing, she'd been through so much lately. Lizzie had seen how washed out and frail Leah looked as a bridesmaid in Naomi's wedding this morning. A wonder she'd managed to get through the wedding service at all!

Heartsick as she was, Leah didn't need to learn that Lizzie, not Ida, was her real mamma . . . not this day. *How awful selfish of me*, Lizzie thought.

Hurrying to the back door of her house, she pushed it open and went straight to the wood stove to begin boiling water. Some strong mint tea would help calm her, if that was possible. She scarcely knew peace at all anymore.

Standing over the pot of hot water, she forced her thoughts away from Leah to Abram's flesh-and-blood daughter. How relieved she was; Sadie's secret was out in the open at last. In spite of the shun the dear girl might be able to get herself some much-needed spiritual help in Millersburg . . . especially if there *was* a godly bishop, as Leah had indicated from Jonas's previous letters. *If only Sadie had never left home,* she thought. If only she'd been repentant *here*, none of this dreadful thing between Sadie and Jonas would have happened.

What gall of Sadie! She poured the water into her prettiest cup and walked to the front room window. Sipping her tea, she looked out toward the depths of the forest, where Sadie had, no doubt, conceived *her* love child.

Lizzie was overcome with despair yet again, recalling the night of her own rumschpringe madness. Things had gotten clean out of hand, beginning with her decision to seek out some New Year's Eve excitement. She had gone to a beauty parlor to have her waist-long hair cut to chin length and parted on the side, with finger waves like the young woman in a Coca-Cola ad she'd seen. Brazen and fun loving, she was ready for anything.

All her life, she had been warned to stay close to home— to avoid fancy Englishers' automobiles—yet defiantly she had tucked a pack of Chesterfields in her pocketbook and walked up to Route 340, thumbing a ride. The handsome young man who picked her up had no idea she was Amish, let alone underage. Grinning a warm greeting, he drove her around Lancaster County, eventually heading to Gobbler's Knob, where he parked his Niagara Blue Roadster near the ditch along the road and shared some moonshine. They laughed and talked and drank too much, then hiked into the cold woods. There, in a hunters' shack hidden deep in the trees, she willingly gave up her viture.

Leah's life began in the shanty that winter night—the worst possible thing that could have happened to young Lizzie, discovering she was with child. Both her mother and father, as well as her older brother, Noah, brought the fact up to her continually, till she thought she might lose her wits. Noah even threatened to haul her away to a big city and force her to abort her baby. "Such a disgrace you are to this family!" he'd said time and again, the color in his face rising to a bright purple.

In desperation, she had written a letter to her big sister, Ida, pleading for help. The next day Abram and Ida came with toddler in arms—fair-haired Sadie—to Hickory Hollow, having ridden all the way from Gobbler's Knob.

A serious scuffle took place in the barn, she learned later. Abram stood up to Noah—even held up his fists—and said under no circumstances was Noah to compound Lizzie's sin with *two* wrongs.

In short order a pact was made involving Abram, Ida, and herself. That very night, Lizzie rode to her new home in Gobbler's Knob.

Lizzie held no grudge toward the handsome stranger. Conceiving his child had been just as much her fault as his. Yet October 2, 1930, the date of Leah's birth, had burned its way into her memory for always.

Abram took her and Ida to talk privately with Bishop

Bontrager, who welcomed Lizzie into the church after she freely repented. She was baptized a year later, along with a number of unsuspecting youths.

So the secret was set, and Leah was raised as Abram's and Ida's own. Altogether plump, Ida didn't have to make much excuse for this new baby showing up three years after Sadie. Only a handful of folk knew much of anything at all, though rumors flew like lightning bugs when Lizzie moved into the Ebersols' Dawdi Haus till her little log house could be built up behind the bank barn.

Lizzie turned away from the window and went to sit for a spell. She was ever so tired all of a sudden. Her head spun with the memory of years.

Setting the teacup down on the floral saucer, she sighed and leaned back a bit, wishing she'd never, ever breathed a word to Abram today, nor this week for that matter. What had she been thinking? Poor Leah needed a respite from sadness and pain. Not a revelation that could cause her further grief.

Closing her eyes, she breathed a prayer for what must surely be happening in Abram's barn this very moment—her dear Leah was being presented with such untimely news.

Tears sprang to her eyes. *What'll happen when Leah hears the truth? Will she distrust me? What of Abram and Ida? Will our girl view us as betrayers, all these years?*

Just how long she had been resting there, she didn't know. Maybe only a few minutes when she heard someone calling in the distance.

"Aunt Lizzie!"

Getting up out of her chair, she flew to the southeast-facing window in the spare bedroom and looked out. There, running up the mule road, was Leah, skirts flying like a kite in a windstorm.

"Aunt Lizzie!" her daughter called.

Oh, Lizzie thought she must be seeing things. Her heart leaped into her throat. How would Leah react to such jolting news?

Lizzie ran to get her shawl and hurried out the back door, down the narrow porch, and past the flower beds, finished for the season. Over the grassy yard she went, past the stone wall and down the hill to the edge of the woods, where the light broke free, clear as glass.

She kept going, fast as she could, though young Leah's pace was far quicker. "Are you all right?" Lizzie called to her, nearly out of breath.

Leah's feet pounded hard against the dirt path, and if Lizzie wasn't mistaken, her face was marked with tears.

And then they were in each other's arms, Leah sobbing and whimpering. "Oh, Aunt Lizzie, it was you all along . . . all these years, 'twas *you*."

Stunned at what she was hearing, she kissed Leah's soft, wet cheek. "The Lord God be praised," she said, breathing much easier now. To think how Leah *might have* responded to the news. Well, she dared not dwell on that. Not now. She wanted to soak up all the love, capture the brightness in Leah's eyes, the pure delight she saw in them, reflected in her own. Truly, she was more than relieved; she was brimming with utter gladness.

Leah stepped back and fixed her eyes on Lizzie. "Ach, I can scarcely believe it . . . you gave me life, Aunt Lizzie. How on earth could it be that I never guessed such a wonderful-gut thing!" Then she threw her arms around Lizzie again.

Why, oh why, did I ever worry? Lizzie thought, truly grateful. "How I love you, Leah." This she whispered, clinging to her daughter for dearest life.

Then, arm in arm, they strolled toward the log house, all the while Lizzie feeling her heart might burst apart. "I could only pray you might feel this way," she managed to say. "Honestly, I have to say I worried you might—"

"But how else *could* I feel? Goodness, I've loved you all along—nearly like a daughter loves her mamma, ya must surely know," declared Leah. "Of course I told Mamma and Dat, 'I am and always will be your girl, too.'" Leah was wearing the first true smile Lizzie had seen on her pretty face in weeks.

"Well, of course, you're theirs for always." She was unable to keep from looking . . . no, staring at Leah's lovely face.

"And I'm *your* honey-girl, Aunt Lizzie. To think I've had two mammas all along. Guess I'm double-blessed, ain't?"

Lizzie agreed wholeheartedly. *O Lord God, thank you for making it so.*

———————◆———————

On November 25, the Tuesday she and Jonas had planned to wed, Leah skirted a sharp, rock-strewn bank scattered here and there with moss, picking her way through the woods. She rather liked the feeling of being overwhelmed by age-old trees and their intertwined branches above, along with the leafy labyrinth below.

Once again, she found herself pondering Catharina Meylin, slain at the hands of God's cruel enemies. Dat's ancestor had given up her life freely for her devout faith. Leah wondered, *Did I lose Jonas in exchange for my obedience to the Lord God?*

For sure and for certain, she hadn't lost her physical life . . . but she felt as if she'd lost her heart. Daring to do what was right and good in the sight of the Almighty, she'd made her lifelong covenant with the church, regardless of the harsh consequences.

Locating the honey locust tree, she stood tall and determined beneath its cold and leafless branches, leaning back to peer up through the web of bough and stem to the blue sky. Somehow, her future would be bright with or without Jonas. If they must be apart—no matter what lay before her—she was determined to trust in God.

Aunt Lizzie had often talked of "praying from one's heart." But not until this moment had Leah ever attempted to do so. She bowed her head, faltering at first, and began to address her heavenly Father. "O Lord, I stand here . . . heartbroken before you. Hear my prayer, dear God."

She poured out her sorrow, even her bitterness, in the timbered stillness. She went so far as to speak aloud Sadie's name . . . and the betrayal, placing it all before the Throne of Grace. "I must find the strength to forgive both my sister—"and here she stopped, struggling with tears—"and . . . Jonas. O Lord and heavenly Father, help me to do this difficult thing."

Drawing in a deep breath, she began to feel an undeniable peace. She wept with strange relief, confident that the God of Moses, who had parted the roaring waves of the Red Sea, could make a path where there had been none before. This same Jehovah God would make plain and straight the path of her own life, wherever it might lead.

Walking toward home, she looked ahead to the wood's edge, where beams of sunlight flooded the opening that led to Dat's pastureland . . . and the mule road. Then and there she knew she was no longer Abram's Leah, although the People would continue to reckon it so. Neither was she Jonas's Leah. In this clear moment of understanding, she knew she was wholly the Lord's. From tip to toe.

"I belong to you, Lord God," she whispered, quickening her pace. "Forever and always, I am your faithful Leah."

Acknowledgments

The procedure for the baptismal service described in this book was adapted from the Amish ministers' manual, *Handbuch*. I am especially thankful for Plain church members in both Lancaster, Pennsylvania, and Holmes County, Ohio, who were willing and gracious, indeed, to verify essential information regarding baptismal instruction and the baptism service itself.

I offer my truest gratitude to Carol Johnson, my editor and dear friend, along with Rochelle Glöege, Barbara Lilland, and David Horton, all vital members of Bethany's expert editorial team.

My deep appreciation also goes to my husband, David Lewis, who encourages me daily with his prayers, love, and keen interest in my many writing "journeys."

My brother-in-law, Dale Birch, was a wealth of information regarding the work of a master carpenter. And an unexpected blessing came from Larry Quiring, retired U.S. postal worker, who eagerly answered my questions regarding mail delivery in 1947.

To my partners in prayer, a heartfelt thank you! I value your ongoing spiritual encouragement. May the Lord bless you abundantly for your faithfulness.

———◆———

For readers who wish to probe deeper into the Plain culture, I recommend the following books:

Amish Society, by John A. Hostetler

The Riddle of the Amish, by Donald B. Kraybill

Strangers at Home, Amish and Mennonite Women in History, edited by Kimberly D. Schmidt, Diane Zimmerman Umble, and Steven D. Reschly

Plain and Amish, An Alternative to Modern Pessimism, by Bernd G. Langin

Martyrs Mirror of the Defenseless Christians, or The Bloody Theatre, compiled by Thieleman J. van Braght

———◆———

Watch for ABRAM'S DAUGHTERS Book Three, *The Sacrifice*, in May 2004 at your local bookstore!

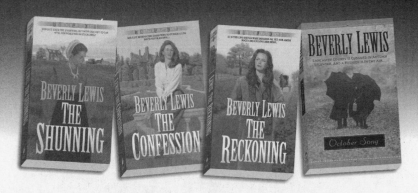
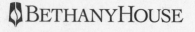

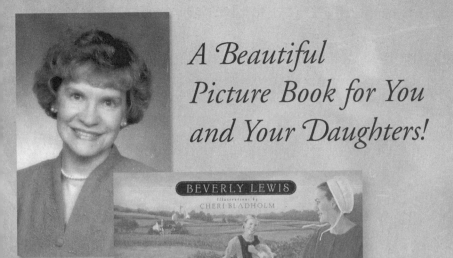

A Lancaster County Series Just For You!

SummerHill Secrets

Heartwarming and uplifting, this series from Beverly Lewis will take you to the heart of Pennsylvania's Amish farmland. You'll meet thirteen-year-old Merry Hanson and her Amish friend Rachel Zook, and follow along on all their adventures. These girls, like you, are facing struggles and joys at home, school, and with friends. If you long for fun mysteries and a glimpse into another world, come unlock the SUMMERHILL SECRETS!

1. *Whispers Down the Lane*

2. *Secret in the Willows*

3. *Catch a Falling Star*

4. *Night of the Fireflies*

5. *A Cry in the Dark*

6. *House of Secrets*

7. *Echoes in the Wind*

8. *Hide Behind the Moon*

9. *Windows on the Hill*

10. *Shadows Beyond the Gate*

SOMETIMES YOU HAVE NO CHOICE BUT TO MAKE A DIFFERENCE

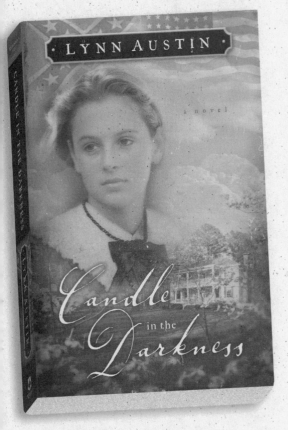

*C*aught between her Richmond home, her awakening abolitionist beliefs, and the Southern man she loves, Caroline Fletcher finds her eyes open to the hard world around her. Will she choose love and the comfort of home, or sacrifice everything for the truth that burns in her heart?

www.lynnaustin.org

Lynn Austin—Stories of Unforgettable Women

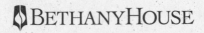